The Lions of the North

RA RIDLEY

Cover art by the author
Cover image by alanf/Shutterstock.com
Copyright © RA Ridley 2018
ISBN: 9781724107480
ISBN-13: 9781724107480

1

JUNE 1963

Mike Armstrong drove the Jensen gently along a narrow sandy track that followed the curves of the red sandstone cliffs falling abruptly away to his right. Hundreds of feet below, the North Sea was in a benign mood as it withdrew from Tantallon Bay on the ebb tide. The sea had left behind a shiny expanse of wet sand, with the odd protruding rock sticking up through the surface. The beach was very easy to cross at night, assuming you could find a way down the curtain walls that surrounded the bay. Much larger formations of jagged rock lined the edges of the water, especially along the north edge. The sheer cliff there created a seemingly impenetrable barrier to anyone approaching from the sea. Sitting atop the cliff was 700-year-old Tantallon Castle, Mike's intended objective.

Night had finally fallen on the last day of June 1963 and a waxing moon provided just enough light to drive without the headlights. Libby Kembrey sat silently in the passenger seat. Her eyes focused way ahead on the headland in case she had to warn Mike of trouble. His concentration was completely taken up with staying on the track.

Both Mike and Libby had wound down their windows to listen out for other vehicles moving on the cliff that night. A difficult task, as the car's rumbling exhaust drowned out most other sounds. The Jensen CV8 preferred its engine to be worked hard on the open road, not trickled along on a country track.

The gentle incoming breeze of sea air helped to relax the car's occupants. They had spent the day pretending to be tourists, after leaving a small hotel in Dunbar and driving north to Tantallon Bay. They had reconnoitred the track earlier in the day and found a path that wound down the cliff face to the beach, where they spent some time sunbathing. Mike had brought with him a pair of Zeiss Jena binoculars to try and spot a route up the north cliffs with which they could reach the base of the castle wall. Thankfully the elements had done their worst with the castle wall, and he could make out plenty of handholds and footholds he could use to ascend the vertical face, though he could see this task was going to be far from easy.

Once the pair had finished their daytime reconnaissance, they retraced their steps back up the cliff and returned to the car, which was parked at the end of the track, almost a mile away. All they had to do was wait for darkness to fall. Before leaving the hotel, Mike had ordered some sandwiches and two flasks full of coffee while Libby had remained in their room, cleaning and double-checking their Smith and Wesson 9mm pistols along with the Uzi sub-machine gun Mike was to carry on his climb. Now they were back at the car, a travel rug was spread out on the ground and they got as much as sleep as possible during the late afternoon and early evening.

By dusk the pair were on their feet, looking around to make sure any remaining tourists and hikers had left for the day. The remaining sandwiches were eaten and washed down by the still-hot coffee before the pair unpacked their weapons and checked them over once more.

Mike pulled out a long length of climbing rope from the car. He hoped he would not have to use it, but he couldn't be sure and would rather be prepared. Mike then changed into a pair of drab olive combat trousers and put on an old Denison smock. He carefully applied some camouflage cream to his face, neck and hands before pulling on a black woollen commando cap.

Both were tense, and neither spoke during what seemed like an age as they waited for darkness to properly fall.

Eventually Mike squeezed Libby's hand and she knew the time had come. She slipped into the passenger seat and Mike took his place behind the steering wheel. He cursed instantly, regretting his decision to drive wearing his walking boots. The cumbersome soles touched the brakes when he wanted the clutch, and vice versa. There was no way he could deftly press on the accelerator to maintain proper control of the back end of the powerful car in these things.

'It's no good, Libby. You look on ahead and I'll concentrate on keeping this thing on the track,' said Mike with irritation.

Eventually, still not having heard a single sound of anyone else nearby, they reached the point on the track where Mike could make his descent into the bay. He stopped the car and they both got out. After checking that his pistol was secure in its shoulder holster, he looped the coil of rope over his shoulder. The Uzi was slung over his chest, with the butt folded and a full magazine of ammunition fitted. Spare magazines full of ammunition cluttered his spare pockets. He also carried a small red mountain-rescue flare. Without another word, he gave Libby a hug before heading down the path into Tantallon Bay.

* * *

With a sinking heart, Libby looked on as Mike melted into the darkness. The man she loved so dearly was yet again risking life and limb under the duress of blackmail. How she wished she could end Wesley's shadowy life of secrets and escape his hold over herself and Mike.

Suddenly she felt alone, cold and afraid. Her stomach churned, and the cool evening air seemed to have an edge to it. The distant waves far below her somehow sounded menacing now that she was by herself. *Get a grip of yourself*, she thought, trying to overcome her fears.

As part of their plan, Libby maintained a surveillance of the area. She used Mike's light-gathering binoculars to scan the clifftops and the various approaches to the castle. She also had a perfect view of the beach that Mike had to cross to reach the vast stone building. She was surprised by how well the binoculars worked and marvelled at the in-flight acrobatics of the odd seagull passing below her. Depending on Mike's progress, she could warn him of approaching danger using the car horn or the headlights. If the worst came to the worst, she would fire warning shots using her pistol. Should she see the red flare Mike carried, she would know it was all over and would need to drive away to safety. Their emergency rendezvous was

Waverley Station in Edinburgh, thirty miles to the west of Tantallon.

Libby also listened out for anything that might be a danger to Mike and unconsciously placed her free hand on the pistol that was resting on the roof of the Jensen. Her eyes had become accustomed to the darkness and she was able to make full use of the meagre moonlight. More quickly than she had expected, she glimpsed Mike's tiny dark figure moving across the sand. She picked him out easily using the binoculars; his movements were fluid and purposeful as he jogged swiftly towards the northern cliff wall. She scanned ahead of the running figure, but there was nothing to see. Her heart was hammering, but not out of fear for herself. It was knowing that Mike may be minutes from death.

She focussed once more on her task. It was no use tracking him so closely; she had to be his long-distance eyes and ears. Just then, a single light became visible from a castle window set high up in the walls. Libby wondered if the man Mike was going to surprise was already in that room. There were no other lights visible, but that did not necessarily mean the man was alone.

A terrible thought crossed her mind: that Mike was heading into a trap and was going to be killed. It was too late now. All she could do was wait in powerless hope. She hoped Mike had seen the light come on and that he would be more cautious in his ascent of the cliff.

* * *

Libby was not the only one feeling the pressure. Mike also felt the pangs of despair and separation as he headed into the darkness, leaving her alone by the car. He already knew from the time he had spent with Libby how precious a person she was; if this was love, he had found it.

Given the chance, he would shoot Wesley on sight, but the cost would be too great. Mike had let Wesley find him and drag him back into his clutches. Now, not only was he forced to work for the man, but Libby was also now in his purview. Mike was angry at himself for his stupidity in allowing that to happen.

By the time he reached the edge of the north cliffs, Mike put all his distracting thoughts aside. If he was to return safely to Libby, he had to concentrate on the task at hand.

Although largely hidden from view, the path to the beach proved easy to follow now that he was accustomed to the darkness. He took an easy jog down to the sands and began to feel the benefit of wearing his walking boots. Once on to the wide expanse he glanced back up the cliff towards Libby. He could see nothing. Despite the extra weight of the weapons, ammunition and rope, he was still able to easily jog towards the cliff to his north. His physical training in Canada was paying off.

Mike glanced back a second time, and now that he was further away he could make out the clifftop where Libby remained. More accurately, he was able to see the car because the moonlight was momentarily reflected off its windscreen. This worried him – if he could see the reflection, so could others. It was too late to do anything about it now, so he pushed the worry to the back of his mind.

Within minutes Mike was at the foot of the curtain wall. At first it seemed impenetrable. He tried to pick out the formations he had spotted earlier in the day as possible points to start his climb. It was no use – he was too close, and it was too dark.

After wasting precious time making failed attempts to start his climb, he retreated onto the beach. From there he noticed a few possible routes up the cliff. He also saw that a light had come on, visible high up on the castle wall. That had to be his target.

He moved forward to what appeared to be a route up to the base of the castle wall. Ensuring the Uzi was still slung securely across his back to avoid it being damaged, he began to climb. He found himself having to ascend, rock by vertical rock, digging his boots into the available crevices. He crammed his fingertips into any handhold he could find whilst trying to ignore the pain as his skin became torn and bloody.

Every time he slipped, Mike believed he was about to plunge into the abyss of jagged rock far below him, but every time he somehow managed to hold on. His knees and elbows were battered and bruised to the point where he needed to rest, but there was nowhere safe to be found on the rock-face.

Then he felt a tuft of grass above him and looked up in desperation. He had finally reached the grassy shelf that marked the base of the castle wall. He made one last effort and pulled himself on to the safety of the verge. From his new vantage point he was able to look back across the bay towards Libby and the car. He hoped she was unable to see how desperate the first part of the climb had been. There was no sound from her direction and no flashing headlights, so he had to assume she was still safe, and so was he.

Lying on his back, Mike took in the expanse of wall standing before him. Up close he could see that a large section was not perpendicular; it sloped back at a slight angle to form a buttress for the adjacent walls that led off from it. The lit window was only a few yards to the right of the sloping section. Mike decided he would climb the sloping section then complete a traverse that took him to just below the window – what happened next was anybody's guess. Before completing the final stage of the climb, Mike glanced around the large grassy shelf to see if there was a point to attach his climbing rope, should he need to escape quickly.

At one end of the area where he was standing, another section of wall reached vertically into the night. The opposite end had some rocks projecting from the grass like a set of disordered teeth. He gave them a hard push with his boot to see if they were as stable as they looked. He was not disappointed. Mike uncoiled the rope and set about tying a self-release knot, then threw the remaining length of rope out into the darkness. The knot meant that he could descend using just half of the rope. The remaining parallel half was for pulling on the release knot. He gave it a good tug and the knot held, as he hoped it would do later. If not, he would fall to his death.

With his escape route secured, Mike turned his attention back to the final section of the climb. The few minutes' rest had given him enough energy to climb up the slightly sloping section of the wall. However, within seconds his calves were objecting painfully to their exertions. He gritted his teeth and continued. Apart from the pain, the traverse was relatively simple as the castle wall was cracked and weathered from centuries of neglect, providing numerous hand- and footholds.

Finally, Mike reached the window ledge. A glazed metal frame set a few feet inside the thick castle wall was easily accessible, so he carefully crawled forward to look inside.

The view was hazy, as a residue of sea salt covered the glass panels. He rubbed at a panel to get a better view of the room. Inside, to Mike's left, was a huge well-set log fire and an open hearth. The stone walls were festooned with weaponry from a bygone age – fighting swords, claymores and daggers of all types were mounted in circular patterns, held in place centrally by shiny buckler shields or tartan-covered rosettes. He noticed a small rosette was missing some of its daggers. In the centre of the room a long, polished wooden table had been set for dinner for one. A huge candelabra on top of it was augmented by other lit candles on escutcheons around the room. A grand meal with wine had been served, Mike presumed by staff that worked at the castle.

The sole diner, wearing an army brigadier's mess dress, sat motionless in a baronial chair. A dagger pierced each wrist, driving down all the way into the arms of the heavy wooden chair. A third dagger pierced the man's chest, buried into his heart. A miniature version of the three other blades acted as a pin to keep the man's tongue protruding from his open mouth. Blood still dripped from the brigadier's wounds.

Mike shivered as the man's bulging eyes appeared to lock on to his. It was too late; the man he had come to warn was dead. All he could do now was try to find any information he could take away with him.

A few stout kicks made the window fly open as the small metal latch gave way. Mike jumped down on to the floor with his Uzi at the ready. Apart from the dead man, he was alone. He rushed over to lock the main door to the room before scanning around for anything that might contain files or other documents belonging to the brigadier. It appeared to be clear, so Mike made his way to a side door that stood ajar. A light was on in the next room, which contained a made-up bed. On the bed was a brown leather suitcase and a matching briefcase. The latter appeared to have been torn open, its contents strewn over the counterpane. Mike rifled through the papers then noticed a scarlet-coloured file discarded on the floor. He hurriedly picked it up and flicked through the pages. A sheet had been torn out; only a corner of the paper remained. He swore quietly. The killer – or killers – had taken the exact thing Mike needed to retrieve from the brigadier.

Suddenly there was a knock on the door Mike had locked just minutes earlier. It sounded like a member of staff was trying to get the attention of the now-dead brigadier.

Time was up. Mike raced over to the window and climbed back outside. He carefully pulled the window shut behind him before he made a hasty traverse back to the sloping buttress. In his haste he slipped, almost losing his grip. Once he was six feet above the grassy ledge he took the risk of dropping down on to it. He landed heavily and only just managed to stop himself rolling over the edge into oblivion.

Lying on his back, winded, Mike looked back up to the window. He could only imagine the mayhem in the room as members of staff broke open the locked door. Tugging the climbing rope once more to check it was safe, he lowered himself hand over hand as quickly as he dared. Halfway down he found a thin ledge to balance on as he tugged to release the rope. After many hurried attempts, the release knot finally gave way and the rope fell towards a relieved Mike. He swiftly tied a rough knot in the rope and jammed it into the first crevice he could find. A hard tug confirmed once more that he was safe to descend, so the rope was thrown clear with the end thankfully landing on the sand way below with a dull thud.

Hand over blistered hand, Mike lowered himself safely down the rock-face. As soon as he reached the beach he abandoned the rope and ran back across the sand, glancing briefly over his shoulder to the castle window. Nothing. It seemed he had escaped unseen.

He increased his pace and was breathing heavily when he reached the far side of the bay to begin his final climb back up to Libby. The gruff roar of the Jensen's engine starting reached his ears, letting him know she had spotted him returning. The sound spurred him on as he stumbled back up the cliff path, and minutes later they were reunited.

Libby threw her arms around him and held him close. He showed her his blistered and bloody hands.

'I think you had better drive,' he said.

2
MARCH 1963

The lone figure stood on the outside of the heavy wooden churchyard gate. His features were obscured in the shadow of two huge yew trees that flanked the entrance, their green bulk suggesting they may have been growing there for many hundreds of years. In comparison, the man was as transient as a drop of summer dew on a blade of grass.

The weather was miserably wet and windy on that March morning in 1963 and water dripped off the trees on to the man's already soaked trilby hat. The wet made the dark blue Irish-linen material of the hat seem darker than ever. The man turned up the collar of his soaked mackintosh in a failed attempt to repel the falling rain and howling wind. The combined effect made him look like an archetypal police detective.

He became motionless once more, as if the two trees were gate guardians mysteriously preventing him from entering the Christian churchyard. The man glanced up impatiently at the source of the irritating drips. A malevolent smile appeared on his face. He thought how ironic it was that these evergreens, long regarded as a symbol of eternal life, contained a poison that could kill someone – assuming they were stupid enough to eat a sufficient quantity of the fine green leaves, of course.

As he looked up, a large drip of water landed on his lips. *You will have to try harder than that*, he thought to himself. The man pulled out a once crisp and pristine white cotton handkerchief and wiped his mouth. He wasn't about to test any theories about yew-tree poison. The persistent rain had penetrated through to his pockets, making the handkerchief damp.

A short, gravelled path wound to the right and away from the gate before curving back to the church entrance. Looking to the south east from the gate, a group of mourners were visible between ancient lichen-covered gravestones. The group huddled around a coffin that was about to be lowered into the thawed and sodden earth. The sky, a wash of black and grey fast-moving clouds, darkened further, threatening to contribute sleet and snow to the already miserable occasion, though its appearance was doubtful. A thaw had finally set in, following the freezing winter of 1962 and into 1963, but no one had told the snow showers that still occasionally fell over north Norfolk. A forecast of more heavy rain added to the continuing meteorological misery of England's eastern counties.

Most of the attendees at the grave were formally dressed in the uniform black of mourners. The man standing outside the gate wondered how many of them believed in God, and he included the minister in his thoughts. He noticed that the only person dressed differently was an attractive woman who had arrived late to the funeral. Her red miniskirt and short fur coat with white knee-high boots contrasted sharply with the clothes worn by the other mourners, but no one seemed to notice. She struggled to control her fashionable clear plastic umbrella as the wind mischievously sent gusts to try and wrest it from her. The other mourners had given up the struggle to use their own umbrellas and stood closely together as if they were a herd of animals trying to block out the worst of the wind and rain.

The man pulled out a small pair of service binoculars from inside his mackintosh and carefully scanned the faces of each mourner. Lastly, he looked at the woman doing battle with the wind-buffeted plastic umbrella. She wiped her eyes with a tiny red handkerchief as the coffin was lowered into the grave. A few moments after it disappeared into the ground, she left the group and headed in his direction. He returned the binoculars to the pocket of his mackintosh and as the woman brushed past him at the gate, she glanced up at him in a way that was hopeful. The instant disappointment that he was not the man she was expecting clearly showed on her face.

The man turned and continued to watch where she went. His unblinking eyes followed her as she walked around the village pond to the nearby public house. She unlocked the front door to the pub before disappearing inside.

Wesley assumed, correctly, that the woman had been hoping he was Mike Armstrong. In fact, the only reason for Wesley being present on the day of Simone Powell's funeral was the remote chance that Armstrong might foolishly turn up to pay his last respects. Clearly this was not to be, so another day had been wasted. *Chasing shadows*, Wesley thought to himself. He had unfinished business with Armstrong and the worm of frustration about this constantly found its way into his consciousness. Wherever Armstrong was, and whatever he was doing, there would come a time when the man would make an error; a tiny slip that would expose both himself and the Kembrey woman, who had apparently run off with him. Wesley hoped the woman would be Armstrong's undoing, just as Simone Powell had almost been only the month before.

* * *

Canute Simpson stood in his black robes, watching the coffin settling into the ground in front of him. He always knew that Simone could never rest in her war against the residue of Nazi scum that still lurked in some of Europe's darkest corners. He also knew this crusade would be the death of her, and that even someone like Mike Armstrong was unable to cure her dangerous fanaticism. Canute, however, had to admit that Simone had been right all along about that lunatic, Mazarin. Despite the fact the man was now dead, Canute felt the world remained neither a safer nor a better place as a result. Certainly not with men like Wesley Macdonald acting as gamekeeper for world peace and security.

The action of Wesley wiping his face with his white handkerchief caught Canute's eye. The outline of the figure standing between the yew trees told him straight away that an unwelcome visitor was keeping his jaundiced eye on proceedings.

Reverend Simpson completed his sad duties, unperturbed by the presence of an unknown figure in the church grounds. Like Julie Stenson, who had left the service early and passed right by

Wesley, Canute, just for a split second, hoped it might be Mike Armstrong standing at the gate. Surely Wesley was too cold and ruthless to attend Simone's funeral for personal reasons, even though she acted as his agent… But it would make sense for the man to be hoping to catch Mike Armstrong appearing unannounced, and yet he had been disappointed. *Good*, thought Canute.

* * *

The funeral service ended, and the group of mourners slowly threaded their way over the rain-soaked grass between the gravestones in Wesley's direction. He turned on his heel and walked back to a large black car parked nearby. The Humber Sceptre saloon was brand new and on loan to Wesley's department for testing ahead of its official launch later that year. He preferred using a Jaguar, but his department was under financial scrutiny once more and he'd been told he had to make do.

The Humber had been fitted with a VHF radio transmitter by his technical department, and once back inside the car he sent a message to his watchers, who were scattered around the vicinity of the churchyard. They were ordered to regroup with him, and minutes later several grim-faced men formed up beside the Humber. Wesley partially wound down his rain-spattered window and gave his orders. One man was sent to maintain surveillance on Simone's grave whilst the others were redeployed around the three small roads that crossed through Little Stratton village. There was no chance anyone could enter or exit without being seen.

The mourners followed in Julie Stenson's footsteps back to her pub, glancing in curiosity at the black car parked at the side of the road. The only person who recognised the man inside it was Canute. Walking past, he glared at Wesley who looked back at him, his face made unreadable by the distortions of the heavy rain running down the glass.

Wesley wondered what ungodly thoughts might be running through Canute's mind. He also wondered how a killer of men such as him seemed to think he stood on the moral high ground in comparison to Wesley himself. He knew this man of the cloth had once been a killer, and no amount of dog collar could erase that fact.

Wesley regarded Canute as a self-righteous hypocrite who was responsible for the deaths of many men and women during the war. Putting on a cleric's robes had not miraculously provided him with redemption. Instead, the man's hypocrisy justified everything Wesley was doing to maintain the status quo in the brave new world in which they found themselves.

There was nothing Canute could gain from blaming Wesley for the death of Simone. She had rewritten her role in a clearly set-out plan and went off on a tangent that got her killed. It was her own foolishness, not his orders, that led to her death. Remorse was a wasted emotion as far as Wesley was concerned. He believed the man who should carry the guilt for Simone's death was Canute.

* * *

Julie Stenson had rushed away from the funeral to make sure all the final arrangements were in place for the wake, which was being held at the Stratton Arms pub. Cold cuts of meat, cheeses, sandwiches, flans and simple canapés crowded platters set out on the trestle tables around the walls of the bar area. Pristine white cotton sheets doubled as tablecloths for the occasion. She hoped the wake would be an occasion to drown mourners' sorrows in a prelude to celebrating the life and times of Simone.

For Julie, the food was almost a secondary issue. She continued to wait, in excited anticipation, for the return of Mike Armstrong. She was positive he hadn't run off with Libby Kembrey, as the local rumour mill suggested. Her guess was that the woman had finally taken her priggish self away to London, leaving her husband Dicky all the happier for her departure. She was sure that Dicky, like Mike, had been sweet on Simone. Any connection with Libby just had to be nonsense.

The whole business of Simone's death had stimulated Julie's mind considerably. Simone getting caught up in the big military exercise at the old airbase was incredibly bad luck. How she had been killed in such a bad car accident had not been fully explained, and nor had Mike's abrupt disappearance. Julie must have driven past his house a dozen times to see if his car had moved, but there had been no sign of him. She had, however, encountered Canute Simpson visiting the house and had asked him if everything was all right. He'd told her he was keeping an eye on the place until Mike returned. After that encounter, she noticed that Mike's car disappeared, but Canute said he had no idea where it was. Julie surmised that Mike had fled, but why? She was determined to hang on to every word spoken that night in her pub, to try to find out what really happened at the airbase, and to Simone and Mike.

Dicky Kembrey entered the pub first. He looked troubled and said very little. He was followed in by the usual gang of friends that made up Simone's 'Masters of the Chandelle' gang. They stood in small clusters, saying very little before Canute arrived through the door last, looking unusually angry.

Subdued conversation continued at a trickle before Dicky gave the first toast in honour of Simone. As the evening wore on, the alcohol seemed to lift everyone's spirits and the group ate the food set out on the trestle tables. Julie was surprised that no one talked of Mike, or how and why he had disappeared. Dicky soon got through a large amount of whisky but made no mention of Mike or Libby either. This intrigued Julie greatly, but by the end of the night she knew no more than before.

Wesley was unable to infiltrate either himself or his men into the pub as Julie had closed it for the wake, as a private event only for those who had attended the funeral. In any case, he would have stood out as a stranger, as would his men. Instead, Wesley and his men maintained a cold and very wet vigil in and around the village.

Well after midnight, the mourners began to stumble out of the pub and head back to their homes. Only Canute and Dicky were left inside, propping up the bar. A bottle of Laphroaig whisky sat between them on the counter and each man filled the other's glass as it emptied. Julie sat on a stool behind the bar, pretending to snooze as she listened intently to their conversation. She was sure that now was the time to hear something interesting being said.

'How are you getting on, Dicky?' asked Canute.

'Oh, just fine. I have a buyer for the estate and will move into my cottage just outside Binham. The buyer wants me to stay on as the estate manager.'

'That's not what I meant,' replied Canute quietly.

'Oh, you mean Libby... Well, I'm sure she will get in touch when she's ready,' said Dicky, appearing to play down the situation.

'You don't seem very worried. She is your missing wife, after all,' said Canute, trying to get some idea of how Dicky was really feeling.

'I think we have been "missing" each other for some time, Canute. There is nothing going on that I wasn't expecting,' said Dicky, evading the questions as best as he could.

Canute remained unconvinced. Family privacy was one thing but sweeping such a matter under the carpet solved nothing. He could only guess at what Dicky knew or surmised regarding the disappearance of his wife. Canute's dilemma was whether to tell Dicky the truth. He guessed that his friend had a fair idea about Libby and Mike and that he wanted to keep the affair private. As Canute had no idea where the pair were, he decided not to throw petrol on to the dying embers of Dicky's collapsed marriage.

Once the whisky bottle was empty the two men said goodnight to an apparently sleepy Julie. Canute said he would be round in the morning to settle the bar bill. Dicky mumbled something similar, but Julie knew he hadn't the funds to do so. The men went on their way, leaving a disappointed Julie bereft of valuable gossip.

* * *

Wesley lay across the back seat of the Humber, wrapped up in a travel rug. He was stiff, totally uncomfortable and freezing cold. The rain hammering down on the roof of the car removed any last vestige of meaningful sleep. His Webley service revolver lay in a footwell next to the radio transmitter handset. A voice crackled through the speaker, announcing that the last two mourners were heading home. Wesley gave orders for both men to be followed and each of their houses watched for an hour. If nothing happened after that time, the men were to stand down and make ready to return to London.

Two hours later, a small convoy of cars formed up in front of Little Stratton church then moved off, heading south. Wesley sat in the lead car with its heater on full. Torrential rain crashed constantly over the windscreen, obliterating the view ahead in between the sweeps made by the overworked wipers.

His mind was elsewhere as he went over recent events. The cause of Simone Powell's death had been portrayed as a car accident involving a military truck taking part in a snap military exercise at the old RAF base. Even the helicopters destroyed near Sandringham were covered with the same cloak of military deception. The only questions that remained for Wesley were how Mike Armstrong managed to escape from the base unseen, whether anyone helped him, and where he was now. Wesley believed the missing wife, Libby Kembrey, to be Mike's willing accomplice. With all these thoughts spinning around in his head, Wesley finally drifted off to sleep.

* * *

Once Canute Simpson arrived back at his house he went to the sitting room and stoked up the remains of the log fire he had set hours before. Instead of retiring to bed, he sat in front of the blazing warmth and waited. He, like others that night, had hoped to see the return of Mike Armstrong. But Canute knew that Mike would never turn up in broad daylight in case he was apprehended by the police – or Wesley. Either way, Mike would have been spirited away to who-knows-where. His return also depended on whether he was fit enough to travel. The last time Canute had seen him with Libby, as they boarded a train at Peterborough station, Mike had been in a rough state. There was no mention of either of them in the newspapers or on the radio, so he guessed the same could be said of the television news. The positive side to this was that no one could force Canute to divulge information he did not have.

From then on, Canute waited each evening – and late into the night – for the return of Mike Armstrong. He supposed Mike would allow enough time for Wesley and his watchers to tire of waiting for him to show up. He would want to know from Canute if Simone had been cremated or buried, and if it was the latter, where she had been laid to rest. Mike would not write or telephone because of the possibility of interception by Wesley.

By the time spring had passed by, no contact had been made; even Canute finally admitted to himself that Mike was not going to return after all.

Wesley remained in London. He believed that his chance to catch up with Mike Armstrong would occur sooner or later.

3
CANADIAN RETREAT

Eagle Lake lay still, a dark featureless expanse mirroring the pre-dawn Canadian sky. No local knew how deep its waters went and none trusted the deceptive cold water where it quickly ran off from the shallows on the shore side. The same could be said of the many large lakes peppering the granite bedrock and pine landscape around Haliburton, Ontario. Geographically speaking, the area was close to Toronto but was a death trap to anyone careless enough to think they were safely close to civilisation. It was all too easy to set off unprepared into the huge green maze of firs, black spruce, pine and maple – only to get lost, possibly for good.

The north shore rose steeply from the lake, comprising of numerous rocky outcrops with boulders before taking the form of small cliffs where shrubs and young trees desperately held on for life. These features remained in semi-darkness until the June sun climbed high enough to warm the meadowsweet shrubs and red raspberry that attracted bees and butterflies in their droves.

A particularly large outcrop of rock provided the base for a large wooden chalet that was used as a vacation home. The apex of the steep sloping roof towered far above the water-line of the lake, the wood-tiled tip trying to rival the tops of the nearby pine trees. The structure's high, south-facing glazed frontage always caught the first rays of sun and gently heated the rooms within. Below the living area a large enclosed storage area housed a multitude of outdoor equipment, canoes, skis and a skidoo.

Access to this part of the house could only be made through secured external double doors on one side of the area.

The current guests had added a large metal strongbox, which was fixed to the concrete floor and kept secure with an imposing padlock. Another small version of the strongbox was fixed to the granite that made up part of the wall of the storage area. This was also secured with an expensive padlock.

The chalet's interior consisted of a huge living area all on one floor, with stripped pine dominating the décor throughout. The open-plan lounge, kitchen and dining area merged into one. A modern shower and toilet were in a separate box extension at the back of the building. Carefully planted grey dogwood shrubs, displaying a mass of white flower clusters and berries that distracted the eye, hid the awkwardness of the arrangement. A mezzanine floor formed the sleeping area in lieu of an actual bedroom. On the eastern side of the ground floor was a large open fireplace made of stone and full of cut logs, ready to be lit. It was topped by a brushed steel canopy and a metal flue that projected through the sloped ceiling.

A parking area at the rear of the building led to the end of an unmetalled track, winding its way through the trees to a small highway three miles distant. A brand new pale blue Jeep Wagoneer displaying registration plates embossed with white numbers on a black background was parked to one side of the rudimentary clearing. The vehicle served to indicate to locals that its owners were visitors up from Toronto on vacation, and its four-wheel drive capability provided a sensible means for getting out along the track back to civilisation.

As the sun slowly began to pierce the tree-line on the south side of Eagle Lake, its rays illuminated the mezzanine floor of the chalet, a large bed, and its two occupants. The gently rising light level woke the man, and he carefully stepped out from under the sheets. His warm naked body had lost the heavy bruising and cuts it had received a few months before, back in England. As soon as he had been able to, Mike Armstrong began exercising hard to regain his physical fitness. He quietly dressed in running shorts, vest and athletic shoes before making his way outside into the beautiful morning coolness of the forest.

Running at a steady pace and controlling his breathing, he followed the track that led away from the chalet. Small clouds of brown dust exploded from beneath his footfalls as he gradually increased his speed. As Mike followed the undulating track along its six-mile distance, he let his mind wander whilst he ran. Thoughts of his recent past flowed by and he wondered where his future would take him next. He also thought about whether Libby was part of that future; he dearly hoped so.

Despite the apparent emptiness and remoteness of the forest, Mike felt safe and secure here. He had been told that the timber wolves kept away from the encroachment of humans, making it very unlikely he would encounter any such creature. There was more likelihood of encountering a black bear or a moose, but the noise of his running hopefully ensured these animals would hear him coming and stay out of the way. Predators of the human kind were the real concern to him, especially the kind he had left behind in England.

Mike raced along the final mile of the return leg of the track, finishing back in the chalet car park. With his head held high, he leant with his back against the Jeep as his heart hammered angrily, protesting at its rough treatment. Within a minute his heart rate had returned to normal and he breathed normally. Each day of exercise had seen his recovery rate improve in leaps and bounds.

He ambled back inside the chalet and downed a pint of cool water straight from the refrigerator. Twenty minutes later, he sat outside on the wooden veranda after having showered and shaved. He wore a long-sleeved olive-coloured bush shirt and matching trousers.

Shortly afterwards, and naked under the cream cotton sheet she had wrapped around herself, Libby Kembrey made her way carefully down the steps from the mezzanine floor. She crossed the large rug-strewn floor and exited through the single glazed door that led out to the veranda. The sun had already reached the area where Mike sat with his eyes closed. He was listening to the whisper of the surrounding trees and soothing birdsong.

She kissed him gently on the lips before sitting in his lap. He took her in his arms and held her closely. Still not fully awake, she nestled against him and closed her eyes once more.

Using their assumed identities, Mike and Libby had travelled overland from Zurich, Switzerland to Rome, Italy three months before. They hoped that travelling by train rather than by air would be more discreet, making them a very small needle in the global haystack. The account at the Banca Albani in central Rome had proven to be as financially well stocked as the Odermatt in Zurich. From Rome, they transferred on to a passenger ship heading for Cape Town, South Africa and then onwards to Sydney, Australia. Posing as the now-dead Victor Mazarin, Mike discovered that banks in both these cities also contained huge cash deposits. Mazarin had unintentionally made Mike and Libby life-long millionaires. This also proved true at the Toronto Trust Bank, from which Mike withdrew sufficient cash to fund their time spent in Canada.

After some time, Libby roused herself and without a word stood up and walked to a set of wooden steps leading off from the veranda. She continued down a steep and roughly finished path to a wooden jetty directly below the chalet. She seemed unaware of the stony ground beneath her bare feet. Mike followed her down without saying a word.

As Libby neared the end of the jetty she dropped the sheet. With her porcelain white skin exposed to the early morning coolness, she took a few more steps until she stood at the end of the jetty. Her dive into the water was perfect, causing only a few ripples that dissipated almost immediately. Mike watched her seemingly translucent body slip through the water. Eventually, she surfaced and struck out in strong regular strokes. Her style was relaxed, but this impression was deceptive as she was soon quite far from the water's edge.

Mike jumped into a rowing boat that was tethered to the jetty. Once the boat was loosed, he set the oars and began to pursue Libby. She maintained her focus on swimming as if Mike didn't exist and continued ever forward out into the deep water. His concern was that the cold water might catch her out and that she might get into difficulties far from shore. Since they had first arrived here he had insisted he followed closely in the rowing boat whenever she swam.

As a child on holiday in Scotland, Libby used to go skinny-dipping in the local loch. Her parents had strongly disapproved but were unable to stop her sneaking off early every morning. It was by accident that she found long-distance swimming gave her a calming focus, and she was glad to be able to indulge herself in such a positive way.

Mike had noticed how much more relaxed Libby had become after taking up her swimming once more. Although she had no weight to lose, her muscles had become more defined, emphasising the lines of her figure even more; this was especially noticeable when she was naked.

A lone pine stood out on a promontory to the north of them and marked the point where Libby turned to swim back to the jetty. They had purchased a detailed map of the local area and used it to identify a point almost exactly one mile from the chalet. Libby upended herself and dived deep before turning around underwater and surfacing to start the completion of the home stretch. She had told Mike the water was so dark she was unable to see the lake bed far below her.

Libby swam back towards the jetty at the same pace, with Mike following her in the rowing boat only yards behind. The jetty had no steps, so Libby hauled herself up as elegantly and demurely as she could. As she did so she glanced at Mike, who was enjoying her moment of exposure. She gave him a look as if to say she would like him to do better in the circumstances. The previously discarded bedsheet was picked up and wrapped around her body. Mike smiled and wondered how he could have dismissed her as a frumpy bore when he first meeting her. Libby headed back up to the chalet to shower and dress before having breakfast.

When Libby reappeared, she was wearing an olive-green long-sleeved poplin shirt and matching full-length trousers that were obviously cut for a man rather than a woman. The owner of the hunting shop where they had bought the clothes had done his best to accommodate her, but said he seldom had any need to stock ladies' sizes. She had to roll up the sleeves of the shirt, while the trouser legs had been shortened by a local seamstress. Her feet remained bare and her hair, still damp, was tied back in a business-like ponytail. She would put on her thick socks and hiking boots later when they headed out into the forest.

Mike had prepared bacon, scrambled eggs and what the Canadians called 'toast'. He found the toast a little too crunchy compared to English toast. A small bottle of local maple syrup also sat on the side, to add sweetness to the crisped bacon. He fetched out a jug of freshly squeezed orange juice from the refrigerator and placed it on the small Formica-topped breakfast table.

He had taken the precaution of bringing roasted coffee beans with him as the pair travelled across the world from

Rome. After checking out the coffee grinder he found at the chalet, he was pleased to find it was a burr grinder, so he knew the beans would be ground evenly. Rather than using the percolator that was also provided in the chalet, Mike had purchased a French press whilst on a visit to Toronto. In both his and Libby's opinion, the percolator only served to dull the rich flavours of the coffee. They both wished that Mike had brought more of the Italian coffee beans with him, as neither had found any they liked locally.

Libby sat down opposite Mike, who poured her a glass of orange juice before joining her at the table. She rested her feet on top of his and studied his face. They were spending twenty-four hours a day with each other and had gotten to the point where talking was often unnecessary. The small talk had been taken over by an intimacy that extended far beyond the bedroom. The touches and gestures of the two made-for-each-other lovers expressed far more than words or any idea of superficial romantic togetherness. Mike thought it was something akin to the relationship of Bonnie and Clyde, or Edward and Mrs Simpson, but Libby did not care for such comparisons.

'What's on your mind?' she asked, gently rubbing her feet on his as she held him in her gaze.

He stared back into her ever-challenging dark brown eyes, which he had so easily come to love.

'I want to return to Norfolk. To find out about Simone. I have no idea what was done with her body – buried, cremated or what. I want to know,' he said earnestly.

Libby was now confident enough in their love not to feel threatened by this. She was more worried about Mike being caught by Wesley, someone she had reason to fear.

'Do you really have to go? You know that awful man Wesley or the police will want to get their hands on you,' she said, trying to place doubt in his mind about returning to England.

'I want to go, but I have to be sure our future is not going to be wrecked by any possible return,' he replied.

'Perhaps you ought to wait a while longer – make them think you're never going to go back,' she offered.

'Perhaps.' Mike knew Libby was right, and he tried to push the thought away from his immediate consciousness. They continued their breakfast in a comfortable silence, leaving Libby to wonder when he would raise the subject again.

Mike used some more of the dwindling supply of coffee beans to make up a flask of coffee they could share later when they were deep in the forest. Libby prepared some ham sandwiches then packed them in a knapsack alongside the flask of coffee, some apples and the boxes of ammunition they would need that day. She had noticed that her clothes matched those worn by Mike, and she could not help but find this slightly twee and amusing. The reality was that it helped to keep the bloodthirsty midges and ticks at bay as they moved through the undergrowth of the forest.

They pulled on their walking socks and boots then made their way down to the strongboxes secured to the floor of the storeroom beneath the chalet. There was no need to lock the chalet doors, as the only possible intruders were insects and raccoons. They did, however, check that no windows were left open.

Mike unlocked the padlock securing the larger of the two strongboxes and lifted the lid. Inside lay two olive-coloured canvas gun slips. Each slip contained a .270 Winchester Model 70 sporting rifle, zeroed using open iron sights. Mike preferred a 26-inch barrel, whilst Libby opted for the 24-inch version. The gun slips were carefully lifted out and placed to one side and the strongbox was padlocked once more.

The second, smaller box was opened; it contained two 9mm Smith and Wesson Model 39 automatic pistols. These were supplied from the same gun dealer as the rifles, prompting the owner to ask if Mike and his 'good lady' also drove his-and-her cars. Libby had not been amused.

The last weapon was kept in a zipped canvas bag and was not bought from the local gun dealer. Mike, armed with a bag full of US dollars as well as a pistol, had found a supplier in the Toronto underworld to provide an Uzi 9mm sub-machine gun. Mike wanted to extend Libby's experience of shooting to include pistols and small automatic weapons. Although unsurprised, he was quietly satisfied to find that she took just as easily to firing a pistol and sub-machine gun as she did to hunting rifles.

The maps they bought served another purpose in addition to finding a distance point for Libby's swim. Mike used them to assess where it would be possible to practise firing their recently acquired weapons. Checking a map, he had found a tiny valley about one third of a mile long, running north to south. The valley, according to the map, appeared to have a box-shaped cliff at its northernmost end, providing a natural backstop for bullets where it rose abruptly from the valley floor.

The valley was miles from any local road or habitation, so they could shoot unseen although perhaps not unheard by hikers. Two weeks previously they had hiked for three hours to the southern end of the valley. The line of sight for shooting extended along the whole of the valley, so Mike knew they had found the best location. Each day after that the pair had returned and built rudimentary targets on which to practise their shooting skills. Both Mike and Libby benefited from making the daily trek to and from the valley as they improved their physical fitness. They also became increasingly proficient in using the different firearms.

Mike carried the pistols and the Uzi in a large army surplus backpack. He also carried extra water for the day, as well as a basic first-aid kit. Each carried their own rifle, loaded and ready for use in case they encountered any troublesome wildlife. Libby led the way, as Mike wanted to her to practise her navigation skills. She found this irritating, but as Mike explained, if something were to happen to him then she needed to know how to get herself back to safety.

After eight long and sweat-soaked hours, they arrived back at the chalet. At Mike's insistence, the weapons were immediately cleaned, oiled and returned to the strongboxes before the two of them showered and ate.

Now that Mike was back to full fitness, he had decided that it *was* time for him to visit Norfolk for the last time. Libby knew this time would eventually come and sensed his need to return to Little Stratton. It came as no surprise to her that evening as he broached the subject once more. His plan was to cross the US border and drive to New York, where they could get a flight to Paris. Libby was to stay there whilst he travelled to London by train and ferry. Once in England, he would hire a car to allow him to get to and from Norfolk. Afterwards he would return to Paris, using the same route in reverse. Libby's instincts told her that Mike's plan of action was risky, but she chose to remain silent.

4
DOUBLE WHISKY

Canute Simpson's hopes of seeing Mike again had long faded away by the end of June that year. The weather over the past month had been mediocre at best and this reflected in his mood; dull and damp. It was night-time now, and a gale hammered at the rectory windows, keeping him awake. There hadn't been a day when he didn't wonder about the whereabouts of Mike and Libby. If the pair had been caught there was no doubt in his mind that Wesley would be unable to resist sending a gloating message to say so.

Instead of trying to get some sleep, Canute climbed out of bed and went downstairs. A large wall-mounted pendulum clock ticked away, indicating that the time was twenty minutes past midnight as he entered the kitchen to make himself a mug of cocoa. He opened a packet of chocolate-covered ginger biscuits and took out two of them to eat with his drink. When the drink was ready he sat down at the small wooden kitchen table before taking a sip of the cocoa. He absentmindedly bit into one of the biscuits, almost lost within his huge hand.

'Mind if I have one?' asked a man's voice from behind him. Canute jumped out of his chair, uttering irreligious expletives. As he rounded on the night-time intruder his chair went flying across the kitchen.

'Mike! Thank God you're alive! This is marvellous, I had given up hope of ever seeing you again,' he said with great feeling.

Mike collected the knocked-over chair and put it back in its place. Canute was looking over Mike's shoulder to see if he had brought Libby.

'Libby is elsewhere, Canute. She's safe and you don't need to know more than that.'

Canute nodded, understanding the situation at once. He then looked relieved and concerned at the same time before the moment passed and he took Mike's hand with a tight grasp. His face suddenly lit up as if something had just come to mind.

'Wait here,' he said with a broad grin on his face, before disappearing from the kitchen. His bear-like figure filled the doorway as he bowled back through, carrying an unopened bottle of scotch whisky and two glasses.

'Laphroaig – I kept it safe for when you returned,' he said, beaming.

Mike smiled back momentarily and sat down at the table. He realised his visit would take longer than he'd planned.

'Take off that wet coat and hang it up over there. We need to talk,' said Canute.

'This is only a flying visit, Canute, and I intend it to be my last. I came to pay my last respects to Simone. It was good to see you had her buried in the village churchyard,' said Mike.

'Indeed, so you have already been to her grave?' asked Canute, searching Mike's face to try and discern his emotions.

'Yes, it was not too difficult to find despite this awful weather making things so dark and miserable.'

'Least I could do for her. A most sad day, made worse by Wesley and his men hanging around to see if you would turn up for her funeral.'

Mike was unsurprised to hear this and explained that it was why he had stayed away for so long. By chance, he had used the bad weather to his advantage. It was almost impossible for Wesley to maintain any credible surveillance on the village. In any case, Mike was sure that Wesley had realised he was never going to catch him in Little Stratton. Canute had to agree, as he too had almost given up on seeing Mike again.

Canute poured out two large shots of the whisky and the men toasted Simone for the final time. Rather than ask Mike questions he wouldn't answer, Canute focused on events since he had left. He told Mike that Simone had died intestate. Her house and its contents had been auctioned off at unseemly speed, with the proceeds going to the state as she had no next of kin. This all took place so very quickly that Canute suspected Wesley was pulling some strings to close off the Mazarin affair for good.

The very same thing had happened to Mike's house, and his car. Canute had tried to find out what was going on, but someone – Wesley again, he surmised – had a court order put in place. It was alleged that both Mike's house and car had been bought with the proceeds of crime. The rector's voice trailed off at that point, indicating that he was awaiting a response.

Mike eyed the canny man-mountain sat opposite him. Whisky in hand, Canute wore a tatty tartan dressing gown that strained to cover his large and muscular frame. Blue-striped flannel pyjamas, fraying at the edges, were visible poking out at the extremities of the arms, neck and legs. A huge pair of wine-coloured corduroy slippers covered his firmly planted feet. Mike took a sip of the whisky to give himself a little time to decide how much he was going to say.

'The money I stole from banks was used to finance the purchase of a house. It allowed me to run a small business buying and selling antiques. My old house became a restoration and refurbishment project, to sell when the time came. The sale of the house and the antiques paid for my new house in Little Stratton,' explained Mike.

'You must have stolen a lot of money,' said Canute, pushing Mike to divulge more than he might like.

'The real fortune came from selling the house and the antiques,' responded Mike, neatly evading the question. He hoped his friend would drop the subject, but the rector persisted.

'So how do you and Libby keep heart and soul together? Aren't Libby's expensive expectations difficult to meet?' asked Canute.

Mike smiled to himself; Canute knew the old Libby so well. The fact was, the boredom and frustration that had filled her previous life had evaporated. Canute could not be told that the pair were now as rich as any of the 'jet set' he read about in the newspapers. Mike now found it ironic that any careless or ostentatious display of this wealth might attract the attention of the authorities. All the same, he and Libby lived very well, and she had accepted the situation without argument.

'Everything I've told you is probably well known to Wesley already. If I tell you too much, our future will be compromised,' said Mike, trying to close the subject once more.

Canute heard the hard edge growing in Mike's voice. He realised that if his friend told him too much, there was a danger that Canute himself may be forced to give information to Wesley, who would use it to try to trap Mike. It was better not to know how they were able to make ends meet. Canute decided to change tack and addressed a more pastoral issue.

'Libby is still married to Dicky, you know, even if she is not a part of his life any more,' said Canute in an even tone.

Mike was relieved that the rector had changed the subject. He didn't hesitate to answer him fully and truthfully.

'We both know the marriage was really a financial arrangement that damaged both Dicky and Libby. Dicky really wanted to marry Simone if given the chance,' Mike said with a defensive undertone.

Canute knew he was not lying. Following Libby's disappearance, Dicky had busied himself in other matters. He wasted no time selling his farm and estate, even though it was Libby's family money that had kept them both going. Nor had he hesitated in moving out to the house outside the village, where he stored all his family furniture and personal belongings. Dicky had moved on with the certainty that Libby had gone for good. In some ways, Mike felt relieved that Dicky had quickly moved on to a new chapter in his life. Canute decided to let the matter go; nothing was going to change.

Switching the subject once more, Canute spoke again about the auctioning of Mike's car. According to Canute, the high bidder at the auction for the Maserati was a shifty-looking character who wore a trilby hat and a sheepskin driving coat.
'From Peterborough,' he added, somewhat disparagingly. 'The Maserati will be wasted on him. He bought your car for a song,' he growled.

'I could never have kept it anyway,' replied Mike, knowing that driving the car would inevitably get him arrested and delivered into Wesley's clutches. 'What about Simone's Jensen?' he asked casually, glad to be on safer grounds of discussion with the wily rector. Canute's eyes sparkled mischievously.

'Ah, bought at the same auction by a real rogue,' he said, unable to hold back the broadest of smiles.

'You outbid the car dealer from Peterborough?' asked Mike, unsurprised. Canute looked a little disappointed that Mike had guessed straight away what had happened.

'Well, yes, I just kept outbidding him. He got very annoyed with me,' said Canute, with the tiniest hint of satisfaction laced with a dash of cruelty. Mike asked what he would do with the car and Canute admitted he had no idea. The thought of someone else mistreating such a thoroughbred had appalled Canute; he preferred not to admit that he, along with Dicky, had not yet got over the loss of Simone. It had crossed his mind that Mike might like to have the Jensen, but it appeared the circumstances were against that.

'Make sure you keep the thing in good order,' said Mike, and the rector promised he would do his best. This pleased Mike, as he knew that meant the car would be in pristine condition at least for the time Canute had it in his possession.

'Well, this it. I have paid my respects to Simone and I have to say goodbye to you for the last time,' said Mike, feeling more downhearted than he had expected. He stood up and offered his hand to Canute, who promptly ignored Mike's little speech and poured another large slug of whisky.

'Surely you have a few more minutes, Mike.'

This was a statement rather than a question. Mike sat down, guessing Canute had one or two more things to say.

Canute was keen to make the goodbye last until he finished what needed to be said.

'As long as Wesley breathes, he will never give up on finding you. For all you know, he could be waiting for you outside my house right now. How well have you covered your tracks?' he asked with a serious face.

'Well enough,' Mike replied. 'It has been months, and there has been nothing to suggest that Libby and I are in danger. No suspect encounters. Not a shred of interest from the authorities. The man can't possibly have the time, resources or influence to continue to hunt a mere bank-robber suspect on the run.'

'Mike, on paper you might be a criminal on the run, but if you talk about what happened here you will become a huge political liability. That is the prime reason for him to keep coming after you. You must not underestimate your importance. All he is doing is waiting for your first slip,' said Canute, more worried than ever.

'Why would I be so stupid to talk to anyone about Mazarin?' asked Mike.

'Because sooner or later you will run out of money. You know all your assets have been auctioned off.'

'Trust me, Canute, I won't need to run my mouth off to anyone for money,' said Mike.

'So, you are well looked-after financially?' asked Canute, again fishing for information. Mike could see where the conversation was going.

'Libby and I are never going to have to worry about money again,' he said smoothly, trying to reassure his friend without giving too much away.

'But Wesley doesn't know that. He will not take a risk even if he did,' Canute argued.

'Then I'm on his hit-list until either I'm dead or he is. There is nothing more to be done about it,' Mike said, trying to end the line of discussion.

Canute knew that Mike was right. Dead men cannot divulge their secrets, and Wesley had to be sure Mike wouldn't talk. There was a short silence before Mike spoke first.

'Look, Canute, I know you mean well but we have lived flawed lives and we survive through compromise. Thanks for the warning – you are right, Wesley will come after me to make sure I won't talk. But I am going to make some arrangements that will make sure he leaves us alone, you included,' said Mike firmly.

'You can do that?' asked Canute.

'Wesley can't afford word getting out to the press, so that is exactly what I can threaten. If anything happens to me, Libby or yourself, the papers are going be the first to know. Trust me on this,' said Mike firmly.

Canute decided to let the matter rest. The two men said their goodbyes as Mike made it clear once more that he had no intention of making any further visits to Little Stratton.

Once the pair shook hands for a final time, Mike put on his waterproof coat and took a black commando cap from one of the pockets. He pulled the woollen hat down over his ears and flipped up the collar of his coat. Before Mike stepped out into the bleak rain- and wind-strewn night, Canute switched off the kitchen light to minimise the chances of his friend being seen leaving the rectory.

Unseen rain clouds rampaged high above the Norfolk landscape as Mike began the long walk back to the rental car he had hidden well away from the village. His legs felt leaden with the effect of the whisky and his heart was heavy from having to say farewell to a good friend. His trousers were soon soaking wet as he trudged along tracks muddied by tractors moving between fields and roads. He remained confident that no one had seen him entering or leaving Canute's house and felt he had little need to move covertly across the land any more.

Eventually Mike reached the heathland where he had parked the car earlier that night. He had found some large gorse bushes that provided a spiky patch of cover to reverse behind. Once back at the car, he unlocked the boot and pulled out a bag that contained some spare clothing. After changing into dry trousers, socks and driving shoes, he climbed on to the back seat and wrapped a car blanket around himself. He needed to get a few hours' sleep before making his way back to London.

* * *

When Mike awoke the rain and wind had blown out into the North Sea, leaving the countryside smelling fresh and damp. He unwrapped himself from the blanket and stepped out of the car into the early-morning fresh air. The sun, unfettered by clouds, was already warming his exposed skin. He felt good to be alive. Saying goodbye to Canute was the final act to end the trauma of a few months earlier. He had seen Simone's final resting place and now he felt able to move on from the recent past.

After a short walk around the heath to get his blood flowing, and to check he was not being observed, Mike returned to the car. He set off on a circuitous route back to London, all the time looking for anything that might indicate he was being followed. A few uneventful hours later, Mike was in north London and returning the rental car. He took a taxi to Finchley Central and travelled on the Underground to Oxford Circus before disappearing into the crowds of shoppers on Oxford Street. He headed west towards Hyde Park to kill time until the evening. He constantly kept on the move, only too aware that he was probably perilously close to where Wesley was based.

As early evening approached, Mike crisscrossed the streets of Belgravia, heading for Victoria station. His evening meal was taken at a small restaurant near the station before he found the nearest bar in which to pass the final hour. Time slowly ebbed away until the point was reached when he returned to a left-luggage locker at the station. Inside the locker was a smart green leather suitcase. Taking it out, he then made his way to platform 2 to board the Night Ferry to Paris, which was due to depart at nine o'clock. With customs checks complete, the train departed on time for Dover. Drifting in and out of sleep, Mike travelled comfortably in a First Class sleeping car. First Class passengers were allowed to remain in their carriage and avoid having to walk on and off the ferry at either Dover or Calais.

The next morning at nine thirty, and half an hour later than scheduled, the train arrived at the Gare du Nord, Paris. Mike stepped down from his carriage wearing fresh clothes taken from a small brown leather suitcase that had been concealed within the larger green leather case. The green case lay discarded in the sleeping car with the clothes he had worn in England. Instead of breakfasting on the train, he was looking forward to eating in Paris. He jumped into the first taxi waiting in the queue outside the station and asked to be taken to the Hotel Picard on the Rue de Berri, just off the Avenue de Champs-Élysées. As soon as the taxi was out of sight, Mike walked away from the hotel and deposited the now-empty suitcase in a dustbin.

The dry continental heat began to warm his bones after the largely damp trip to England. Mike took an indirect route to the Hotel George V on the avenue of the same name. After Canute's warning, he avoided getting careless about security and made sure he wasn't being followed, despite his impatience to be reunited with Libby. His pace quickened as he eventually approached the hotel, knowing Libby was waiting for him in the duplex suite they had taken for their short stay in Paris. On reflection, he realised how suffocating his return to Norfolk had been without her by his side.

Minutes later they were reunited. For Mike and Libby, it was true that absence made the heart grow fonder. His later-than-expected arrival had set her nerves on edge. As soon as they were behind the closed doors of the hotel suite they held each other closely, with actions speaking louder than words. She was in no hurry to find out what had happened on his trip to England. Instead she sat serenely silent, watching Mike quickly despatch a continental breakfast delivered by room service. He revelled in the superb-tasting coffee that had been so absent from the past few days, almost suggesting they fly to Rome to stock up on more beans instead of flying to New York that afternoon. They spent their last hours in Paris making love.

5
AN UNWELCOME VISIT

Mike and Libby found getting through US customs then crossing the border back into Canada as uneventful as the flight from Paris. Their ease of passing through both customs and immigration resulted from discovering the contact details of a Swiss master forger in the safety-deposit box held at the Odermatt bank in Zurich. The telephone number belonged to an intermediary, the intermediary turned out to be the nephew of the forger, and the forger had been extremely cautious in dealing with Mike – and this reassured him. Eventually, Mike purchased a collection of expertly forged passports that allowed the two of them to travel through countries unhindered.

Victor Mazarin had amassed a vast storehouse of wealth from which he and his partner, Carla Mancuso, were destined never to benefit from. The thought put a grim smile on Mike's face as he and Libby travelled from bank to bank, transferring Victor's money into new accounts. As a demonstration of trust, he gave Libby joint access to the accounts. At first, there had been no way of knowing if his show of faith would backfire on him; she could have cut and run at any time. Both he and Libby had to give serious thought as to how they were going to live in a way that kept them at arm's length from Wesley and any potential gold-diggers they might encounter.

Renting the chalet in Haliburton gave them the chance to withdraw from the world and its distractions. Mike was all too aware that they could still be enjoying a honeymoon period in their relationship. If their feelings for each other were to cool, what would happen next? Mike had tried to make the experience as claustrophobic as possible for Libby to see if the fascination she had for him would wear off. So far, it seemed the opposite had taken place. He felt they were closer than ever in their relationship, and Libby became increasingly relaxed and loving towards him. Sooner or later they needed to decide if they were going to remain financial nomads or find somewhere safe enough to live permanently. Mike knew that his in-depth thinking about these choices showed how serious he felt about his future with Libby.

Once back at Eagle Lake, the pair resumed their daily routine. They occasionally drove the Jeep into Haliburton when they needed to stock up on food and drink, and to avoid the weekend influx of visitors to the area, these trips were restricted to weekdays. Libby also dropped swimming at weekends, when the lake came to life with tourist boats and locals out fishing for panfish, lake trout or the rarer muskie. Instead of regular trips to their makeshift shooting range, they began spending time together on hiking trips. They still carried their rifles and pistols in case the local wildlife took too much of an interest in them, and they remained defenceless against the no-see-um midge bites. Libby appeared to have moved on from her previous life and expressed no desire to return to England.

The last weekend in June was a longer break than usual, as the locals were celebrating Canada Day on the Monday. While they were relaxing in the chalet, Mike heard a radio news bulletin announcing that an MI6 spy called Kim Philby had defected to the Soviet Union. He smiled to himself, hoping that Wesley had his hands full with this Philby affair rather than concerning himself with tracking down Mike and Libby.

A quick glance from the chalet veranda at the activities on the lake confirmed that the twists and turns of the Cold War held little interest to the locals. The world had not stopped turning and Ontario was safe that afternoon. Libby was relaxing on a sun lounger and showed no interest in the news. Mike could see from the gentle rise and fall of her chest that she was asleep.

The afternoon passed quietly by into evening and the traffic on the lake gradually abated. Somewhere overhead a single-engine aircraft lazily droned across the cloudless sky. Mike had lit a barbecue, ready for two large tenderloin steaks. He had also followed a local recipe for steak spice and looked forward to trying it. When the charcoal was ready, he slapped the steaks on the grill. There was a satisfying sizzle and the smell of seared meat permeated the atmosphere to excite any saliva gland in range.

Libby had prepared a salad of freshly cooked black beans, lentils, pearl barley, arugula, red peppers, dried cranberries and a green onion. In addition to vinaigrette, she had a small amount of locally produced maple syrup on the side. She had also found some bottles of Gamay Noir in the local LCBO store; the red wine originated from the not-so-distant Niagaran Peninsula and she was keen to have a complete Canadian dinner. Mike had readily agreed in the hope that the wine was better than anything they had come across so far. Neither of them expected to be left hungry enough to need dessert, so none had been prepared.

* * *

The small aircraft that had droned across the sky earlier overflew the lake a second time before disappearing behind the distant trees on the horizon. Out of sight, the aircraft made a final turn, heading for the lake. The pilot throttled back gently and partially lowered the 'flaperons' on the high mounted wings to prepare for landing. As Eagle Lake was long and large, the pilot knew his de Havilland Canada Beaver aircraft had way more water than was needed for the floatplane to land. He used the full length of the lake to complete his shallow glide on to the surface of the water. Once the aircraft had softly alighted, the engine was set to idle. Throughout the manoeuvre the pilot kept a lookout for lake users or floating debris in the water. The silver metal bird continued to drift quietly along to the jetty outside Mike and Libby's chalet.

Libby joined Mike to inquisitively watch the slowly approaching aircraft. This was the first floatplane they had seen on the lake since they had arrived in Haliburton. Its polished metal surfaces gleamed attractively, enhanced by the sun's lower angle in the sky. The scene looked like something out of a vacation advert for Americans. The floatplane's drift slowed almost to a stop and a man stepped out on to a float, carrying a short rope to attach to the jetty. After lightly stepping on to the jetty, the man tied the rope off. He looked up, smiling, whilst the pilot remained in the cockpit, seemingly busying himself with shutting down the engine.

Apart from the water lapping against the floats and the jetty, everything became overly quiet once the plane's engine was shut off. Mike noted that the aircraft had a Canadian registration, but that could have meant anything. The man on the jetty was a stranger, but again, that meant nothing.

The steaks were pulled off the grill and set to one side on a plate. Libby glanced around and slowly placed her hand over the handle of a small meat knife. The pistols and Uzi were too far away, secure in the storeroom along with the rifles. As far as Mike could see, the man was unarmed.

'Can I help you?' Mike asked from the veranda. There was no response from the man, who kept looking at him and smiling. Mike asked again, but more loudly this time. The man smirked and pointed between Mike and Libby, making them both turn around to see what he was pointing at.

Wesley stood behind them, flanked by two men who each held a Browning 9mm automatic pistol. One was pointed at Mike, the other at Libby.

'Hello, Armstrong. Did you really expect to get away from me?' said Wesley with a self-satisfied smile on his face. Mike said nothing. Libby followed his lead.

'I suppose I ought to be asking how a common thief can afford to live on the run, and in a place like this,' continued Wesley, picking up one of the steaks with a fork and examining it carefully. The meat fell off the fork and dropped on to the wooden decking.

'Oops, sorry about that. Easily remedied with a quick wipe,' he said, waiting for Mike's reaction.

Mike remained silent, waiting for Wesley to finish his pointless needling. The man on the jetty made his way up to the veranda and slipped handcuffs on Mike, then on Libby. The couple were pushed inside the chalet and left standing whilst Wesley took a seat.

'I will get straight to the point, Armstrong. You are going to carry out some work on my behalf. If you refuse, your little trip ends today, and she will die,' he said, nodding his head towards Libby.

'You can't do that,' said Mike defiantly.

'You are so naïve, Armstrong. I can do exactly what I like. You cannot stop me. Right now, you are the best man available to me but if you refuse to cooperate I will simply find someone else,' said Wesley, sounding relaxed and confident.

Mike had to think fast to give himself time to understand what was happening. He had to play along with Wesley until an opportunity arose that would allow both himself and Libby to make their escape.

'Do you really need to be waving guns around, Wesley?' he asked.

'Not if you and your good lady are prepared to behave.'

Mike glanced over to Libby to reassure her. He could see from her face that it wasn't reassurance she needed, it was restraint.

'Fine. Libby and I are going to take a seat, then you are going to tell us what you want,' said Mike, looking at Libby and willing her to do as he suggested.

She sat down reluctantly on the couch. She had wisely left the small knife behind. Mike sat down beside her. The two heavies accompanying Wesley remained standing, with their attention fixed on Mike and Libby. Wesley smiled, giving the impression of someone in effortless control.

Canute Simpson once told Mike that Wesley was as slippery as a snake in wet grass. Mike was also being reminded of how arrogant the man was. He looked incredibly smug at having successfully caught up with them. His characteristics were weaknesses, and Mike was going to pander to Wesley in an effort to try to use them against him.

Wesley was casually dressed and presented a very different image to the 'secret policeman' image he personified. Despite this, the brogues and cavalry twill trousers shouted out his Englishness. His open-necked shirt and blouson jacket fooled no one and were not items he would wear back in England. *No, he was never going to pass himself off as someone on holiday*, thought Mike. Instead, he was overdoing his effortless in-control act in an attempt at misdirection. Wesley's open jacket also partially revealed the pistol he was carrying. The man was taking no chances, so perhaps he was not as confident as he made out.

Mike's attention then focused on the two heavies. The men were dressed casually, but in a more authentic way. Their contrast to Wesley became more marked as he studied them.

The haircuts were in the American crew-cut style and not English at all. From the neck down they were north American; even their boots were Western in style. It had only been the Browning pistols that made him think they were British military, or secret service. Thinking back to the man on the jetty, Mike was in no doubt that he was Canadian. *There are so many inconsistencies*, thought Mike, and he found this reassuring.

'Right, Wesley, what are you up to? You didn't travel all this way just to put me under arrest,' said Mike, leading the conversation.

Wesley bristled at the transparency. He was reminded why he so disliked the man he regarded as a northern thug sitting before him.

'A little more respect, or she will pay the price,' he snapped, glancing at Libby. 'You are going to do a little sniffing around for me. Something you seem to be good at. Your—' Wesley paused to smirk, '—lady friend can assist and keep you warm at night.'

Mike was unmoved by the insult, but Libby looked ready to strangle the man.

'Who keeps you warm at night, Wesley – your dog?' asked Mike.

Wesley's eyes poured venom as one of his men sniggered. He gave the man a sharp look and silence fell.

'Don't push your luck, Armstrong. I can put you in Wormwood Scrubs any time I choose,' said Wesley in an angry tone.

Mike doubted that very much, as it seemed Wesley wanted him on the outside to do some dirty work for him, rather than on the inside. 'So, are you going to tell me what you want now, or later?' he asked.

'You have twenty-four hours to get the first available flight back to London. Don't think about trying to get away from me. You have been found and I can do it again. The only difference is that next time you will both be shot. A surveillance team will keep an eye on you until you are on the plane. Use this number to give me the flight details,' said Wesley, handing over a card with a number handwritten on the back. Mike recognised the area code as a London number.

Wesley stood up, signifying the meeting was at an end. Mike realised that he was not going to hear any more until he and Libby arrived in London.

'Don't do anything foolish,' repeated Wesley in a menacing tone, as he walked out on to the veranda. Mike and Libby followed him outside.

The Beaver had been turned around to point back down the lake. The pilot, standing next to the man on the jetty, nervously flicked a cigarette into the water before climbing back into the plane. Seconds later, the engine had been fired up. Wesley made his way down the steps and without a backwards glance, disappeared inside the floatplane. The other man undid the rope and passed it inside before jumping aboard.

The roar of the Pratt and Whitney radial engine subsided as the pilot throttled back after taking off. The familiar drone returned, then faded, as the Beaver disappeared over the horizon of trees. Mike guessed the remaining three-man team were to be Mike and Libby's watchers until they departed for London.

'You heard what the guy said, and don't ever think we aren't watching you,' said one of the men.

Mike didn't. He was told that he and Libby could stay in and around the chalet, but to go no further until they left for good in the Jeep. The three men left and headed down the track. Mike waited to see if an engine started up. As this never happened, he knew they had company for the duration. As a precaution, he searched the chalet from top to bottom in case listening devices had been left in place by Wesley's men. He came up with nothing and felt able to talk freely with Libby.

'Don't be taken in by Wesley. There is something not right about this,' said Mike.

'He seems to have us well and truly under his thumb,' she replied, looking concerned.

Mike shook his head. 'His heavies are Canadian or American for a start.'

'Meaning what?' she asked.

'He always uses his own people, not hired hands. Those men would be an unacceptable security risk for legitimate intelligence work. If Wesley was working with departmental approval, then he would have us taken away in custody and flown straight back to London. Instead, he's left us to find our own way there. This is a risk he has been forced to take because he is probably hiding his activities from his superiors. All he needed to do was arrest us, but that's not what happened,' said Mike.

'That all seems too far-fetched to me. Perhaps he really does want us to do something for his department – whatever that may be.'

'I never did find out who he works for. He could be MI5 – or 6. I am sure he works somewhere within the British intelligence set-up, though,' said Mike.

'So, we could make a run for it and he couldn't touch us?'

'Hardly. I am a criminal, so all he has to do is keep looking for us then tip off the local police. He caught up with us once, so he can do it again. No, we should play along with him and take our chances. The alternative will leave us looking over our shoulders until we die,' he said resignedly.

'How do you think he caught up with us?' asked Libby.

'Well, our passports didn't let us down or we would never have got through immigration at the airports. It could have been when I was over in England, but the only person I met there was Canute Simpson.'

'Do you think he betrayed you?' Libby hardly believed her own words.

'Canute detests Wesley, and for that reason alone I know he would never sell us out. Anyhow, he had no idea what my plans were when I left Little Stratton,' Mike replied.

As Mike and Libby packed their bags, they continued to speculate about how Wesley had caught up with them. They left the chalet early the next morning and drove straight for the US border before heading on to New York to find the next available flight for London. Throughout their journey they were followed by a dark Mercury Monterey sedan containing three occupants. Mike noticed the Monterey had New York plates, but was unsure if this was a coincidence or not. They decided Idlewild airport was their best bet, and soon found a flight leaving for London Heathrow that evening. He purchased First Class seats on a Pan-American Boeing 707. As he and Libby made their way through to the departure lounge, Mike glanced over his shoulder. Three pairs of eyes coldly watched their progress.

6
A FLYING VISIT

Mike and Libby ate a light continental-style breakfast from the Pan-American Clipper menu. The chilled orange juice and petits pains with butter and cheese, followed by a fresh fruit salad, was intended to tide them over until they booked themselves into a good hotel in London. Neither had slept well during the eight-hour overnight flight, and both looked forward to getting some sleep in a comfortable bed following a long lunch.

As soon as they were in the airport baggage area, Mike headed for the nearest telephone kiosk. He flicked through the directory until he found the number for Greene's Hotel on Albemarle Street, Mayfair. The hotel confirmed that a taxi would be sent to pick up the couple and take them across London once they had collected their baggage.

Libby's return to London played on her mind because of the off-chance of running into friends – or worse, family. She knew the likelihood was remote, but she had to admit to Mike that she would be embarrassed if any such encounter occurred. News of her apparently brazen reappearance in London with another man would inflict a cruel embarrassment on Dicky. She believed he had suffered enough from their marriage of convenience.

Mike had already anticipated Libby's worries. He requested any available suite, as they wanted to avoid using public areas within the hotel. He was also sure they would not be in London for long. Wesley had plans for them and that probably included travel away from the capital.

By the time the taxi pulled up outside the front door of the hotel, Libby had tied a green patterned silk scarf over her hair and put on sunglasses. She stepped straight out from the taxi, paying no attention to the large Victorian frontage of the hotel, and swept through the double doors that were opened by the top-hatted porter on duty. Mike followed at a slower pace, scanning up and down the street to see if anyone might be following them. Relieved, he saw nothing suspicious.

Minutes later the couple were shown into a large and luxurious L-shaped suite, situated on the top floor of the hotel.

'I had no idea you had such expensive tastes, Mike,' said Libby, moving from room to room and taking in the opulent furnishings.

'How on earth did you find this place?' she asked incredulously.

'I didn't know about the suite. We're just lucky it happened to be available,' he replied, smiling.

'But you knew about Greene's?' she asked.

'Yes. I once had dealings with a gangster who used this place all the time. He told me that if I ever wanted somewhere posh and discreet I should come here. The old boy even brought me here to meet his mistress.' *Who knows, he might still show up here with her*, he thought.

Libby shuddered at the thought of dining with a gangster, and Mike read her mind.

'Don't worry, that was a long time ago and he was an old man even then. The chances of bumping into him are non-existent. Anyway, we will be dining in here, not the restaurant,' said Mike reassuringly.

Now they were in London and hidden away from prying eyes, Mike and Libby began to relax. They showered and ate a lunch of chicken pappardelle and cime di rapa accompanied by a chilled bottle of pinot grigio. The pair were still in their bathrobes as they intended to catch up with some sleep after they had eaten. Feeling relaxed, they slept well. It was late afternoon when they woke up to get dressed. Mike had tea and coffee sent up. They sat in the suite's lounge area, waiting to see what would happen next.

Along one wall were three windows that looked out on to the street. The ceiling stretched well above the windows and was finished throughout with an Acanthus cornice. Panels of reproduction French Reveillon wallpaper decorated the walls. Mike found the style a little too fussy and distracting. The furniture was in the style of Louis XIV and covered in a satin material with wide plum and silver striping. Mike reflected that the furniture was also not to his taste and mentioned this to Libby, who gave no opinion. As Mike assumed they would not be staying in the suite for too long, there was probably no need to be so judgmental about it.

One welcome feature of the lounge area were the three windows, all fitted with privacy glass. This allowed Mike to use them as one-way mirrors to observe the street from time to time, knowing he remained unseen from below. If Wesley did harbour some sinister intention, there was no guarantee he would openly approach the hotel. He had previously taken great precautions when meeting Mike in the past and he guessed nothing had changed. All the same, Mike remained vigilant.

'How will Wesley know where to find us?' asked Libby.

'Probably the same way he found us in Canada. Luck, an informant, or he had us followed everywhere we went. Maybe it was a combination of all those things. I'm as interested as you are in finding out,' said Mike, continuing to look down into the street.

'Well, if he did know where we had gone then why take so long to contact us and not have us arrested?' she asked.

This troubled Mike, because being taken into custody meant his usefulness to Wesley would be over. It was apparent to him that Wesley had some questionable task for him that had to remain secret. He knew he remained an expendable pawn and that Wesley would not hesitate to sacrifice him for his own gain. Mike decided to play along until he could spot a way out.

'I don't know, Libby. He's up to something and to get our cooperation he will have to tell us what it is,' said Mike. He sat down next to her and began flicking impatiently through the latest edition of the *Illustrated London News*.

* * *

Wesley MacDonald spent months trying to find Mike Armstrong. Now, in front of him on his desk lay a file stamped 'SECRET' followed by the letters 'PSI' in brackets. Mike

Armstrong had been classified as a Person of Significant Interest. This meant that MI5, MI6 and Special Branch were all required to report his movements to Wesley. He was not to be approached or contacted in any way other than by Wesley's department, which consisted of an ad-hoc team of ten men, including himself, and had no official title.

Despite the small size of the department, Wesley had direct access to the Prime Minister, the Foreign Secretary and the Home Secretary. No other government minister knew about Wesley or his activities. Outside this political triumvirate, only the Heads of MI5 and MI6 officially knew of his existence. Special Branch were only allowed to send reports to him via an obscure contact hidden by the bureaucracy of Whitehall. It was assumed, correctly, that he led a non-accountable 'dirty tricks' department that had managed to survive closure following the end of the Second World War.

In addition to the security services, Wesley had contacted Interpol and requested reports on any sightings of Mike. Despite all his efforts to keep track of his prey, he had been unable to uncover Mike's whereabouts. The red file on the desk only told Wesley what he already knew. The time between Mike's speedy disappearance from Norfolk and his recent reappearance at Victoria station remained unexplained. Wesley was also surprised to find that Mike still had the Kembrey woman with him. He assumed that when he'd been spotted at the station, he was on his own.

Mike had been unlucky in choosing the Night Ferry train to Paris. By chance, a Special Branch officer had been following a suspect linked to a left-wing revolutionary group, also based in Paris. The officer had glimpsed Mike's face as he boarded the train and he later reported that he thought he had seen a man who looked just like a mugshot on the latest PSI watch-list. The message had eventually reached Wesley, who was at first unconvinced that it was Mike. However, Wesley alerted Interpol and officers were sent to the Gare du Nord to meet the Night Ferry train. Mike was spotted and photographed without his knowledge before he left the station. Following strict orders, the Interpol officers tailed Mike to try to find out where he was heading.

The taxi Mike had boarded soon disappeared in the chaotic Paris traffic. The officers caught up with the taxi driver later that day and questioned him. It was soon clear that Mike was not staying at the hotel where he had been dropped off. Frustrated, the officers had to admit they had lost their man. The photograph of Mike was sent to London by radiofax, then couriered to Wesley. The image, now contained in the file on Wesley's desk, was clear enough for him to recognise Mike.

With only limited resources, Wesley gambled on having the airports watched by Interpol officers and his own rapidly assembled team of men, who flew over to Paris. The gamble paid off as Mike, along with Libby, was spotted entering the Departures lounge of Orly international airport, to the south of Paris. Wesley was contacted by one of his men immediately after the New York flight had departed. The man confirmed that the suspect plus a woman were onboard the aircraft. Wesley terminated the surveillance operation then ordered his men to return to London. Unwittingly, Mike and Libby had played right into Wesley's hands.

Wesley needed to act quickly to ensure that Mike and Libby would be under surveillance once their flight landed at Idlewild. It was impossible for him to find a flight leaving London to arrive ahead of them. He faced the choice of getting the first available flight to New York and trying to pick up their trail the following day or going to the FBI in New York to ask them to provide surveillance until he arrived and could take over. For Wesley, the decision had to be based on whichever was the lesser of two evils. The former almost certainly meant losing track of the fugitives, whilst the latter meant having the FBI sniffing around asking awkward questions.

Wesley reluctantly decided to contact the FBI to alert them that Mike and Libby were possible Soviet spies who were heading for New York via London and Paris. A carefully worded diplomatic signal was sent to Washington before being forwarded on to the New York FBI field office. The signal emphasised that neither individual should be approached, thus keeping them completely unaware they were under surveillance. The spy subterfuge gave Wesley the time he needed to get a flight to New York. He hoped that the mentioning of Soviet spies ensured that the usually less-than-friendly FBI would take an interest in his 'Limey' surveillance operation.

The subterfuge worked, and two FBI Special Agents were in position at the Arrivals hall in Idlewild airport thirty minutes before Mike and Libby's flight touched down on American soil. The Special Agents followed the couple as they collected their suitcases, before going through customs and walking out to the taxi rank. The agents had correctly anticipated there would be no reception party for the suspects, who rather convincingly made themselves out to be British tourists. A third Special Agent was waiting nearby in a black Chrysler 300 sedan. On seeing the agents at the taxi rank, he engaged the TorqueFlite three-speed automatic transmission, allowing the 300 to surge forward towards his colleagues.

With the three men onboard, the powerful sedan easily cut through the midday traffic to keep in touch with Mike and Libby's taxi. The taxi headed west for Lower Manhattan, then briefly north before heading west again, following the Holland Tunnel west under the Hudson River. Once the taxi emerged from the tunnel it headed to a large multi-storey car park next to Journal Square in Jersey City. The taxi pulled into a street-level waiting bay where the driver offloaded the suitcases. The driver was paid by the male passenger, who then headed inside the car park. The female passenger waited on the sidewalk with the offloaded suitcases.

One of the FBI men was dropped off further down the street and took a leisurely walk towards the woman. Just past the waiting bay was a bus stop that the agent headed for whilst getting a closer at the woman. She appeared to take no notice of him as she was preoccupied with scanning inside the car park, looking for someone. The agent then lit a cigarette and made out as if he was waiting for his bus. A few minutes later a pale blue Jeep Wagoneer pulled up alongside the woman. The agent memorised the vehicle's number plate and the dealer sticker in the rear window. The couple loaded up the Jeep and continued their journey.

The Jeep was driven at a steady pace heading west on Interstate 80 before heading north. The agents tailed a long distance behind, hoping not to be noticed by the couple in the Jeep. After a couple of hours, the Jeep pulled up at a diner and its occupants went inside for a rest and some coffee. One of the agents took advantage of the halt to call New York and pass on the vehicle details. The men had a fair idea that the Jeep was heading for Canada, as the plates and dealer sticker indicated the Jeep was from Toronto.

Wesley knew the agents would not cross the border into Canada, so once more he had to move fast. He managed to charter a small plane to get him to Toronto and hopefully ahead of Mike and Libby. This was another massive gamble. For all he knew, the plates could be changed on the Jeep before it was driven on to somewhere entirely different.

Wesley later sat at the bar of a Toronto motel, nursing a large bourbon. The pressure on him had subsided when one of the agents reported that the fugitives were heading west and had checked into a motel off Interstate 86. The FBI agents and Wesley were sure the Jeep would be heading for Niagara Falls the next day and would be in Toronto soon afterwards.

Wasting no time, Wesley had rented a Ford 500 sedan in Toronto and drove to a motel near the border crossing point. All he had to do was park up on the Canadian side of the border and wait for Mike and Libby to cross. He had also found himself a private investigator who asked no awkward questions and could bring along with him some dubious associates to act as muscle once he caught up with Mike.

For reasons of his own, Wesley wanted no more official security agency involvement. As a last resort, he had been forced to use the FBI and was now more than happy for them to remain on the American side of the border. Allowing the Canadian Directorate of Security and Intelligence to get involved also meant too many complicated questions he preferred not to answer. Once Mike and Libby were in Canada, the private investigator and his goons could take over the surveillance.

The next day a Mercury Monterey sedan took up its station well behind the Jeep, which was now being driven by Libby. On the back seat of the Mercury sat Wesley, next to one of his hired men. He took out his small binoculars and allowed himself the luxury of getting a closer look at the Jeep and its occupants. To his immense relief, he was just able to make out Libby Kembrey driving and Mike Armstrong sitting in the front passenger seat.

A few hours later the Jeep turned off a backwoods metalled road on to the rough track that led to their rented chalet. The Mercury stopped momentarily to allow two of the men to get out to follow the trail on foot. The sedan was then parked a short distance away amongst the trees and out of sight of the road. After half an hour, the men returned and confirmed that the Jeep had reached its destination.

Wesley wasted no time. The Mercury was driven to the local town of Haliburton to find out if he could hire someone with a floatplane to fly him around the local area. As he was prepared to pay cash, he soon found both a pilot and a floatplane.

The pilot was shown a local map and asked if he could put the aircraft down on the lake where Mike and Libby's hideout was situated. Wesley made out he wanted to surprise his friends by literally making a flying visit. The pilot thought the Englishman could surprise his friends in less expensive ways but was more than happy to take the money.

The Beaver floatplane took off that evening and headed for Eagle Lake. There were two passengers, neither of which was the Englishman the pilot had expected. When he remarked upon this he was brusquely told by one of the men to get on with the job he had been paid to do. The pilot guessed the safest thing was to ask no further questions.

Once at the lake, the pilot made an overflight to check the dark, glass-like surface was clear of obstructions and people before making his final approach. After the smooth and skilful landing on the lake, the pilot was directed to the jetty below the holiday home where Mike and Libby were having a barbecue.

When the pilot saw his English customer standing at the chalet with two armed men alongside him, he felt a rising panic. Guns meant trouble and he was up to his neck in it. The first of his passengers stepped out on to the jetty whilst the other remained on the aircraft, keeping an eye on him. Sometime later, Wesley made his way down from the chalet and then leisurely walked down the jetty to the aircraft. Once aboard the aircraft, Wesley offered to triple the original cash payment if the pilot flew him to the Toronto City airport that was located on Lake Ontario. The pilot grabbed at the payment in advance and prepared for take-off.

The aircraft arrived at the Toronto waterfront airport just before dark. The pilot was given a menacing warning not to talk about his movements or what he had seen that day. He instantly agreed and was more than relieved to see the back of the seemingly rich Englishman and his heavies. Once he paid his landing fees, the pilot headed for the nearest phone, wondering how to explain to his wife where he was and that he intended to stay in Toronto that night.

Once in Toronto proper, Wesley paid off the two heavies and set about making plans to travel back to London. He would need to set up surveillance in readiness for Mike and Libby's return. He found himself a good hotel where he could get a decent night's sleep before travelling back to London the next day. That night he continued to ponder over how Mike and Libby continued to support themselves so easily. Asking them outright would have shown his hand. He fell asleep, going over in his mind the possibilities of how to access what must be a considerable sum of money.

7
BRIGHTON

Mike and Libby spent the night at the hotel waiting impatiently for Wesley to contact them. Over breakfast on the second day, they both expressed their irritation with the man. Libby believed that Wesley and his men had failed to maintain a proper surveillance on them and did not have any idea where they were. Her concern was that Wesley's inability to find them again might lead to the police being tasked with finding and arresting them.

Mike thought differently; he knew they had complied in every way with Wesley and the man knew exactly where they were in London. Mike was sure the waiting game was Wesley's way of making sure they understood who was in charge. It was something he regarded as a childish and pointless delay.

Wesley had organised a team of watchers to follow Mike and Libby the moment they stepped off the BOAC Boeing 707 at Heathrow airport. The team leader reported that the pair had used assumed names and flown First Class. Wesley had been provided with a copy of the flight manifest and an extract of the passenger list. Despite his best efforts, he failed to find any irregularities regarding passengers and crew that might raise suspicion. He was also piqued that Mike and the Kembrey woman could change identities so quickly and easily. Their documentation must have been perfect to get them through immigration without a hitch at Heathrow. Such documents did not come cheaply, and nor did First Class seats on a BOAC transatlantic flight. How, he pondered, did Mike have the funds and the connections to do this?

The outcome of Wesley's team's investigation after the best part of twenty-four hours had produced nothing, except for the fact that Mike and Libby had assumed yet another set of identities to that used on their flight to London. To add to Wesley's irritation, he had been unable to link either Mike or Libby to any bank accounts at home or abroad. He hoped that making the pair wait for him to get in contact might serve to unnerve them. There was nothing to be gained from leaving them to stew in the luxury hotel for too long, though, so Wesley decided to continue with his plans.

* * *

Mid-morning, the concierge telephoned Mike and Libby to say an unnamed gentleman had left an envelope for the occupants of the Parisian suite; the suite Mike and Libby were staying in. Mike asked for the envelope to be sent up, and minutes later, he and Libby sat down to read the single piece of paper inside the envelope. There was a typewritten address plus an instruction to take the train and arrive that afternoon. The terse message could only have originated from Wesley. They both committed the address to memory before readying themselves for their journey.

Mike knew it was a waste of time trying to get a description of the person that delivered the note. A non-descript individual with non-descript clothing with no clear accent would have been part of a set-piece that would have diverted the concierge long enough to ensure he had no clear memory of what had occurred at the time. *Typical Wesley*, Mike thought to himself. He called the concierge and asked him to order a taxi to Victoria station. No sooner had they stepped out from the lift in the hotel lobby, they were ushered across the pavement and into a waiting taxi that immediately threaded its way through the busy London traffic to the station.

Libby had long since dispensed with the old wardrobe of tweed and wool she had worn in Norfolk. Instead she wore a modern outfit – a sleeveless longline button-fronted blazer with pale grey patterning and matching trousers. Smart black patent-leather heels with large matching buckles replaced her old and practical brown leather country shoes. Her large black rattan-box handbag contained a shawl and scarf, in case the June weather cooled later that afternoon. She put away the sunglasses she had worn on arrival at the hotel once the taxi got moving. Mike wore a navy blazer, a dark grey roll-neck sweater, skinny-fit charcoal-coloured trousers and a pair of smart black leather Chelsea boots.

At Victoria station Mike paid the driver and gave him a generous tip. The couple made straight for WH Smith & Son to try and find themselves an A-Z map of Brighton. The typewritten note from Wesley had been ripped to shreds and lay in anonymous tatters at the bottom of the first waste bin Mike could find.

Mike hurriedly bought two First Class return tickets before he and Libby dashed away to catch the train. Their carriage was almost empty, allowing them to be as comfortable as possible for the hour and forty minutes it would take for them to reach Brighton.

Mike thought the whole trip was a waste of time resulting from Wesley's phobia of being seen by the 'wrong people'. A meeting could just as easily have been arranged almost anywhere in London but making a journey by train made the situation much easier for Wesley to monitor and control. He could ensure that Mike and Libby were not being followed and, equally, that they did not bring uninvited guests.

The train carried few passengers that lunchtime, and the number of other people in the First Class carriage could be counted on the fingers of one hand. Mike knew that somewhere amongst the passengers there had to be some of Wesley's agents travelling with them. These men would be indistinguishable from the other passengers. As Wesley would think it improper to employ a woman, Mike discounted any females travelling on the train.

The situation made it all too easy for these agents to spot Mike and Libby, and to see if they were being followed out of the station. The agents would have been briefed as to where the couple were heading. That meant the likelihood of another passenger heading precisely to the same address was nil, giving Mike a chance to spot any man who might be following them.

From the precautions Wesley put in place, it seemed to Mike that his adversary took no chances. Mike burned with curiosity as to what was going on. Given the current situation, he guessed Wesley needed him more than he needed Wesley. If

Mike never met him again, and that was his intention, it mattered not in the slightest.

The note originating from Wesley was typical:

Wait to be met at the GPO mail box located on the southern end of Montpelier Street, just off the Seven Dials roundabout in Brighton.

The address meant nothing to Mike, as he had never been to Brighton before. Libby had made several visits to the seaside resort but was equally mystified as to why they had to meet Wesley there. As they were told to wait next to a GPO box, both knew the location of the meeting had to be elsewhere.

Their train gradually reduced speed and the sound from the carriages made a gentle and rhythmic clackity-clack as it neared the terminus. A few of the passengers had made their way into the corridor, some with luggage and some without. Mike gave up trying to work out which were genuine passengers, and which were working for Wesley.

Libby retrieved her scarf and tied it around her hair before donning her sunglasses once more. It was clear she still feared being spotted by someone she knew. Her precaution was not sufficient to fool anyone who really knew her, but Mike said nothing, hoping to allay her fears.

She stepped out on to the platform and put her arm through Mike's before they headed off towards the ticket collector at the exit gate. The station was covered by a double-spanned glass and iron roof, providing a space that was lighter and more spacious than Mike expected. As he seemingly glanced around to take in the architecture, Mike took in the movements of their temporary fellow travellers. Most were moving at a fast pace, as if in a hurry to meet someone, get a taxi, or catch a connecting bus somewhere.

One man, however, remained on the platform looking closely at a wall-mounted timetable. He wore a naval pea coat, dark denim jeans, work boots and a cotton cap. His hands were pushed into the pockets of the jacket. Mike stopped and stared at the man, forcing him to make eye contact. The man realised he had been spotted. He brazenly turned towards them and stared back, knowing the game was up. He maintained a poker face, waiting to see what Mike would do next.

Mike spoke quietly to Libby, who glanced at the man with a withering look of disdain. The man scowled back and maintained his position.

'I hope he's one of Wesley's goons.' said Libby, sounding slightly nervous.

'Don't worry, he must be,' replied Mike, trying to sound certain. He had no idea who else the man could be working for and hoped the meeting with Wesley would remove all doubt.

The couple left the station on foot, heading west. Mike had read the map in the A-Z and was pleased to see that Montpelier Crescent was not far away. After memorising the route, he pocketed the map book. They carried on walking west until they arrived at Dyke Road before turning north on one of the roads radiating out from the roundabout at Seven Dials. Mike was impressed with Wesley's choice, as it meant he could approach from and leave Seven Dials from any direction by car. Once at the roundabout, they took the south-westerly spoke that would eventually end up at the beach.

After one hundred yards, a crescent diverted off to the left in a gentle curve that joined back on to the main road further along. The curved frontage was made up of substantial and immaculate white Victorian villas that faced west, rather than the usual practice of facing towards to the sea. Mike speculated that they might be heading to one of these villas. He made an even wilder speculation that one of the villas was Wesley's second home, where he kept a mistress. He quickly dismissed the thought; Wesley would never compromise his personal security.

Up ahead Mike spotted a red Penfold hexagonal postbox with a black painted base. The villa adjacent to the postbox gave no clue as to who lived there. As far as he could see, the house looked lived-in but seemed unoccupied at that time of day. Mike could find nothing suspicious about the prim piece of Brighton's smart suburbia.

As they neared the postbox a car approached them from behind. No time had been stipulated on the note he had been sent, so Mike had no idea if they had arrived at a suitable time. The car slowed and drew into the kerb slightly ahead of them. Two men sat in the front whilst the rear passenger seat was empty. Mike recognised the car as a black Humber from its badging and guessed it was a new model as he had not seen one like it before.

As the car halted the front passenger door opened and a tall man stepped out on to the pavement. He wore a shabby dark-grey gaberdine car coat and a pinch-front black fedora hat. The man looked Mike up and down then did the same with Libby. He curtly told them to get in the car.

Once seated, the car pulled away sharply with a short squeak of the tyres. *Not very professional,* thought Mike. The driver wore a scuffed black leather motorcycle jacket and seemed totally at odds with the image presented by the passenger. Mike appraised the odd couple. Both were trying hard to look as if they could handle themselves in a fight. The man in the hat had successfully managed to make himself into a pastiche of a hoodlum from a movie. The young leather-jacketed driver was more convincing as the type of greasy motorcycle thug who lurked around Brighton with scooter riders looking for trouble at weekends. On reflection, Mike thought the latter was the more authentic. He also thought the two men were losers.

The incongruity of the men reminded Mike of the heavies they had encountered with Wesley back in Canada. He decided neither pair could be working for the British security services.

Mike asked where they were going. The passenger turned and looked at him. The man's eyes seemed to sneer at Mike, then Libby. He looked as if he hadn't bothered to shave that morning. His breath was foul as it exited his mouth past teeth yellowed through smoking cheap cigarettes. Without a word, he turned back and watched the road ahead.

Mike turned his attention to the driver. His greased-back black hair looked as if it hadn't been washed in weeks. A sweaty unwashed odour drifted from his direction into the back of the car. Both of his heavily scarred hands were visible on the steering wheel.

Mike reassessed the pair and sensed amateurish machismo more than calm professionalism. Street thugs, not ex-coppers or ex-servicemen as he had first thought. He was confused. Why was Wesley employing these lowlifes instead of his usual professionals? The men were out of their league but too stupid to realise it. Mike had seen similar types many times before, back home on the streets of Newcastle. The sort of men that hung around coffee bars, amusement arcades and betting shops, flicking cigarettes on to the pavement in a pointless attempt to intimidate people or eye up an attractive girl passing by. They were losers, and Mike knew he could easily deal with them. The only man he might have to worry about slightly more was the driver, who looked as though he was no stranger to fist fights.

He looked across to Libby and squeezed her hand with renewed confidence. She sensed his appraisal of the situation and smiled back at him. Mike decided to say nothing more until they met up with Wesley.

The driver wound down his side window and leant on to the door with his elbow clumsily sticking out into the air. He spat the gum he had been chewing into the oncoming traffic. Although Libby had been poker-faced during the journey so far, she welcomed the blast of fresh air that entered the car. Anything was preferable to the driver's body odour.

Mike noticed the car had a radio transmitter/receiver fitted, though for some reason the device was switched off and the handset was missing. He hadn't noticed any external antenna on the car when they were picked up. Wesley obviously did not want the men using the radio. Mike checked the passing road signs that told him they were travelling in an easterly direction after initially heading north from Brighton. Several miles after leaving the outskirts of the town, the car was driven up a well-maintained track that led due north for a quarter of a mile. Sign boards indicated that a farm and its estate were due to be auctioned off in a week's time. The straight stretch of track provided an easy way to look back to see if they were being followed before it threaded through a small wood. The car moved through gently dappled green light from the ancient oak trees before re-emerging into sunshine. Seconds later they arrived at a farmyard.

The car was driven to the far end of the yard before stopping outside a large cow barn. They all stepped out of the car and were hit by the stench coming from an overflowing slurry pit to the rear of the open and empty barn. The surroundings were littered with rusty farm machinery and a few ancient-looking tractors.

The two men leant against the front wing of the Humber, ignoring Mike and Libby. It seemed they were waiting for Wesley to arrive. Soon enough, an identical Humber pulled up in front of them. Inside were Wesley, his driver and two other passengers. Wesley said a few quiet words to the two passengers, who then got out and sauntered over to the thugs. The thugs smirked expectantly as one of the other men reached into his jacket as if to fetch out a wallet to pay them.

Their faces dropped as the second man also reached into his jacket but pulled out a Browning automatic pistol from his shoulder holster. The lead man ordered the two thugs to make their way to the back of the barn. The frightened men raised their hands and did exactly as they were told. They stopped at the edge of the slurry pit before turning to face the gunmen. Looking over the shoulders of the two men who had their pistols drawn, the thugs' eyes pleaded wordlessly with Wesley. The man wearing the leather motorcycle jacket finally lost his nerve and a wet patch of urine spread downwards from his groin on to his right leg. The face of the man in the hat was white with fear and he shook visibly.

Two sharp retorts came from each pistol, one quickly followed by the other, and the two hapless thugs were thrown backwards with the impact. They hit the green slimy surface of the slurry with one disgusting splat after the other. The one in the leather jacket was still just alive. His terrified wide-open eyes looked up from the glutinous mire; then he was gone. Crimson splatters of blood contrasted heavily with the green slurry, leaving only a temporary indication of where the bodies had sunk. The older man's hat floated forlornly upside-down on the surface like a tiny boat with no sail.

'Those two will make an interesting addition to the coming auction,' said Wesley without a trace of emotion.

Libby stared in shock at seeing the double murder, her frozen eyes locked on to the spot where the men had disappeared.

'Did you really need to kill them?' asked an incredulous Mike.

'Indeed. The stakes are high,' replied Wesley, 'and I don't want to leave any unnecessary loose ends.'

'What about the car?' asked Mike, looking past Wesley's shoulder.

'That will be cleaned thoroughly inside and out, and the correct number plates will be refitted,' he replied, nodding towards the two armed men, who were now carefully watching Mike and Libby.

'So that means any witness to their disappearance will say that only Libby and I were the last to see them alive,' said Mike.

'Exactly.'

Mike knew that made both himself and Libby prime suspects in any police inquiry. He had forgotten what a solid gold bastard Wesley was. Libby, on the other hand, now understood why Mike had been so careful to try to remain below the radar of the authorities: especially if they were all like the man smiling sardonically back at her right now. It seemed Wesley had them both exactly where he wanted them.

'So, what happens next?' asked Mike.

'We go somewhere with a slightly more pleasant aroma,' said Wesley, glancing back at the slowly congealing surface of the slurry.

8

THE MARTELLO TOWER

Wesley's Humber pulled smoothly away, with the man at the wheel demonstrating the skills of a high-speed driver trained by the police. The car retraced its short journey back down the farm track and sped along, controlled by minimal movements of the steering wheel. The brakes were deftly applied to make minor adjustments for speed on the winding track. Once out of the wood, the car accelerated once more on the straight section that ended at the main road between Brighton and Lewes. Wesley sat unconcerned in the front seat, obviously confident that he had nothing to fear from his unwilling passengers.

Libby's mind was reeling with the shock of witnessing the execution of the two men. She wondered if the heavies Wesley had employed in Canada had suffered a similar fate. For a second, she felt as though she were going to be sick and wound down her passenger window to allow the fresh air to wash over her. Mike glanced at her and saw the colour had gone from her face. She looked shocked, so he gently took her hand.

Libby looked back, trying to force a smile. Even though she had been forced to shoot a man before, that had been with a rifle at long range. This time she had witnessed two brutal killings, up close and personal. The look on the young motorcycle thug's face as a bullet ripped through him, followed by the pleading eyes as he sank in the stinking slime, had the hard edge of a visceral and violent reality. Libby was reminded of the terrible newsreels shown after the war, of Nazis shooting people as they stood in freshly dug pits. She was sickened to the core.

A few seconds later, she squeezed Mike's hand as she regained control of emotions she had never experienced before. It seemed she had been wrapped up and stifled in invisible cotton wool until he had come into her life. The killing of the men was Wesley's doing, and nothing to do with Mike. It was clear to her that Wesley was no stranger to murder. Her contempt and repugnance for him had turned into a bitterness that began to eat into her soul.

She began to fear that the honeymoon period with Mike was over. Now the killing had started, she might not be able to stay the distance with him. She looked at his impassive grey eyes and wondered what he was thinking. The Mike she had so quickly come to love was not an unfeeling psychopath, and yet, just like Wesley he was hardened and seemingly impervious to the act of death.

She thought back to when she had shot Victor Mazarin. There was no thought or consideration to the act, there had been no time. It had been necessary; the slightest hesitation might have led to her missing the shot. Mike would be dead and her dreadful life at Little Stratton would have carried on untouched.

Now, just like Mike and Wesley, she was tainted with the permanent stain of death and memories that could not be erased. Trying to wash away that stain was impossible. Like an angry and stupid word spoken in haste, death could not be undone. She would lose her mind trying to reverse the impossible finality of her actions, and the scene she had witnessed at the farmyard. She took a deep breath and looked out of the open window, wondering how this terrible day might end. She also wondered whether she would be alive to see it.

The driver hurtled along the road, ignoring speed signs and pushing the car just to the limit of its capabilities. The rush of air on to Libby's face soon became unbearable and she wound up the window, leaving a small gap that was just wide enough to allow a small amount of fresh air in.

Mike could see that Libby had mentally taken herself out of the situation. She had that thousand-yard stare he had seen on the face of many wartime veterans as they tried to readjust to the day-to-day trivia of 'civvy street'. Wesley was unaware that Mike had picked up on this same look, momentarily fixed upon his face, during the few times they had met. He regarded this as a chink in Wesley's armour.

Wesley's war continued, even though friend and foe no longer wore uniform. His wartime compatriot, Canute Simpson, had successfully crossed the chasm created by war to find peace. Mike did, however, think it slightly ironic that as a rector Canute continued to wear a uniform of sorts. Wesley, meanwhile, remained partially blinkered by his experiences and retained a cynicism that Mike might be able to use against him.

Mike put his arm around Libby. In the rear-view mirror, he caught Wesley almost sneering at what he thought was a show of weak romanticism.

Still speeding eastwards on the A27, the car continued slicing and dicing its way past lorries, vans and the odd tractor. Salesmen in their overloaded cars could only look on with a hint of envy as the Humber sailed past them. Eventually, the driver took a right and followed the road down to Eastbourne. Neither Mike nor Libby had visited the town before, so they had no idea why they were headed that way.

Mike thought that Wesley was being overly cautious with his choice of meeting places. This turned out to be true. The car was driven through the town streets until they stopped beside a large green that opened out on to the seaside proper. On one side of the green stood a large circular structure overlooking the beach and the sea beyond.

Wesley stepped out of the car and Mike followed.

'You can tell your lady that the conversation we are about to have is not for her ears,' said Wesley flatly to Mike.

Libby, halfway out of the car, looked set to explode. She hated men who talked about her instead of to her. Mike looked at her and shook his head slightly from side to side. She dropped back into the seat and slammed the car door behind her.

Wesley smirked.

'Quite a little fire dragon. Do you think she will stay with you once money becomes tight?'

'That's our business, not yours,' replied Mike, trying to sound as unruffled as possible.

Wesley nodded knowingly, but Mike knew it was a sham on the man's part. Money or no money, Libby had stuck with him and had drawn a line under her previous life.

Wesley strode off, making his way across the grass to the stubby tower standing silently ahead of them. Mike followed, already bored. The journey to Eastbourne had provided a means to shake off or expose any car that might have tried to follow them from Brighton. Any driver would have needed to undertake some very risky manoeuvres to keep up and would have easily been spotted.

Mike looked back towards the parked Humber. The driver had got out and now stood by the roadside, casually smoking but really looking up and down the road for anything suspicious. Libby sat ramrod straight in the back seat of the car, staring straight ahead. Mike had no idea what might be going through her mind at that moment.

The pair entered the tower, and once inside, Wesley came to a standstill. He waited silently, staring down at his feet. Mike looked around at the whitewashed brick walls that curved around them. Although electric lighting brightened up the place, there was a damp smell that made the building feel cold and abandoned. Mike recognised it – it was common to all old abandoned military installations that had been repurposed in some way. He knew the building was a Martello tower dating back to Napoleonic times, built to protect the south-east and London from invasion by Bonaparte.

A man trotted down some steps and approached Wesley. He confirmed they had the tower to themselves and said he would wait at the entrance to keep out any unwanted sightseers. Wesley nodded and waited for the man to leave.

With the man out of the way, Wesley made his way up to the next floor and entered one of the two rooms that made up the upper floor. Mike followed. He noticed a small sign that indicated he was entering the officer's quarters. The room was plain, empty and much the same as the ground floor. There was nowhere to conceal microphones or mount cameras without them being seen. Mike had no recording equipment with him and he guessed the same applied to Wesley. No one would see or hear anything of the conversation they were about to have. *Typical Wesley* thought Mike.

'I would have preferred to have tipped off the police about where you were and let them arrest you. I believe you to be a murderer and nothing but a common thief,' said Wesley, turning and facing Mike directly.

Mike stood silent, knowing Wesley would have an impossible job to prove either allegation. His silent grey eyes challenged Wesley, whose irritation at failing to intimidate Mike was obvious. In one respect, Mike believed Wesley to be no better than himself – he knew how to kill and had done so before. The only real difference was that the police would never come looking for Wesley, a man shielded by the power of the British security services. Mike was not so lucky. He waited, unruffled by Wesley's weak threats. Soon he would have to explain why he had not taken Mike and Libby into captivity.

On the journey to Eastbourne, Mike had had plenty of time to think about the situation. Once Wesley had finally caught up with him in Canada, he had personally travelled there to deliver the message that he and Libby had been found, and they had been kept under strict surveillance ever since. This suggested to Mike that Wesley needed him more than he cared to admit. He anticipated that he was going to be offered a choice; go to prison or follow orders. Something needed to be done that, like the Victor Mazarin affair, was unofficial and completely deniable by the authorities. The next time he was out of Wesley's clutches would be the last. No more risky trips back home, ever again.

Wesley looked coldly at Mike. There was a pause, as if he was letting the tension build before announcing some shocking news. He had succeeded in getting Mike's attention, though Mike fought not to let Wesley see any signs of overwhelming curiosity.

'I want you to be Victor Mazarin,' said Wesley finally, in a flat and unemotional tone.

Mike was aghast. This was the very last thing he believed would ever be asked of him. His jaw dropped before he laughed involuntarily. What possible purpose was there in resurrecting the sociopathic killer?

'You have lost your mind! You want me to impersonate the very man you blackmailed me into destroying only a few months ago?' asked Mike with incredulity. He was about to ask why but Wesley got in before him.

'I know it sounds crazy, but things have come to light since Mazarin's death. He had been approached by some very important people and was asked to join them in a significant venture that I want to know about. If I knew at the time that he was my only means to get to these people and discover their plans, he might still be alive.'

'This is madness, Wesley. I don't look or sound anything like the man! Surely these people you are talking about know him personally. It's ridiculous! I can't help you – surely you can see that?' asked Mike with rising desperation.

'You are wrong, Armstrong. Mazarin was only approached via intermediaries and cut-offs. There was never any direct contact between him and the group in whom I am interested. All they know is that he is a naturalised Briton with a female partner. You can tell any lie you wish to pass yourself off as Mazarin, because there is no way for them to check your story,' Wesley responded firmly.

'No, I can't do it. As soon as they hear me speak it will be obvious I am no corporate businessman,' said Mike.

'You can't say no to me, Armstrong! You will do as I say, or you and your woman will pay the price,' said Wesley, with menacing emphasis on the word 'woman'.

Mike's mind reeled. He knew Wesley would deliver on his threat, and instinct told him there was no way he could wriggle out of this for now.

'I hold all the cards, Armstrong, because you are nothing but a criminal. You have no option and you know it,' said Wesley with a huge amount of self-satisfaction.

Mike looked at him. It seemed he was right. Mike had no options at that moment – *but who knows what opportunities to get away might arise later*, he thought.

'All right. I just don't see how me masquerading as Mazarin can achieve anything apart from probably getting me killed,' said Mike, with the resignation of a man with no choice.

'Good. Now that you are being reasonable, I can give you this.' Wesley pulled out a plain folded manila envelope from an inside pocket of his overcoat. He handed it to Mike.

'Read the contents and make all the arrangements you think necessary. The woman will need to know everything as well.'

Mike nodded. He wondered just what he was agreeing to and how dangerous this might be for Libby. Just then, Wesley grabbed his wrist.

'Don't lose the document or even think of making a copy. I want the entire thing returned to me next time we meet,' said Wesley, using his menacing tone from before.

Mike angrily pulled his wrist away then turned on his heel to leave. As he made his way back outside he could hear Wesley shout: 'A word of this to anyone and you will be committing treason!' He thought this was an odd choice of words for Wesley to use and assumed this would become clear once he had read the file.

Mike strode purposefully back to the car. By now, a second Humber was parked behind the first. Libby now sat in the back seat of the second car, which on closer inspection proved to be the one that had picked them up in Brighton. Mike supposed the real number plates had been refitted, noting that the car now sported its radio antenna.

He opened the rear passenger door and sat down beside Libby. Wesley had followed at a distance behind Mike but made for his own car. The radio transmitter in the second car had been powered up and a handset connected, ready to use. Libby was looking at him questioningly and Mike wondered how he was going to explain what had happened.

The two men who had acted as executioners at the farm earlier that day slid into the front seats. The driver turned to look at Mike and Libby. His chiselled features, strong nose, slightly over-length hair and extended sideburns indicated to Mike that the man was probably still in the armed forces. How special or not, Mike couldn't tell. The man slowly looked over Libby from head to toe as if he were appraising her with his slate-grey eyes. She shuddered slightly and felt exposed somehow; she tried to close her already closed legs further if she could and pulled her jacket as closely as possible around her neck. The actions were involuntary, but she could not help herself because of the way the man looked at her. He then looked over towards Mike.

'We'll drop you off near Hyde Park barracks. That's on orders from the boss, so don't argue. OK?' He made it a statement rather than a question. 'You can have your domestic with her after we drop you off. So, no talking from now on, understand?' Again, an order rather than a request.

Mike nodded. There was no point making enemies. The man in the passenger seat continued to act as if neither Mike nor

Libby were there, and he and the driver made no small talk between themselves.

The journey felt extremely unpleasant and over-long for Mike and Libby. The evening rush hour was in full swing when the Humber pulled over to a stop on the Kensington Road. The two men in front sat wordlessly looking ahead, waiting for Mike and Libby to get out. As soon as the couple were on the pavement and the back doors were shut the car pulled away into the traffic.

Mike and Libby unconsciously breathed a sigh of relief.

'Why did that man look me over in that way?' was Libby's first question. 'I felt so embarrassed. It was as if he was undressing me.'

Mike shrugged.

'We probably need to read this first to understand why,' he said, holding up the manila envelope.

'I get the feeling I am not going to like this,' she replied.

'That makes two of us,' said Mike as he waved down the first taxi that came along.

Once the pair were back in their suite at the hotel they relaxed a little. Both felt hungry and thirsty, so they decided to have a meal before sating their curiosity about the contents of the envelope. Mike and Libby also agreed they would be better able to deal with their situation on full stomachs. Once they had eaten they went and sat side by side on a sofa next to the coffee table. Placed on the surface was the manila envelope. Mike held a glass containing a generous slug of Laphroaig whisky and Libby a glass containing a Gordon's gin and tonic. They each took a steady sip of their drinks, then Mike opened the envelope.

9
UNLUCKY FOR SOME

Wesley gratefully took his seat on the train that was about to leave King's Cross. He always got off at the thirteenth stop, as he had done for nearly twenty years. Anyone else using the stop knew it as Welwyn Garden City, but Wesley had counted the stops when he first started using the service and it was the supposedly unlucky number that had stuck in his mind ever since. It never occurred to him that King's Cross was also the thirteenth stop going in the reverse direction from Welwyn. This might have been because it did not matter if he fell asleep going into London, as the train terminated there anyway. He *had* fallen asleep a few times before when travelling on the train, but only when he was returning home. On all these occasions, he awoke as the train was pulling into Cambridge. This gave him the idea that he and Evelyn, his wife, ought to have settled in Cambridge and not Welwyn. The trouble was, he used Cambridge as one of his places to meet with people like Armstrong, and this was a problem for Wesley when it came to the proximity of his public and private lives.

Wesley's mind began to wander down familiar paths, as it usually did on the journey home. As an Oxford graduate he had also felt that settling in Cambridge was inappropriate, for the same reason he had always sided with Oxford when the annual boat race took place against Cambridge on the River Thames. He had, however, never bothered to attend as he had no interest in sport of any kind. Messing about in those needle-like boats seemed an unnecessary thing to do as far as he was concerned. For Wesley, Oxford had merely been a stepping stone in his grand plan, a way to get on in life. Gaining a degree from Oxford or Cambridge opened many doors for graduates like Wesley that were ordinarily closed to the rest of the population. His plan was simple: get a degree to enable him to escape his life and parents in Virginia Water; find and marry a suitable girl; have a long career in the Civil Service that will pay for a nice house in suburbia and a comfortable pension on retirement. Wesley even had plans for motoring around the continent on holiday every year. Although he had achieved his aims in life, the lived reality fell way short of his expectations. He believed life had been cruel to him, giving him all he wanted but in ways that prevented him from enjoying any of it.

In the run-up to the war with the Nazis, a recruiter in Oxford had snapped up Wesley as the right sort of man to help wage a more secret kind of war. The recruiter easily persuaded him that working for military intelligence involved educated gentlemen and not the masses. Even the 'dirty tricks' missions carried out during the war by Wesley were for 'gentlemen' and not thugs like the commandos.

When the war ended he was thankful that there was much post-war work to be done because of the continued threat from the Soviet Union. Wesley was also thankful that the only real rival to him in the service had left and now wore a cleric's dog collar. Even more conveniently, the man had hidden himself away in north Norfolk following the end of hostilities in 1945. Wesley still hated Canute Simpson. Canute gave the impression of having found a contentment in life that Wesley still searched for in vain. *How could such a ruthless killing machine have found contentment?* he asked himself. Canute irritated him even more for his still-unproven complicity in assisting Mike Armstrong during the Mazarin affair.

Wesley had kept Canute under surveillance when Armstrong had disappeared. He received regular reports indicating that Canute enjoyed his new life in post-war Norfolk. The man lived in a form of self-imposed seclusion, abandoning contact with past friends or associates and concentrating on his parishioners instead. In turn no one had tried to contact Canute, so, annoyingly for Wesley, there was no evidence of Armstrong or any other kind of intermediary.

Wesley, on the other hand, was far from content because he was the only one who had not benefited in some way from the destruction of Mazarin. Unlike the men watching Canute, he knew he was still highly spoken of within the corridors and offices of MI6. But even Wesley's support of Simone Powell, the woman he had recruited personally, merited no recognition for himself. He found it typical that because he was not part of MI5 or 6, a Chinese wall existed, preventing him and his department from being acknowledged in the affair.

Wesley's work also led to him identifying both politicians and members of 5 and 6 who presented a high security risk. He was convinced that his claims were continually rebutted or ignored simply because he was not recognised as being one of them anymore. He believed the inferred message was that such matters would be dealt with in-house and not by the head of an unnamed 'dirty tricks' department that was still barely hanging on from the war. He knew his warnings had been brushed under the carpet and subsequently forgotten. It seemed to Wesley that whistle-blowers were not wanted even if national security was at stake.

The services had protected their own and were currently paying the price for their arrogance. Revelations in the newspapers confirmed how right he had been. He also assumed – correctly – that there would be no message or phone call containing an appropriately worded apology. Wesley also believed that if you were a member of Britain's social elite, a graduate of Cambridge or Oxford, sexually promiscuous and – ideally – homosexual, then you were perfect recruitment material for the Soviets.

Looking back, Wesley was firmly convinced he had been dealt an unfortunate hand in life. He had a security role so secret that no one was able to acknowledge his achievements. Each day when he caught the train to London, he looked around at the other passengers in the First Class compartment. He wondered how many of these men – there were no women – in their well-cut suits with pinstripe trousers and bowler hats were as important as they wished to appear. *What had they contributed to national security as opposed to their personal security?* he wondered. He had no idea what they did, as small talk during the rail journey was non-existent. Completing a crossword or reading the paper were the chief pastimes conducted by these men each morning and evening. This did not matter to Wesley, as the Official Secrets Act prevented him from talking about himself or his work anyway. He had painted himself into a professional corner and the paint was never going to dry. When the time came for him to retire, there would be no mention of him in the New Year's honours list or a cosy sinecure post at some university or college. Once he retired, his department would be closed, and his men reassigned elsewhere.

Wesley and Evelyn were childless but even if they weren't he would be unable to tell his wife and children about his work. He recognised that the latter was perhaps a blessing in disguise, despite the secrecy between himself and Evelyn. They had married in 1940 and after a honeymoon weekend saw almost nothing of each other for the next five years. Once the war had ended, she was no longer needed as a reservist Sub-Lieutenant in the Women's Royal Navy, where she had been working in the War Office. As both Wesley and Evelyn were desperate to escape the grime and bomb sites of the ravaged post-war capital, they had moved out to Welwyn Garden City. The irony was not lost on Wesley that his domestic arrangements mirrored that of his parents. Instead of finding freedom, Evelyn found herself marooned in what she described to Wesley as 'a green and pleasant wilderness'. It was a wilderness because their home was a place where one day they would die with no one around to notice. He had no counter to her observation.

Wesley thought it inappropriate that she should go out to work, since he was the breadwinner. Because of his work they made no friends and it never occurred to him to ask her what she did with her time. Evelyn told him she had long since tired of the few women she had met in Welwyn pressing her to tell them about his work. In time she lost contact with them all and lived in faded insular elegance. Like a forlorn wraith, she visited the library and posted letters to her sister before doing her shopping on the way home. Wesley carelessly let the crushing daily routine and the claustrophobia of the house smother her. She often spent extended periods staying with her sister in Tunbridge Wells.

Wesley kept many secrets from Evelyn, and Anja Ukraden was the bittersweet one he wanted to keep hidden the most. He was less worried about the unhappiness he would cause Evelyn, but just by having to admit that he had fallen in love with another woman. Wesley knew Evelyn would sue for a divorce, despite the huge amount of embarrassment it would cause, so he was desperate not to allow such a thing to happen.

The only other person who knew about the Yugoslav beauty and her relationship with Wesley was Canute Simpson. This gave Wesley an added reason to hate and, though he would never admit it, fear Canute.

Wesley had met Anja whilst working with partisans in the Balkans during the war. At first, he had been opposed to allowing a woman to join their combat group fighting the Nazis. Canute, who operated alongside Wesley, persuaded him to change his mind. Other partisans had many stories to tell of how fiercely she had fought and killed the soldiers of the occupation forces. The partisans insisted she would be an asset. Her beauty and ruthlessness in the face of the enemy also made excellent propaganda for the Yugoslav National Liberation Army. On both counts, they were correct.

Anja was as lethal as she was beautiful. She kept her long dark hair tucked under a field cap, dressed as a man and carried a Soviet PPS-43 submachinegun. She also used a Tokarev TT-33 automatic pistol as a back-up. She never explained how she had been able to get the Soviet weapons or their ammunition, but no one cared as long as she kept killing German soldiers with them. With her hair let down and her clothes discarded, she was able to twist any man around her finger. Wesley and Canute were no exceptions, but it was the former she fell in love with. Their affair lasted until Wesley returned home to England in 1945. She soon involved herself in a political war, helping to oust the monarchy and keeping the Catholic church under control in Yugoslavia. As her political strength grew, she made enemies who were publicly blamed for her being shot to death in the winter of 1950.

Unknown to Wesley, MI6 had identified Anja as a Soviet agent in 1946. The department also knew of their wartime relationship. The summer before her death, she came to London as part of a Yugoslav trade delegation. Wesley was routinely supplied with the details of visiting delegates from Soviet bloc countries. This was in case he was able to provide 5 or 6 with information for exploiting individuals. He experienced a mixture of surprise, elation and desire as he read Anja's name on the list. He had no reason to report her to other departments, so he made a snap decision to contact her and they arranged to meet in Battersea Park. The summer's day was bright and sunny as they walked along the banks of the Thames in the direction of the Albert Bridge. Unfortunately for Wesley, things had changed.

The memory continued to make him feel deeply uncomfortable as he looked out of the grubby train window at suburbia flashing by. With her hair down, and wearing a dingy leaden-styled Soviet bloc blouse, straight skirt and flat shoes, Anja calmly attempted to recruit him to spy for the KGB. Her beauty was undiminished and for a moment he had been ready to succumb. He knew she was playing on his wartime memories, but her intent was clear and the outcome more so. The meeting was not a reconciliation of old lovers and his choices were obvious. Agree with the remote chance of seeing her again or cut off the conversation there and then.

Wesley walked away, having chosen the latter to avoid compromising his future. He reported the contact with her to both 5 and 6 and then waited to see what would happen. Despite himself, he wanted to see her again. Months later came word that she had been shot during a purge of political suspects by the UBD, the Yugoslav equivalent of the KGB.

Wesley knew he had made the right decision that summer and had narrowly avoided destroying his career. It was not until her reported death that British intelligence departments were sure that Wesley could not be persuaded by Anja to spy for the Soviet Union. With a heavy heart, he also recognised that he had thrown away his only opportunity to try and entice Anja to defect. His two greatest decisions in life had been careless, rushed and emotional. They had led to him being reunited with, and then losing, the love of his life. He had vowed from then on to never again make snap decisions that were not calculated to be as risk-free as possible, with all outcomes considered.

Then Mike Armstrong entered his life.

Wesley considered Mike Armstrong to be an expendable pawn that his agent, Simone Powell, had recruited to spy on Mazarin. Instead, the man had become a wilful and overly independent thorn in Wesley's side. He knew too much about Mazarin and presented a security risk. Now that Wesley had Armstrong back under control, he was going to make sure the man's life ended once he had outlived his usefulness. For the sake of completeness, Wesley had also planned that Libby Kembrey would have the same fate as Armstrong.

What happened over the next few weeks would determine Wesley's future once and for all. He would exploit Armstrong to the maximum to get the information he needed and the recognition he was so long overdue. Wesley smiled to himself as he imagined the looks on the faces of his long-time critics and rivals when he finally proved himself to be better than all of them. Very soon all those sitting around him in the train compartment would learn who he was; they would know his name. He was coming out of the shadows at last – there was to be no turning back.

The train slowed to a gentle stop at Welwyn Garden City, bringing Wesley back from his thoughts about what had been and what was going to be. His mind came back to the present as he stood up to join the other passengers waiting in the carriage corridor before alighting at the station. Once on the platform he became just another face amongst the throng of commuters dispersing from the station. Glancing round, he noted the sense of urgency as people rushed off in all directions. Bodies were pushing past him, but he resisted the group's urge for haste. Some people were greeted by their loved ones; most others rushed on alone until they could meet their own at home or disappear behind the door to their inner sanctuary.

Wesley stood alone at the station entrance. A few taxis had arrived to tout for business and gleaned the last of the commuters off the pavement. A green double-decker half-cab bus pulled away in a cloud of diesel smoke. The noxious fumes assaulted Wesley's nose and reminded him why he lived in Welwyn. He only had to walk a few steps and he was back in the fresh summer evening air.

This was his favourite time of day. If he smoked, he would have lit a cigarette and stood alone to take in the stillness and returned calm of the station frontage. Instead, Wesley set off at an even pace towards Parkway and home. Counter-intuitively for someone working in intelligence, he never varied the final leg of his journey home. Attentive people would notice if he took an erratic pattern of routes over the short distance from the station to his home. He felt it wise instead to keep to a routine that attracted no interest to the casual observer. A professional would soon work out his method anyway.

Their large black front door was looking shabby, noted Wesley, as he pushed the key into the lock. An extra effort was needed to push it open and the hinges grated through lack of oil. The smell of recently cooked liver and onions depressively pervaded the inside of the hallway as he took off his jacket and hung it on the coat rack.

Wesley sat on the single chair and proceeded to take off his shoes before putting on his slippers. He popped his head round the door of the sitting room and smiled at Evelyn, who was sitting in her favourite Waring & Gillow armchair. She smiled back. The smiles were those of people who had nothing left to say to each other. Their routine and lack of intimacy overwhelmed any needless communication. They would talk later, they always did. His dinner was waiting in the oven, getting slightly dry at the edges; he knew that. Evelyn continued to read Hardy's *Tess of the d'Urbervilles* whilst listening to the BBC Home Service on the wireless.

Eating alone in the dining room, Wesley's mind began to wander once more. He was looking forward to next Christmas. He expected to be in the south of France, in a hotel room looking out on to the Mediterranean enjoying decent food and decent wine. Evelyn would not be there to share his European tour, but this was not an issue. No, he would be literally in the driving seat of his new life. He did not like the word 'retirement', even though that was exactly what he planned to do. Evelyn could do as she pleased once he was out of the way. The surprise to him was that she never had tried to do that before.

Her voice interrupted his thoughts. 'The door hinges need a bit of oil.'

'Indeed,' he replied as he began to cut through the cooked liver.

10
VICTOR'S RETURN

The contents of Wesley's manila envelope contained little in the way of paper, and no photographs either. This gave no indication of what Mike and Libby were about to get involved in. There were just a few close-typed pages of foolscap that Mike read before passing each page, one by one, to Libby. Afterwards he poured himself another large whisky and waited for Libby to finish reading.

They glanced at each other in shock and disbelief. No words passed between them as the import of the documents sank in. There was no maniac with an outlandish plan, nor was there a secret base in Norfolk that Mike had to penetrate and steal documents from. Instead Mike had to *be* the maniac; he had to impersonate Victor Mazarin, the man Libby had shot to death only months before.

'I don't believe it, Mike! How can you be expected to do this? You don't even look like Mazarin. You can't speak German and your accent belongs to someone from the north of England. What if one of these people knows Mazarin is dead? This is madness!' Libby exclaimed, looking alarmed and perplexed.

'We can come up with a cover story in the time we have left. I'm assuming Wesley's information is correct,' said Mike, desperate to placate her.

'What are you going to do? Dye your hair blond and learn pidgin German?' she asked, almost shouting.

Mike looked at her calmly. This was not about Wesley's crazy task for him, but about her being reminded that she had killed a man in cold blood. Mike put his arms around her.

'It's all too much and too soon,' she said, calm once more.

'You're right, and I don't think we should assume this is the beginning and the end of the matter.'

'You mean once we find out what Wesley wants he will force us to carry on?' asked Libby.

'Yes, I think so. He's no different to any other blackmailer and is keeping his overall objective hidden from us for now. Once we get a full picture of what he is up to we might get an idea of how to escape from his clutches. We have to play along for now,' he replied.

Libby took a sip from her drink and began thinking about their situation. Wesley had neatly linked them to the murder of the two men back at the farmyard. There was no doubt the bodies of the two thugs would be found once the slurry pit was emptied. Even if no witnesses could be found in Brighton, she was sure Wesley had ways of getting herself and Mike implicated in the killings.

'Fine, we play along, but I don't see how we can come out of this alive,' she said, pointing towards the envelope and its contents. 'Where is this town in Germany where the meeting is going to take place?'

'Bielefeld is in North Rhine-Westphalia. It's halfway between Dortmund and Hanover,' he explained.

Libby looked at him quizzically. She had little idea about the locations and even less of an understanding of their relevance.

'Bielefeld is the headquarters of 1(BR) Corps of the British Army of the Rhine. I was posted there for a few months when I was in the army,' he explained.

'So that's why all those names on that list belong to army men,' she replied.

'Exactly, and not just any old soldiers. They are all senior-ranking officers; the lowest rank is a brigadier whilst the rest are generals. This is one hell of a meeting that Wesley wants us to attend. There must also be a very good reason why they have chosen to meet off-base, as Steinhagen is well outside the town.'

'What would Mazarin have been doing with these men?' asked Libby, keen to explore their situation now it was unavoidable.

'They want something from him they can use. I bet when we get there we are not the only business types attending this meeting,' mused Mike.

'Hmm. Another thing: Mazarin's woman was Italian. How am I going to pass myself off as Carla Mancuso? I can't speak any Italian.'

'I'm sure Canute will help us to come up with a cover story,' replied Mike.

'Canute Simpson? I've heard it all now. What on earth has he got to do with all of this?' she asked, with a face resembling thunder. 'You know we can't go back to Little Stratton!'

'Why not? We don't have to worry about Wesley any more, he has already caught up with us,' said Mike.

'He is only half the problem. What about Dicky? He's still my husband, remember? What if he sees us?' she asked, searching Mike's face with her eyes.

'I will approach Canute on my own and we can make plans from there. You don't need to be with me when I speak to him,' he replied.

Libby knew he was right, though she wondered how Canute was going to be able to help them. She decided to put her trust in Mike, as they had no sound alternative plan other than to cooperate with Wesley. *After all*, she thought to herself, *Canute might be the wild card that unbalances Wesley's plan.* Libby also found herself feeling relieved that she need not face up to the responsibilities she had left behind in Little Stratton.

'I have to telephone Canute and arrange a meeting in Norfolk,' said Mike, interrupting her thoughts.

'Why can't he meet us here?'

'He won't budge unless it is absolutely necessary. You know what he's like,' Mike replied.

Libby nodded.

'Do you think we could meet him without the rest of the village knowing?'

'Of course, he would never say a word to anyone,' said Mike encouragingly.

'Right, I will come with you,' said Libby in a decisive tone.

Mike was glad she had decided to go with him. He hated being apart from her and she felt the same way too, even if returning to Little Stratton was going to be uncomfortable for them both.

Mike rang Canute in the hope that he would be at home late in the evening. Canute was surprised to hear from him, but from the tone of his voice appeared very interested to hear that both Mike and Libby wanted to meet. Mike made it clear the meeting was not a parochial matter. He also asked if the Jensen was usable. With unconcealed pride Canute confirmed that the car was in perfect condition.

Soon after the call finished, Mike and Libby went to bed having decided to discuss their plans first thing in the morning, to see if they still believed cooperating with Wesley was their only option.

* * *

Once Mike had rung off, Canute returned to his favourite armchair and unconsciously rotated a full whisky tumbler in his huge hand. He had to admit to himself that hearing Mike's voice again, and so soon, could only mean one thing: the man must need his help. Though surprised to hear that Libby would be accompanying Mike, he guessed the matter must be serious enough to make her return to the village. Mike had told him they planned to arrive at the rectory after dark to avoid being seen. Canute felt this to be a wise precaution – if the pair were seen, the village rumour mill would swing into operation straight away, something Libby would hate.

Glass in hand, Canute went outside and ambled over to his large garage. He went inside and pulled the dustcover back from the Jensen CV8 that had once belonged to Simone Powell. The exposed front end of the vehicle shouted muscularity and contempt in its lines. Canute could see his reflection in the deeply polished dark blue paint that Simone had ordered specially. The twin sets of halogen headlights angled aggressively inwards towards the narrow grille nestling behind the chromium bumper. A small air scoop sat centrally and slightly back from the front of the bonnet, and underneath that sat a modified V8 engine and gearbox. Temporarily inert and silent, the engine waited to voraciously feed upon the copious amounts of petrol that would allow it to release its bellicose roar. Canute wondered how such a bestial car could be of use to Mike and Libby.

* * *

The next morning Mike and Libby sat opposite each other, eating breakfast. Mike was relaxed and ate well, whilst Libby's appetite was muted.

'Still worried about going to Little Stratton?' he asked in a gentle voice.

'No, I suppose not,' she replied. Mike waited for her to carry on, as it was obvious to him that something was clouding her thoughts.

'I'm worried about what will happen when all this is over. Wesley is going to kill you and I think you already know that. What are we going to do?'

'You are not going to achieve anything through worrying about Wesley,' he replied. 'Let's meet up with Canute first and go from there.'

'Don't you think you put too much faith in him?' asked Libby.

'Who else knows Wesley better?' countered Mike.

Libby had to agree that Canute really was the only man they knew who could help them.

Following breakfast, they packed their overnight bags and checked their automatic pistols. The pair had shoulder holsters, allowing easy carriage of the weapons during their journey north back to Norfolk. They sat passing the time away in their hotel suite. There was no point getting a train that delivered them to Norfolk in daylight. But by late morning both had had enough of sitting around in the hotel and they headed out to have a light lunch. Mike suggested they eat near Regents Park, so they could go for a walk and relax afterwards. Libby readily agreed. By the time they returned to the hotel it was evening. They skipped having an early dinner and headed to King's Cross station.

Unknown to Mike or Libby, had they waited any longer they would have caught the same train used by Wesley for commuting. If Wesley did see them he would have been anxious to know where they were headed and furious about who they were going to meet.

The train journey to King's Lynn was uneventful and on time. As they made their way to the taxi rank outside the station, Mike looked up at the persistently bright June sky. They still had time to kill before it would be dark. Mike told the taxi driver to take a slow drive around the coast road before dropping south and inland to Little Stratton. When he hesitated, Mike let him know there would be a substantial tip when he dropped them off. The driver set off once it was clear a good earner was in the offing.

The taxi arrived at Little Stratton as the last vestige of light quickly receded from the countryside. Libby shrank in her seat and avoided looking out of her window as they passed the few houses situated on the road that led from the village to the rectory. Their lateness meant the dog walkers had long gone home and evening visitors to the nearby churchyard had completed their business, spiritual or otherwise. Mike directed the taxi driver into the rectory's drive. The approaching taxi headlights reflected off the windows, alerting anyone inside that a vehicle was approaching. Mike quickly paid the driver before they hurriedly fetched their overnight bags from the boot of the car.

Canute had opened his front door before the taxi had even stopped and he ushered his guests through, closing the door quickly behind them. All three relaxed now that they were in the sanctuary of the rectory. The overnight bags were placed down to one side, then both Mike and Libby pulled out their Smith & Wesson pistols and placed them on top of their respective bags. This told Canute a lot, even though he made no comment.

'This is a most pleasant and interesting surprise,' he said, starting the conversation with a large warm smile. Mike returned the gesture, but Libby was hesitant. Canute touched her elbow gently with a powerful hand.

'There are no moral judgements to be made in my home, Libby. You are as welcome as anyone else, you should know that,' he said encouragingly.

'Thank you. I'm not so sure that everyone around here holds the same view,' she said, though she relaxed slightly.

'Shall we go through to the kitchen to see what we can find to eat?' said Canute. 'Your old housekeeper, Mrs Rudd, works for me now, Mike. She is a fine woman and tells me all the local gossip just as she did with Simone. A most useful lady.'

'I employed her on the basis that she minded no one else's business and on the recommendation of Simone. It seems I was misled,' Mike replied.

'She is a tight-lipped lady when it comes to talking to the rest of the village, though. Thoroughly reliable. No questions at all when I asked her to prepare food for extra guests tonight,' Canute replied with a twinkle in his eye.

Mike returned the smile whilst a look of alarm crossed Libby's face. 'You don't think she's worked out who your guests are, do you, Canute?' she asked worriedly.

'Not a clue. I gave her the rest of the afternoon off and as soon as she had finished preparing the meal she was straight out the door to visit her sister,' he responded, trying to dispel Libby's fears.

Canute noted that the haughty Mrs Kembrey had softened considerably. Before taking up with Mike, her superior manner had given the impression that she cared little about what others thought of her. He approved of the change.

The rector and his guests talked amiably as they ate dinner. Mrs Rudd's interpretation of a quiche Lorraine with a mixed salad and lemon mayonnaise went down very well with the threesome. Canute opened a well-chilled bottle of Alsace Riesling to accompany the meal.

When they had finished eating, Canute led the others through to his parlour. He double-checked the curtains were closed properly and the three sat around a wooden coffee table. Canute had anticipated they would need a space to work on, so had cleared the table of everything except a new bottle of Laphroaig whisky and three pristine tumblers.

Mike laid out the typed papers that were given to him by Wesley. Without touching them, Canute read each sheet one by one as they lay on the table. By sharing the documents with an unauthorised person, Mike knew he was going directly against Wesley's orders. However, as he believed there was more to this plan than Wesley was letting on, Mike didn't hesitate in showing them to Canute.

The big man finished reading the documents then purposefully opened the bottle of whisky. He poured three large drinks and passed one glass to Mike and another to Libby before settling back into his chair.

'If my summation is correct, you two must travel to West Germany posing as Victor Mazarin and Carla Mancuso to attend a meeting arranged by a group of senior British army officers. Wesley wants you to find out what they are up to, identify the weakest link within the group and exploit him,' said Canute.

'Exactly,' Mike replied.

'An impossible task,' added Libby firmly.

Canute glanced at her with interest. 'Why do you say that, Libby?' he asked, putting up his hand to prevent Mike's interjection.

Libby took a sip of the whisky and placed her glass down on the coffee table. 'Neither of us look anything like the people we are supposed to be, and if any of these officers know what Mazarin or Mancuso look like then we are in big trouble. Neither of us can speak a foreign language, so how can we pass ourselves off as originating from Austria and Italy? That's just for starters,' she said.

Canute sat back, whisky in hand, and thought for a moment. Mike chose to remain silent, as Libby had put his thoughts into words perfectly.

'I cannot believe that Wesley would risk sending you to a meeting where people might know instantly that you are not who you claim to be. He has nothing to gain by doing that,' said Canute thoughtfully.

'I agree,' said Mike, backing his friend. 'All we need do is come up with a good cover story and we will be fine.'

'Simply tell them a lie that's salted with the truth, if asked,' added Canute cryptically.

'Meaning what?' asked Mike.

'You were a child refugee from the war who was brought up by an English family in the north-east of England. You are too young to remember anything else, hence you only speak with a Geordie accent. Use your personal knowledge to answer any questions about the north-east should the need arise,' replied Canute.

'What about me?' asked Libby.

'Your Italian parents sent you to English relatives living in London when the war started, with the intention of joining you later and travelling to America. Events overtook your parents in 1940 when Italy took up with Germany, so they were unable to travel to London. They were killed during the hostilities and you have remained in London with your relatives ever since,' said Canute.

'You think these stories will hold up?' challenged Mike.

'Yes, there will be no time for anyone to check the details. The fact that you have been sent by Wesley will establish your bona fides, so you will be accepted without question,' replied Canute, smiling.

'But we have no documents to prove we are Mazarin and Mancuso,' said Libby.

'Of course not, you are sensibly travelling under false names.'

'I still don't know what they are expecting to get from a madman like Mazarin,' said Mike.

'When they ask, simply lie and promise them all they need. Just don't overdo things,' replied Canute.

'Do you know any of the army officers on the list Wesley provided?' asked Mike.

'Yes, it's an intriguing list of individuals. The few I know all originate from the Scottish and Border regiments of the British army. They were junior officers when I knew them during the war. They all seem to have done spectacularly well in achieving their exalted ranks. The brigadier, in particular, has been promoted well past his capabilities. A real loose cannon with very dubious politics, as I remember. He runs off at the mouth when he gets a drink inside him, so may be a good starting point for you,' said Canute.

Mike checked the list: Brigadier Iain Thomson, 3rd Earl of Tantallon.

'Now, what are your immediate plans?' asked Canute.

'We need to get some sleep and then head off before first light,' said Mike, checking his watch and realising it was already after midnight.

'The Jensen is ready to go. The keys are in the ignition,' said Canute.

11
STEINHAGEN

Libby looked at the deep blue, almost black pre-dawn Norfolk sky as she stood alone in the unlit doorway of the rectory with the overnight bags at her feet. Mike and Canute had gone around to the garage for the car, leaving her to her thoughts for a few moments. A few stars were still visible and shining like tiny diamonds dotted across the velvety swathe of inky sky. She could hear the opening notes of the dawn chorus beginning to sound around her.

The night had been warm and quiet, allowing her to sleep easily as she had done in faraway Canada. The chalet by the lake seemed to be in the distant past now, and she felt her life before meeting Mike was a fiction. *Was she once a respectable landowner's wife who wore tweed, pearls and sensible shoes?* She shuddered at the thought of returning to her dull pre-existence.

Her pistol weighed heavy against her side, pulling the shoulder holster downwards. The slight discomfort would disappear once they were on the move, she knew that.

Libby snapped out of her reverie as she heard the Jensen roar into life. She remembered the sound from before, when Simone Powell had been the owner of the car. The rumbling offbeat notes of the engine quickly settled, then she heard the car pull away before appearing around the corner of the building. The headlights flashed across her face, forcing her to squint.

Mike stepped out of the car and flipped open the boot lid. Libby placed their overnight bags inside and Mike reclosed the lid. Canute joined them to say his goodbyes. He shook Mike's hand and gave Libby a hug. He only needed to smile now – they had said all they needed to say during breakfast.

Mike drove out along the same back lane the taxi had taken the evening before. No words were spoken as they roamed around in the solitude of their thoughts. Libby searched her memory to see if anyone she once knew might be around at that time of the morning. She thankfully drew a blank.

A tiny piece of Mike expected to glance over to the passenger seat and see Simone sitting there, casually smoking a cigarette as she had done when he first drove the Jensen that night in February – a time that was now as distant as Libby's previous life with Dicky. Their past was known and immutable, just as their future was unknown and open to change. Mike stole a glance at Libby. He sensed there was an aura of vulnerability around her that morning and he almost stopped the car to hold her tightly. She noticed his glance and smiled, evaporating any worries he had.

'When do I get to drive this thing?' she asked mischievously.

'How about now?' replied Mike as he pulled over to the side of the empty road. The pair swapped seats. Mike watched as she adjusted the seat and mirrors until they were to her liking. Last of all, she pulled her skirt back from her knees before selecting first gear and accelerating away with a slight screech coming from the rear tyres.

'This is fabulous, Mike! So much more powerful than Canute's Rover,' she enthused as she took control of the surging power coming from the engine.

Mike grinned at the thought of her driving Canute's Rover in the same manner. 'You're taking to driving this very well,' he said. 'Did Simone ever let you drive it?'

'She never let anyone within ten paces of this monster,' she replied.

Except me, he thought. He wondered if Simone had deliberately used the car to draw him into her conspiracy against Mazarin, and if she really trusted him as much as he believed.

'So, where did you learn to handle a car like this?' asked an intrigued Mike.

'My cousin has an Aston Martin, a DB4 he calls it, and he used to let me drive it to Sandown Park to watch the horse racing. He had the car tuned and uses it for circuit racing. Very fast, noisy and very uncomfortable,' she replied as she changed up through the car's gears using the precise gear shift.

'Do you want to drive the rest of the way back to London?'

'Of course, this car is fun to drive!' she replied enthusiastically.

'How about driving to Germany too?' he asked, this time watching for her reaction.

Libby looked over and gave him a coy smile. 'As long as you are with me,' she replied.

Mike's memories of Simone evaporated as he reached over to momentarily rest the back of his hand against Libby's cheek. His eyes lingered across her exposed knees. He was rewarded with another coy smile.

* * *

A few hours later they were back at the hotel, the Jensen left to cool its heels in the hotel's underground car park. When they arrived at the reception desk the concierge passed an envelope to Mike. The small sheet of paper inside it was plain and unsigned. A typed sentence tersely informed them that the meeting was taking place a day earlier than previously notified. The note meant nothing to anyone other than the person for whom it was intended, and Mike knew it could only have originated from Wesley. He had no doubt the note had been delivered in such a way that the on-duty concierge would have no clear memory of the person delivering it.

'We'd better pack and head off as soon as we can,' Mike said to Libby.

Before leaving reception, he asked the concierge to contact British United Air Ferries and find out if the next flight to Le Touquet in France had space for them and the Jensen. They then went up to their suite and started packing in the hope of an early departure. The concierge called up to tell them they could be squeezed on to a late-morning flight the next day, if Mike could supply their passport and car details. Mike passed on the information and left the concierge to finalise the arrangements.

'That leaves us plenty of time to pack,' said Libby airily.

'This isn't a holiday,' replied Mike in a cautious tone.

Libby put her arms around his neck and kissed him deeply, leaving Mike no option other than to respond. She kicked off her shoes before slowly walking backwards towards the bedroom, pushing open the door whilst pulling Mike in with her. He deftly undid the back of her skirt and pulled the zip down until it fell away to the floor, then he undid her back-buttoned blouse to leave her wearing only her underwear. By this time, she had slipped off Mike's jacket and undone his tie before removing his shirt. A little more hurriedly than intended, she undid Mike's belt and trousers. Fully aroused by her sensual provocations, he stepped away from his fallen trousers and pushed her gently over on to the large bed. As their eyes locked in desire he thought it might be good for her to drive the Jensen when they were on the continent.

* * *

The next morning Mike rang the reception desk to find out if the hotel would hold the suite for him whilst he was away for a few days on a business trip. The concierge was happy to oblige as Mike would continue to pay in full for the suite. He had originally planned to check out of the hotel, but had realised it would be far easier to leave their belongings, especially the rifles, in situ. The rifle cases were left locked and out of sight in case an overly curious housekeeper or maid decided to have a look around.

Both Mike and Libby had packed enough clothes for an excursion on the continent lasting several days. After they had finished, they ate a leisurely breakfast. Mike wondered what Libby would make of the next few days in Germany, where breakfasts consisted of coffee, black bread, cold meats and cheeses.

Mike wore a two-piece business suit in grey lightweight wool and a well-polished pair of black Oxford shoes with closed lacing. Libby decided to complement him by wearing a grey tweed peacoat jacket with a matching fitted skirt and high heels. The jacket was perfectly tailored to her figure and had six oversize black buttons. The tweed she wore now, compare to in her previous life, was light, fashionable and designed to show off her figure instead of hiding it away beneath unflattering heavy pleats.

Neither of them carried their Smith & Wesson pistol. Instead, the firearms were carefully stowed away by Mike under each of the front seats of the Jensen. He reckoned the chance of such a pair of respectable-looking individuals having their car stopped and searched was nil. Once through the border crossing at Venlo and in West Germany proper the pistols would be reunited with their owners.

The pair had their leather Ventura suitcases taken to the basement garage and placed in the boot of the Jensen. Once the keys to the car were returned to Mike, he and Libby headed downstairs. Despite being underground, Libby insisted on wearing her black Paulette Guinet sunglasses and a grey silk headscarf. Mike thought she was still being overly cautious about running into someone from her past in London. His Persol sunglasses remained in his breast pocket until they drove out into the bright sunshine.

Once through the choking morning traffic of west London, Mike began to push the Jensen harder. It was strangely satisfying that no matter how he drove, English roads prevented him from finding these limits. *Things will be different on the German autobahns*, he thought to himself.

They arrived at Lydd airport in Kent with plenty of time to spare. The Jensen's now-inert engine ticked quietly to itself as they left to find the departure desk in the small airport complex. An hour later, the car was strapped ignominiously to the floor at the front of the main hold in a Bristol Superfreighter air ferry. The twin clamshell doors of the Bristol began to close, as if it were about to slowly digest the Jensen. Further back, Mike and Libby sat side by side in the boxlike structure of the passenger cabin. Around them the seats were full of excited passengers looking forward to their visit to France and the continent. The short flight of 47 miles was soon completed, with the cars swiftly unloaded and the passengers dispersing soon after landing.

Mike and Libby noticed the change in climate the moment the doors to the aircraft opened. The flight over the English Channel had been breezy and cool, as the air had found its way through the large, barely sealed clamshell doors of the Superfreighter. As they stepped out of the aircraft the pair literally warmed to the change in weather. The dry continental heat contrasted with the temperate nature of the British climate. Straight away Mike thought of driving off into the countryside to find a village where they could share a bottle of chilled white wine. As it was already well into the afternoon, though, he knew they needed to get on; they had a long road trip ahead of them and he wanted to reach Steinhagen before dark.

The route Mike planned to take from Le Touquet was close to 600 miles and would take over six hours, excluding stops, to complete. Mike drove the first stint, to Ghent in Belgium. Libby drove the second stint, through Antwerp and up to the German border at Venlo. The Jensen took the long journey in its stride, allowing the pair to travel at much higher speeds than they could on English roads. Once through the Dutch–German border near Venlo, Mike pulled into the first *parkplatz* they came across and waited a few minutes to ensure that they were alone. The area was as deserted as they had hoped, so they reached under their seats to get at their pistols. Minutes later, they moved on.

As Mike drove the Jensen back on to the *autobahn*, Libby suggested they split the last part of the journey between them. He could see how much she enjoyed driving the car and her suggestion made sense. By late evening they would both be getting tired from the long drive, and as neither of them knew the local roads around Steinhagen, the more alert they were the less likely it was for them to make a wrong turning.

As they got closer to Bielefeld, Mike purchased a local map when they stopped for petrol. This meant they could easily find Steinhagen even if it was dark. The hotel where the meeting was planned to take place was called the Bauernhaus, and although it did not appear on the map, Mike assumed that when they were in Steinhagen proper, finding it would not be a major problem.

He was right not to have worried. The hotel was the largest one around and, for Steinhagen, the most prestigious. Small signs with the Bauernhaus name on them pointed the way to the hotel, which was situated on the south-west edge of town. A large well-manicured garden and car park separated the building, which appeared to be a huge barn converted into a hotel, from the road. The extensive shingle roof was supported by black-painted wooden-framed walls with white panels of stucco between the uprights. Windows had been inserted along the length of the walls and there appeared to be no upper floor. The end of the building was at right angles to the road and each side had further provision for parking. The end nearest the road had double doors with a large sign above, indicating in traditional German: *Kurrentschrift*; they had reached the Bauernhaus Hotel.

Libby had driven the last stint of the journey. She pulled into the hotel car park and chose a space close to the entrance. The pair glanced around at the collection of expensive cars parked nearby and noted that many of them had British number plates. They collected their suitcases from the boot and made their way into reception.

The hotel had the feel of an old hunting lodge, with a collection of varying sizes of deer antlers hanging from the walls. Numerous electric lights, in the form of faux candles and a heavy chandelier hanging from the roof apex, made the reception area feel surprisingly light and airy.

At the reception desk stood a smartly dressed young man. His jacket, white shirt and tie were in the latest style and contradicted the traditional setting in which he worked. He smiled and greeted them in English, telling them his name was Stefan. The accent was only slightly Germanic, and to Mike's surprised consternation, he addressed him as Herr Mazarin. They were invited to sign the hotel register and to allow reception to hold their passports for safe-keeping.

'Do you require a double room or two singles?' he asked, after seeing that the names on the passports differed from those on the booking.

'A double. How did you know my name?' asked Mike, holding the young man's gaze.

'There is nothing to worry about, Herr Mazarin. All the staff understand our guests' need for confidentiality. We use your real names to avoid unnecessary confusion,' replied Stefan. 'You are the last of our English guests to arrive – and I can see you are both English from the way you dress,' he added, smiling.

Mike laughed. 'Do we dress that badly?' he asked.

'No, not at all. The English style is getting very popular and is hard to find in Germany unless you live somewhere like Berlin or Hamburg,' Stefan replied as he picked up their suitcases and led them to their room. 'Shall I book you a table for dinner?' he asked as they walked along a lengthy corridor.

'Yes, we will eat at eight,' Mike replied. 'The other guests in our party, will they be eating in the restaurant tonight?'

'I believe they are, sir,' was the reply.

Mike tipped Stefan and the young man left them to their own devices.

The room was larger than Mike had expected, though sparse in the way that a provincial hotel in Germany would be. The décor and furniture were modern, with no antlers to be seen on the white painted walls. Instead there were modernist prints attributed to German artists. On the large wood-framed bed lay duvets contained in crisp white cotton with plumped-up pillows to match. The bathroom was equally modern, suggesting that the barn that made up the hotel had been thoroughly converted to fulfil its new purpose. Fine net curtains protected them from the prying eyes of guests using the car park outside, and the well-lit minimalist lines of the room left little opportunity for the easy sighting of a listening device or a camera, though Mike checked anyway. Once he was happy, they unpacked their suitcases.

Libby announced that she was going to relax in the bath before dinner. She undressed completely, leaving her clothes and pistol strewn on the bed. Mike smiled. She had not even bothered to close the heavy curtains before taking off her clothes. It occurred to Mike that this was something she would never have done back home in England. Libby had noticeably relaxed now that the pressure of feeling hunted had temporarily lifted. It was possible that the thrill of their adventure into Germany was also giving her a feeling of new-found freedom. She had clearly enjoyed driving the Jensen at full throttle on the *autobahn*. The concentration of driving at a three-figure speed appeared to have pushed any worries far from her mind. When they had stopped for a coffee break, she had given Mike a fully relaxed and carefree smile that he had never seen before.

Mike stood by the window and pulled the net curtain back. His mind had been ticking over to the point where he thought he might be drawing totally the wrong conclusions. The hotel was modern and unlikely to draw any local customers unless they were well-heeled. All the cars parked outside with German registrations were top Mercedes models, interspersed with the odd Jaguar and Cadillac. The hotel was remote enough to allow people to come and go inconspicuously, if that was what someone wanted. He was sure the hotel catered for well-off guests who would know their trysts would stay private. Stefan had not batted an eyelid when Mike had confirmed that he and Libby were to stay in the same room. The young man had assumed Herr Mazarin and Miss Mancuso were lovers and, of course, he was right.

The prospect of dinner and perhaps encountering other guests intrigued Mike greatly. He assumed that anyone who was English and possibly travelling alone had arrived for the meeting that was scheduled for the next day. Any German guests who were accompanied by an attractive woman probably had a very different meeting in mind. Dinner was going to be where Mike and Libby's work began for real.

12
A NIGHT OUT

'Did that Mancuso woman dress like a harlot or had she got some style about her?' asked Libby.

'Oh, she had plenty of style. She was a drop-dead gorgeous Italian,' replied Mike.

The comment irked Libby and she did not hide her reaction. Standing naked in front of him with her legs apart, her hair wrapped in one of the crisp white towels belonging to the hotel, she placed her hands on her hips. She looked him in the eye, challenging him to say something more.

Mike found it refreshing that her old snappy and superior manner had become provocatively sassy, making him love her even more. Stepping forward, he cupped her chin in his hand and turned her head left and right as if inspecting her.

'That woman had nothing on you, Libby,' he said.

She gave him that special smile he had seen earlier in the day. 'Well, I suppose I had better get ready for dinner,' she said, turning her back on him and returning to the bathroom.

Mike's eyes lingered on her well-shaped behind before she disappeared from his sight.

Later, with their pistols secured in a suitcase and put away in a locked wardrobe, the pair headed for the dining room. They were both hungry and thirsty from their long journey. Mike wore a dark business suit, a white cotton shirt, a dark blue wool tie and his well-polished black leather Oxfords. Libby wore a simple black cocktail dress by Balmain. The top lay horizontally across her cleavage and was flanked by inch-wide shoulder straps. The dress stopped just short of her knees, suggesting everything and betraying nothing. Instead of wearing a necklace, she wore pendant earrings with large teardrop pearls. She had put on black patent-leather high heels that showed her off her shapely legs. Mike anticipated that Libby would attract side glances from guests as she entered the dining room.

He was to be disappointed. The dining room was at the opposite end to reception and the entrance was via a pair of smoked-glass double doors that ensured privacy for guests sat in the restaurant. As they went through, Mike glanced around for the maître d'.

A young man approached them, dressed in the same smart fashion as Stefan at reception. In faultless English the man asked for Mike and Libby's room number. He then led them to their table in amongst a collection of booths that formed the dining room. Mike had presumed the area would be open plan, allowing him to observe the other guests at their tables. The booths made that impossible, as heavy drape curtains provided a further measure of privacy once the guests had taken their seats. Mike found the arrangement old-fashioned and claustrophobic. He could not, however, fault the privacy the hotel provided for its guests.

No other people were visible, but voices could be overheard, so Mike tuned into these as he and Libby were led to their table. As expected, he could hear lots of German being spoken by both men and women. The hubbub in the room made the voices too indistinct to be heard clearly, but this was not a concern to Mike. He wanted to hear someone speaking in English, because an English voice might well belong to some of the men meeting with Mike and Libby the next day.

No sooner had Mike thought this when they passed a large booth that was much noisier than the rest of the dining room put together, and he knew this would irritate the more restrained German clientele. The group was unmistakably English, with clipped upper-class accents. It seemed the individuals knew each other well, as they seemed to be using first names or nicknames when they spoke to each other.

Mike and Libby took their seats and were politely asked if they would like something to drink before ordering. Mike ordered a bottle of Spätburgunder Blanc de Noir, knowing that Libby avoided overly sweet wine. The young man smiled in appreciation at Mike's choice and left the pair to peruse the menu.

The noise from the large booth continued to pervade the dining room and Mike wondered how long it would be before another guest complained. He need not have worried, though, as shortly afterwards a voice within the group announced that having eaten, they should all visit the nightclub across the road. There was an all-male voicing of agreement and the group of men chatted amiably as they walked by Mike and Libby's booth. Mike noted that, despite the joviality of the group, none of the men appeared to be drunk, nor had any of them said anything that might indicate why they were staying at the hotel.

Without warning, a head popped round the curtain of Mike and Libby's booth.

'Good evening, Mr Mazarin, Miss Mancuso,' said the man, his glance lingering on Libby. 'I am glad to see you have arrived safely. My name is Iain Thomson. I am the man who invited you to join our meeting tomorrow.'

'Good evening, Mr Thomson, and thank you for your invitation,' replied Mike, smiling. 'Carla and I are looking forward to meeting the rest of the invitees in the morning.'

'Oh, don't wait until tomorrow. I'll pop back later after you've eaten and take you to join the others. They are a nice crowd and the club I am taking them to is just across the road.'

Mike looked at Libby, who was giving nothing away. 'Thank you, it would be a pleasure,' he said.

'Excellent, enjoy your meal,' said Thomson, who promptly withdrew his head and disappeared.

'Well, that was a surprise,' said Libby.

'Yes, I think we are the outsiders to this gentlemen's club,' said Mike, referring to the noisy group of men leaving the dining room, 'so if we get a chance to meet them socially it will oil the wheels for tomorrow.'

'Judging by our Mr Thomson's breath, he is already well oiled,' Libby responded dryly.

'Yes, I noticed that too, but the others didn't sound very drunk.'

'Perhaps they are more security conscious than Thomson.'

'Brigadier Thomson, you mean – the one Canute said is holding a rank beyond his capabilities,' he replied.

'Meaning?' quizzed Libby.

'Well, we have a supposedly "secret" meeting tomorrow and Thomson is hardly being discreet about things, is he? A noisy dinner and a trip out to a club the night before. I suspect the only people who don't know the agenda for tomorrow are ourselves. I think the others in the group are already well informed thanks to their talkative friend, the brigadier,' he continued.

'Yes, if I were his boss I would not like having my thunder stolen just before a meeting occurs. Thomson may be the weak link we can exploit tomorrow – or maybe even tonight,' Libby replied.

Mike had noticed the way Thomson's eyes had roved over Libby. Perhaps the man had other weaknesses that could make him vulnerable to saying more than he should. Mike was also sure that the club Thomson referred to must be connected to the hotel other than by geographical position. If businessmen were using the hotel for clandestine meetings with their mistresses, then it must also be possible to seek their entertainment at a conveniently situated establishment. This might explain why the group of men using the large booth were more than happy to decamp across the road.

Mike recommended that he and Libby share a *pfefferpotthast* between them. The delicious peppery stew with lashings of onions and potatoes was very popular in the region and soon sated their hunger. While they were eating he warned her that the club they were being taken to might not be what she expected. He knew from his brief time in Bielefeld that certain nightclubs were bordellos that featured adult entertainment. Libby's eyes widened as Mike explained.

'You mean they do much more than the clubs in Soho?' she asked.

'Well, if I'm right, you will soon see,' he replied.

'You really think they allow women inside?' she exclaimed.

'They are nightclubs, Libby; these are places some women are taken to be seen in,' he said, wondering if Libby would prefer to stay in the hotel until he returned.

'But why?' she asked incredulously.

'Probably the only place for men to relax and show off their catch, or perhaps they just like the adventure. I don't know,' he said.

'Well, I am not going to be put off by your suspicions, Mike. We will go together,' she said, with an edge to her voice.

Once Mike and Libby had eaten they escaped the confines of their booth and sat at the bar. They each had a straight whisky and chatted as if they were like any other guests at the hotel. From the bar they were able to observe the comings and goings of the other diners. Men in formal eveningwear or business suits broke cover occasionally when they went to and from the restrooms. Their female counterparts did the same. Libby noticed straight away that the women were all younger than any of the men. Mike could see her mind working around to his way of thinking about the relationship between the hotel and the nightclub.

'Well, here you are,' said a voice approaching from the dining-room entrance. 'Your meal and drinks are on me tonight and so are any expenses later this evening,' Thomson said, winking at Libby.

She shifted uncomfortably on the bar stool then took a sip of whisky before unconsciously pulling her dress down to try to cover her knees. Mike guessed she was only going to get more uncomfortable as the evening wore on. They downed their drinks then followed Thomson outside and through the car park. The small talk began innocently as they walked. Thomson was on one side of Libby, Mike on the other. As expected, Thomson casually probed them with questions that both had anticipated thanks to Canute Simpson. By the time they had followed the well-maintained path to the nightclub it seemed that Thomson was sure he was talking to Victor Mazarin and Carla Mancuso.

The nightclub gave nothing away other than its name, 'The Windmill', as they approached the large glossy black door. The lack of cars parked nearby might make someone think, mistakenly, that the place was empty. Darkness had fallen as it was getting late, and low-key lighting illuminated their steps as they neared the entrance. On either side were old-fashioned lanterns fitted with low-wattage red bulbs that emitted an inviting glow. *Enough light to see, but not enough to be seen by*, thought Mike. There was no doubt in his mind about the type of club they had been invited to.

Thomson rapped on the door and a small hatch opened inwards. A woman peered through the black painted bars that protected her from the others waiting outside. The hatch snapped shut and the sound of heavy door bolts being opened reached the ears of the waiting trio.

The woman whose eyes they had seen through the small hatch gestured for them to come in through the open door. Her narrowed and inquisitive eyes, as they had been seen through the hatch, had become friendly and welcoming. She smiled at Thomson and said good evening to him. She had auburn hair and wore a bottle-green velvet dress with a plunging neckline that displayed her ample cleavage. Mike guessed that the woman, who had a faultless curvaceous figure, was at least middle-aged but there was no way of knowing her actual age. She welcomed Mike and Libby with a courteous smile then snapped her fingers. An equally attractive but much younger woman appeared and was told to take Thomson and his guests to their table.

As they wound their way to their table, Libby looked around. At first the club looked like any other; small circular tables dotted around the place, each with a small table lamp. Well-dressed guests, both men and women, sat smoking and chatting to each other over drinks, with champagne appearing to be the drink of choice. Background music played through loudspeakers across the large, dimly lit room. There was no dance floor. As they approached a table she noticed some pictures hanging on the wall behind the seats. They depicted men and women making love to each other. Nothing was left to the imagination, though the skill of the artist managed to emphasize the erotic rather than simply present banal crudity to the observer. Once they had sat down at the table, Libby could see similar pictures on all the walls around the room.

She began to understand the nature of the club Thomson had taken them to and coloured slightly. She also felt guilty that her embarrassment was tinged with excitement. The woman who had led them to their table left briefly before returning with a bottle of champagne in an ice bucket. Thomson then took over and poured the drinks.

The noisy group of men from the hotel had commandeered some tables near to a small raised stage at one end of the room and had quietened down now they were sitting down. Mike realised he had no way of joining in to get information from them.

Heavy red curtains hung at the back of the stage, and an older man in an old-fashioned dinner jacket appeared from behind them. Using a microphone, he made an announcement in German and the German guests clapped politely.

'The second part of the show is starting, Carla,' said Thomson, lightly placing his hand on Libby's knee. She pushed his hand away as the lights dimmed.

The stage curtains opened as the music changed to a heady slow beat and Libby witnessed her first striptease artist. She found Mike's hand and held it tightly as the beautiful stripper erotically divested herself of clothing and walked naked amongst the tables, teasing men as she went.

Once the act was complete the lights went out completely and thunderous applause filled the room. As the noise died down the almost inaudible whirr of a movie projector could be heard. A short but professionally made Swedish pornographic movie began. For the rest of the night, more striptease acts took place interspersed with short movies depicting sex and fetishism.

During breaks in the show the lights came on again, allowing guests to make use of the restrooms. Libby quickly excused herself at the first break, leaving Mike alone with Thomson.

Mike got straight to the point and asked what the next day's meeting was about.

'Don't worry, Victor. A friend of mine is going to sound out a group of like-minded people such as yourself. I really cannot see how it will come to anything. I think you will find that your time has been wasted,' said a drunken and resolutely enigmatic Thomson.

'All the same, Iain, I really would appreciate having an idea of what is going on,' Mike persisted.

Thomson hesitated. Mike hoped the alcohol had had enough of an effect to loosen the man's tongue. The brigadier leant over Libby's empty seat and whispered conspiratorially:

'A representative of a very powerful and influential group in England is going to ask a few business types like yourself to bankroll or provide materiel support to a mission that will change our great country for the better. I personally can't see any of this coming to fruition, but what do I know?' said Thomson.

'Are those men over there in business too?' asked Mike, gesturing towards the tables near to the stage, where the men from the hotel were sitting.

'A mix of military and civilians, but all from the same background if you understand me. All went to the same school, that sort of thing,' replied Thomson.

'Do you know who is going to talk to us?'

'I think you know enough for now, Victor. Make the most of tonight and tomorrow afternoon you can leave for England and forget about this nonsense.' Thomson clicked his fingers at a passing waitress who was scantily dressed and ordered another bottle of champagne.

Libby returned and took her seat between the two men. Her face and neck had returned to their normal colour and she appeared more relaxed.

'There will be more of the same until the finale in the small hours,' said Mike to Libby.

'Finale?' she asked.

'I think Victor has attended similar establishments to this one. The finale will be well worth waiting for,' said Thomson, interjecting.

'You must tell me all about these places later,' Libby said to Mike in a non-committal tone.

Mike found it difficult to read her thoughts and her equally non-committal face.

Inconsequential and intermittent small talk between Mike and Thomson continued for the rest of the show. Thomson began suggestive small talk with Libby and at every opportunity his hand repeatedly found its way on to her knee. To her relief, the finale was announced some time later by the elderly compere.

Two of the striptease artists appeared together on stage. Each suggestively undressed the other before they kissed and sank on to the stage floor. When the two women had finished with each other they lay breathless, side by side, on the stage. The guests gave the women a standing ovation with some of the Englishmen cheering. The lights were extinguished for a few seconds and when they came back on, the two women were gone.

'As it is just after three, Carla and I should be getting some sleep. We want to be refreshed and ready for the meeting later today,' said Mike to Thomson.

'The meeting has slipped back to eleven, so there is no rush,' replied Thomson casually.

'All the same, I would like to be fresh and alert,' Mike insisted.

'Very well. You too, Carla?' asked Thomson.

Libby nodded, feigning tiredness.

'In that case, I hope you enjoyed the evening and I will see you in the morning. Goodnight,' responded Thomson with disappointment, before wandering over to join the group from the hotel.

The English men were clustered around the woman in the green dress who had met them when they arrived at the club. She was handing out keys and pointing to a door that was set back on the right-hand side of the stage. The men then walked, some now rather unsteadily, towards the door through which they would find their individual paid-for finale.

Once back in their room at the hotel, Mike and Libby undressed for bed. The room was well heated, so Mike lay comfortably on top of the bed naked. Libby was also naked as she sat astride Mike, her palms pressed gently upon his shoulders.

'I would never have believed such a club existed in such a quiet place as Steinhagen,' she said in a husky voice, nuzzling his neck and letting her hair fall to one side and tickle his ear.

13
WOODVILLE

Breakfasting in the deserted hotel dining room seemed surreal to Mike and Libby. They chose to leave the curtains open on their booth, allowing them to observe other guests when they came through to eat. A few tables were set for breakfast, though their intended users had yet to break cover. Once the pair had finished eating they sipped on their delicious coffee.

'Do you think they are sleeping off their hangovers?' asked Libby, referring to the group of English men.

'Probably. I think the locals have been and gone, assuming they bothered with breakfast at all,' he replied.

Libby nodded. 'Last night was very interesting,' she said.

'For you, or for what little we learnt about the meeting?' asked Mike.

She smiled knowingly at him over her coffee cup. 'For me, of course. I have never been in a nightclub like that before, though I think you have,' she said, fishing for an answer.

'Yes, briefly, when I was over here with the army,' he responded, trying to read her face.

'Did you ever pay to go with a woman?' she asked.

'You mean pay for sex?' he replied.

'Yes,' said Libby, holding his gaze.

Mike was uncertain as to where she was taking the conversation. 'Never had to. There were plenty of girls around and visiting a sex club was a bit of a laugh. A night out with the boys. It was something you did as a young soldier and nothing more. Does it bother you?' he replied, watching her closely.

'A bit,' she said, trying to work out if she felt jealous or perhaps disappointed.

'I was much younger and a lot more naïve. Going to Korea made me grow up,' he said.

Libby pondered on what he said for a short while.

'That's all right then,' she replied breezily, as if drawing a line under the matter.

It seemed to Mike that unimportant, and largely forgotten, events in his life had greater meaning to Libby for some reason. He decided they had to talk about his past some more when they were away from their current entanglement with Wesley.

'We need to focus on why we are here,' he said, 'and I think Thomson can tell us much more. I don't think he is taking things as seriously as he might. The meeting is going to be interesting.'

They finished their coffee and, as no other guests had appeared for breakfast, they returned to their room. After checking their pistols over they left them concealed in an easily accessible suitcase. Mike had no idea if they would be searched before the meeting started, so had decided to take the risk of not being armed. He left a 'do not disturb' sign on the room door to keep the hotel staff out.

As eleven o'clock approached, Mike and Libby made their way to reception to join the other meeting attendees. Mike wore his dark business suit with a white shirt and matching tie, Libby a ribbed wool two-piece suit in pale olive. The long-sleeved top buttoned from the neck to just below the waist, while her pencil skirt reached to her knees. She completed the ensemble with some smart high heels. With detached curiosity, some of the men glanced over towards them.

Thomson emerged from a set of swing doors, above which was a sign indicating that a conference room was just beyond.

'Well, we all seem to be here so please follow me,' he said.

The group was led along a glazed corridor that ran the length of the original barn. As the corridor only emerged halfway down the building it was not easy to see from the hotel car park and Mike had been unaware of it. They carried on to the end and through another set of double doors. The conference room was oblong and austere in a Germanic way. A large dark wooden table devoid of accessories but surrounded with chairs sat in the centre of the room.

'Please, sit where you like,' said Thomson.

As there was no order of precedence, they all took a seat of their choice whilst avoiding what might be regarded as the head of the table. *So much for worrying about being searched*, Mike thought to himself.

The room went quiet, but no one fidgeted or gave away any hint of nervousness. Without announcement, the double doors they had just come through were opened by two men. Mike knew straight away that they were part of someone's personal security team. Flint faced, muscular and carrying weapons that bulged under the arms of their over-tailored suits, the men looked around the room. The larger one signalled to somebody unseen that the room was safe.

In the quiet someone could be heard walking along the carpeted corridor. The deep pile scrunched reassuringly as each step was placed upon it. A man walked through the doors, which were immediately closed after him by the two heavies. They remained in the room, keeping a close watch on all those sat around the table.

The man they had all come to see was over six feet tall. He wore an elegantly tailored dark-blue pinstripe suit and stood at one end of the table. His hair was light grey, making Mike think he was in his sixties. He had an imperious look that suggested he was in charge and expected others to know it. *A born aristocrat*, thought Mike. He also guessed that the man was highly intelligent and to be treated very carefully.

'Good morning, gentlemen,' said the man, adding after a pause, 'and lady.' He continued without waiting for a response. 'I believe that all of you, apart from Mr Mazarin and his assistant, know who I am. So, for Mr Mazarin's benefit, let me introduce myself. My name is Charles Woodville and I act as the head of a group of interested parties seeking to protect the future of the United Kingdom. The fact that I am speaking to you now indicates that plans have advanced to the point where the executive arm – yourselves – can be brought into position to take the decisive action on behalf of those I represent. Those of you in the military will soon receive your individual and final written orders setting out what is expected of you. The security of these documents is paramount, and you must not reveal the contents to anyone, including those attending today. My personal presence here is your authority to proceed.'

Without another word, most of the men got up from their seats and left. Woodville's last words formed the executive order for them to leave and begin their preparations. Mike concluded that these men were the military element of the group. Only five other men remained, in addition to Thomson.

'Please bear with me, Mr Mazarin,' said Woodville before continuing. 'The remainder of you will also receive written instructions appertaining to your role and position in Britain. As private individuals you must be as stringent in your security as your military counterparts. Be in no doubt: your lives depend upon it,' warned Woodville, gazing at each man in turn.

Some nodded their agreement while others looked down, as if Woodville's stony gaze was too much for them. Woodville then told them they could leave. The men got up and left, some more hastily than others.

Woodville looked on until the men were through the doors, then told the two bodyguards to wait outside until they were called for. The only people left in the conference room were Woodville, Thomson, Mike and Libby.

'Mr Mazarin, what an odd fellow you are,' said Woodville.

Mike looked right back at the man's implacable features without allowing a trace of deference that might be mistaken for weakness.

'Why is that, Mr Woodville?' he asked.

'For months you have rebuffed our offer to join us, and suddenly here you are. Why?'

'I made the simple mistake of not taking the offer as genuine. I need to protect my interests as much as you do,' Mike replied, hoping his answer was sufficient to prevent further questions.

'Well, at least you are honest about it,' said Woodville, sounding a little surprised.

'I still have no idea why you need me,' said Mike attempting to find out a little more.

'I am not prepared to tell you everything just yet, Mr Mazarin. However, in principle, I need a well-trained airborne assault force to capture and control a key location in London. I understand you have sufficient manpower and the means to do this.'

This was a clear attempt on Woodville's part to find out about the men and helicopters that the now-dead Mazarin had once had under his control. It was obvious to Mike that the security services had successfully covered up the demise of the real Mazarin, thereby preventing Woodville from knowing the truth.

'Equally, I am not prepared to disclose what assets I am able to employ for such a role,' said Mike.

'Ah, so they do exist,' said Woodville, with a note of triumph that told Mike he had swallowed his bait.

'All I need to know is where the target is, what resistance I should expect and what to do once the target is secured,' replied Mike.

Woodville eyed him with renewed interest. 'You sound as though you have military experience, Mr Mazarin.'

'I learn quickly. What about yourself?' Mike kept his answers brief, trying to evade complicated lies, but Woodville ignored the question.

'How quickly can you ready your force?' the man asked, with increased vehemence.

'All I need is time to train my men specific to the operation. The complexity of the mission will impact on the readiness of my force. When will I receive your orders?' asked Mike, fishing for a timeline.

'In due course, in due course,' was the careful reply.

Mike decided to press Woodville on the matter. 'Why can't the army perform this task of yours? It's clear you have some friends in military positions,' asked Mike as casually as possible
Woodville hesitated, making Mike think he had gone too far. Had he jeopardised himself and Libby?

'The mission is way too sensitive for British soldiers, who are great patriots, Mr Mazarin. A mercenary force will be much more effective. That will become clear when you get your orders,' was the enigmatic response.

'All the same, I need to know what time I have to prepare, Mr Woodville,' said Mike, pushing for an answer.

Woodville, clearly irritated by Mike's persistence, scowled. 'You will receive your orders in three days, and I expect you to be operationally ready seven days after that,' he snapped, angry that he had divulged further information.

'Thank you,' Mike replied, smiling. 'Knowing how much time I have helps me enormously.'

At that point Woodville turned to Thomson and asked him to leave the room so he could discuss a personal matter with his guest. Thomson nodded and made himself scarce.

'There is another matter we need to discuss,' said Woodville, having regained his composure.

'Oh, what's that?' asked Mike.

'I want to apologise for any embarrassment that may have been caused to you last night. Your visit to the nightclub was not part of my plans for you or for the others. That was all Thomson's idea and may have placed the security of the whole operation at risk. Did he say anything that caused any concern?' Woodville asked.

Mike was unsure if he was being tested. If he said no he would be lying – Thomson had told them he thought that nothing would come of the meeting. If he said yes, then he was placing Thomson's life at risk. Mike chose the latter.

'His view was that today's meeting would come to nothing, and nor will your grand plan. He does not appear to understand how advanced this mission is and how determined you are,' said Mike.

'I see,' said Woodville. 'Thomson has been kept on the edge of things regarding the exact details of the plan, but he knows my intentions. Thank you for being frank with me.'

'You are welcome, Mr Woodville. I hope you straighten things out with him. In the meantime, I need to return to England as soon as possible. How will you get your orders to me?'

'The orders will be delivered by an intermediary we have used before.'

'That will be fine,' said Mike, trying not to show panic; he had no idea who that might be.

'Then I think our meeting is at an end, Mr Mazarin,' said Woodville finally.

Mike and Libby stood up. The two men shook hands and Woodville nodded in Libby's direction before walking through the double doors. He was joined by his two bodyguards as he walked along the corridor. Thomson was nowhere to be seen.

'I suppose we had better pack and head home,' said Mike.

'What are we going to do about this intermediary he talked about?' asked Libby with a look of concern.

'That is a problem for Wesley, not us. We have done our bit and I now need to get in touch with him as soon as possible,' said Mike, trying to sound unconcerned.

The pair left the meeting room and headed back to their own room to pack. Libby walked in stony silence alongside Mike before speaking.

'I might as well have been a picture on the wall for all my presence was worth at that meeting,' she said.

'I suppose women have little value in the lives of these men.'

'More like no value,' she seethed.

'Let them underestimate you and you can catch them by surprise,' replied Mike, trying to sound positive.

Back in their room, they had nearly finished packing when there was a knock at the door. Mike and Libby looked at each other then, instinctively, checked their pistols were holstered before Mike opened the door.

Thomson stood in the corridor.

'May I come in?' he asked.

'Of course, we were almost ready to leave so you caught us just in time,' said Mike with an airy tone.

Thomson had a serious look on his face and sat down in the nearest chair.

'I never thought Woodville would find sufficient support for this treasonous adventure of his. All this could go very wrong, with the most serious of consequences for us all,' he said.

'I understand that, Thomson, and I have my own unvoiced concerns. As I must wait for the orders to arrive, I intend to go along with him before making my final decision,' said Mike.

'What will you do if you are unhappy with what Woodville wants you to do?' asked Thomson with a hopeful look.

'Woodville is not the only one with contacts and intermediaries,' replied Mike encouragingly.

'Good; you must use them,' said Thomson. 'I am also returning home today, as my time in Germany has come to an end. I hope to be given more information about the rest of Woodville's plans by another like-minded thinker within the group. Perhaps you might be able to pass this information on in a way that does not implicate me, Mr Mazarin?'

'Yes, I understand why you would want to do things that way. How will you provide this information?' asked Mike.

'I will be at my home, a place called Tantallon Castle, where some files will be delivered to me in person. My address is written down here,' said Thomson, passing Mike a slip of hotel notepaper. 'Can you be there two days from tomorrow?'

Mike read the address quickly and confirmed that he would meet with the brigadier at his castle home. Thomson smiled uncertainly, then said goodbye and left.

'Well, that was a surprise,' said Libby.

'Yes, and it seems he is not alone. It sounds to me as if Woodville's plans are so far advanced that some of his co-conspirators are losing their nerve. Another reason to get in touch with Wesley as soon as possible,' said Mike.

Libby looked at the note Thomson had left.

'His castle is near Edinburgh, Mike. Do you think we can get back to England and then up to Scotland in just three days?' she asked.

'The timings are tight, but we'll make it,' he replied.

* * *

The Jensen fired up eagerly after its day of rest and was driven without mercy back to the French coast. At Calais, Mike and Libby were lucky to get the car on to the first ferry crossing available.

Once they arrived in Dover, Mike left a message for Wesley by telephone using a special number disguising the recipient's location. Mike waited at one of the port's telephone kiosks for a call back from Wesley that came within minutes. Mike updated him on everything they had learnt on the trip to Steinhagen. He also told Wesley of his concern over how Woodville intended to use an intermediary that had previously been in contact with Mazarin.

'Don't worry about the contact not being able to find you. The intermediary works for me,' said Wesley.

'Is there something more I should know?' asked Mike suspiciously.

'Never mind the details. Just get whatever information Thomson has and the name of the other man he mentioned,' said Wesley in an irritated voice before putting the telephone down.

Mike replaced the receiver and returned to Libby, who was sitting in the driver's seat of the Jensen.

'That intermediary is one of Wesley's men, but he never mentioned being in dialogue with Mazarin before. We need to unstitch some of his lies,' said Mike.

'You sound very suspicious of him,' said Libby.

'I am. Canute was right when he said that Wesley was as slippery as a snake in wet grass. He's way closer to the action than he first let on. I wonder how many more hidden links of his will come to light?'

'Where to next?' asked Libby with a smile.

'A place called Wansford, just west of Peterborough. We are going to rendezvous with Canute to pick up some climbing ropes and boots,' replied Mike. He had called Canute straight after the truncated conversation with Wesley, a plan already forming.

Libby flashed him a wicked smile as she briskly accelerated the Jensen towards the port exit.

14
AFTER TANTALLON

Heading south from Tantallon, Libby drove the Jensen as fast as she dared until it was safe to switch on the headlights. The going got easier once she was able to get on to the main road. There was silence between herself and Mike until she had put enough distance between them and Tantallon Bay. Finally, she pulled off the road and switched off the engine. They sat in the cocooned darkness, looking out into the remains of the night.

'What happened in the castle, Mike?' she asked.

'I found Thomson dead. It looked like he had been ritually stabbed to death. His tongue had been pierced, with a tiny dagger forcing it to protrude from his mouth. I think this may have been to signify his punishment for disloyalty, perhaps for talking too much,' he replied.

Libby stared ahead in shocked silence. Mike waited for her to speak.

'Because he talked to us, you mean?' she said.

'I don't know, but it was a horrific way to die.'

'Do you think it was also a trap set up for you?'

'No. Someone wanted Thomson dead and whoever did it was sent to recover whatever he was going to give to us. His rooms had been searched and there was nothing left that may have been of use to Wesley. The dirty work was over by the time I arrived. I will have to call Wesley later this morning,' said Mike with an air of finality.

'Where do we go now?' asked Libby.

'We head inland and then south. I can call Wesley from somewhere and we can get some breakfast as well. Something tells me our troubles are not over yet.'

Sometime later there was an annoyed silence on the other end of the telephone as Mike waited in a call box for Wesley to say something. When Wesley did speak, he sounded as if he was taken aback by the account of what had happened.

'This is all too dramatic and theatrical. Why didn't they just shoot the man and be done with it?' he said, half asking and half musing.

'I don't know, but my job is done,' said Mike, moving the conversation along.

'You are finished when I say so,' Wesley snapped back.

'Meaning what?' asked Mike, with an edge to his voice.

'Thomson was working with another,' said Wesley. 'A man called Dacre. He is a recently promoted Major General posted back to England from Germany. My source tells me the man was mixed up with Thomson and some other generals that attended the meeting in Germany. You can forget about anything else until you find out what he is doing and if there are any others working in sympathy with him.'

'How the hell am I going to find him?' asked Mike angrily.

'You don't need to travel far. He lives on the border between England and Scotland. Like Thomson – or should I say, like Thomson *was* – he is a member of the aristocracy and his family seat is an ancient fortified tower house at a place called Blindburn, south-east of Jedburgh. You can be there within the hour.'

'Very convenient, Wesley. How on earth do you know all this?' asked Mike in a tired tone.

'Haven't you learnt anything, Armstrong? It's my job to know these things and yours is to do as I say. I want an update this evening,' he snapped before disconnecting the call.

With a face like thunder, Mike made his way back to the Jensen.

'What's happening?' Libby asked, taking in his murderous look.

'Wesley is stringing us along. Just as I expected, but for now, I think we have no choice but to carry on.'

'And?' she persisted.

'Someone called General Dacre is holed up in what Wesley called his "family seat" just somewhere south of the border. Wesley says he is, or was, working in sympathy with Thomson and we must find out if anyone else is too. Wesley sounded a little desperate over the phone even though he tried to conceal it. He wants an update tonight.'

'Tonight? We're going to have to move fast in case the same people that killed Thomson try to do the same with this other man,' Libby responded.

'Yes, but we should book into a hotel in Jedburgh first and have some breakfast before getting some sleep. I can get myself cleaned up and then we need to buy some hiking gear,' said Mike as he put together a plan of action.

By the early afternoon, Mike and Libby had sufficiently rested enough to carry on with their task. They wore hiking clothing and footwear, to look as if they were going walking in the nearby fells. Each had a small knapsack to carry pistols and ammunition, plus some food and water. Libby drove the Jensen and Mike gave directions using an Ordnance Survey map; he wanted his painfully blistered hands to have any available time left to recover before their encounter with Dacre. Both wore their sunglasses as the bright afternoon sun bore down on to the heather-clad hills around them.

'Do you still want to carry on with this, Libby?' he asked. 'We don't know what we are going to find at Blindburn.'

Libby carried on looking straight ahead as she drove.

'I'm here, and that means I intend to see things through to the end. Sitting alone somewhere wondering what is happening to you would be worse than anything else I can think of,' she replied.

Although expected, her response gave Mike the moral support he needed to carry on. Using the map, he guided her to a point just short of Dacre's house and she pulled off the road where the ground looked firm enough to take the weight of the car. They were in dead ground and hidden from the house.

Mike made his way up a small rise and took out his binoculars whilst Libby stood guard by the car. Both now kept their Smith & Wessons more accessible under their lightweight zipper tops in case of trouble.

Mike scanned the ground between themselves and Dacre's house. The landscape was devoid of human life, seeming very bleak even in the middle of summer. Sheep were resting where they could as there was no shade from the afternoon sun. Some had congregated along the path of an almost dried-up river that wound its way towards a stone-built structure in the middle distance. Looking through the binoculars, heat shimmers made the stark construction look like a stone mirage. Mike noted that the river wound its way towards the building, which would allow them a covered approach until the last two hundred yards. After that, there was no cover at all from any direction.

Having checked the surrounding area, Mike then concentrated on the 'house' itself. The huge stone tower was, in fact, a simple castle with a single ground-level entrance cut into the south-facing stone wall. The flat curtain walls were dotted with small windows at various levels, once used as gun-ports to defend the tower. The structure was topped with a gable roof, also made of stone and with no obvious access point. Circling the base of the walls was an ancient moat-like ditch designed to impede anyone attacking the tower. The structure sat on its own heather-clad plateau, making it doubly impossible to make a final approach unseen. The forbidding nature of the locale was only slightly lessened by the bright afternoon sunshine and a cloudless sky.

'There is no point trying to make our approach hidden, so we will just have to pretend we are out on an afternoon walk,' said Mike when he returned to the car.

'We don't even know if anyone is in there, or if they are watching,' Libby replied.

'Well, we will soon find out. Make sure you can get to your pistol quickly if you should need it.'

'What makes you think we need our pistols?'

'I don't think Dacre is going to automatically welcome us with open arms, and he probably has a weapon with him too,' said Mike, cocking his pistol.

'So, we are just going to walk up to the door and knock to see if anyone is in?' she asked.

'Yes, that's it. I'll do the talking,' said Mike, and the pair set off.

As they made their way across the moorland, Mike studied the tower house, hoping to see movement in one of the tiny windows. It was hopeless. He still had no idea if there were any occupants in the building, even when they were just yards away from the large wooden door reinforced with iron straps.

Without warning, the door opened inwards and a man stepped out into the sunlight. He carried a shotgun that was ready to use. The closed double barrels were held parallel to the ground, pointed at Mike and Libby. Mike recognised the man as being one of the party of army officers that had attended the meeting in Steinhagen. The man was tall and had thick wavy chestnut-coloured hair that matched his eyes. Although older, he had the broad shoulders of an athlete.

'What do you want?' he asked gruffly, before hesitating when he recognised them from the Steinhagen meeting.

'To talk to you,' replied Mike.

'You are Mazarin – and she is Manaro,' he replied suspiciously.

'Mancuso,' said Libby, correcting the general. He looked at her sharply. Being corrected by a woman obviously annoyed him.

'What do you want to talk about?' asked Dacre, keeping the shotgun pointing at his intruders.

'Woodville and Thomson. Did you know Thomson has been killed?' asked Mike.

Dacre was taken aback with the news. 'Tommo is dead?' he said, half talking to Mike and half to himself.

'I think you might be the next on the hit list and standing outside in the open is not helping your chances,' said Mike.

Dacre hesitated then looked around before nodding. He broke the shotgun open and asked them to come in.

The ground floor of the house consisted of packed earth and was not anything like what Mike and Libby had envisioned. The larger than expected space was dark and cool. There was a residual smell of animal droppings and urine.

'The smell is a lot worse when the sheep are kept in here during the winter,' remarked Dacre as he led Mike and Libby towards a wooden U-shaped staircase set in one corner that led up to the first floor. They climbed the stairs and rose up through a large square gap. Once they were all upstairs, Dacre lowered a heavy trapdoor and secured it with an equally heavy iron bolt.

'There, I think we are safe now. Welcome to the original Dacre family seat,' he said, with a more welcoming tone.

'Original?' asked Libby, sounding curious.

'Yes, Miss Mancuso. My forebears built a larger hall in the sixteenth century. It stands further down the valley, but as taxes are ruinous I sold the place last year to an American. His ancestors were from around here and I was very lucky indeed to find such a buyer,' he said, as his mind seemed to go elsewhere momentarily.

Mike looked around the room at the furniture, ornaments and pictures that hung from the stone walls. 'You managed to hang on to some fine examples of furniture,' he said.

'Yes, all heirlooms,' said Dacre.

'Reminds me of someone I used to know,' said Mike.

Libby squirmed at his reference to her husband, and the home she had left behind in Norfolk.

'So, you think I am in danger,' said Dacre, returning to what Mike had said outside.

'Yes, General Dacre. I suspect Woodville knew that the brigadier was less than enthusiastic about his plans to oust the government and bring stability back to the nation.'

'You sound as though you are supportive of Woodville,' Dacre replied, sounding suspicious.

'His words, not mine. I wanted to meet with the brigadier because he said he had files that the authorities would like to see,' said Mike.

'Files that got him killed. They might do the same to you, Mazarin. What do you hope to get out of this?'

'Freedom,' said Mike. 'Do you have copies of the files Thomson had?'

'I'm sorry, but no. Nor have I seen them. However, I do believe that finding them will provide all the information you need to stop Woodville.'

'It looks like I have hit a dead end, then,' said Mike.

Libby had remained quiet during the exchange between the two men. Now they knew the general had nothing to assist them, it was time to move on. The only question remaining was what role Dacre had to play.

'One last question, General,' said Libby. 'What is your role in the planned coup?'

'My role was comparatively minor. Merely to give my tacit support and turn a blind eye,' he replied simply.

'Turn a blind eye?' asked Libby.

'Some units that were being sent to Aden and the Middle East have been diverted back to the UK. Others have had their postings to English garrisons extended indefinitely. My job was to give the nod to these arrangements. I signed orders that I never read,' said Dacre in a regretful tone.

'Which units are you talking about?' asked Mike, with increased urgency.

'I heard a whisper that they are northern – possibly Scottish regiments,' said Dacre.

'Which ones exactly?' Mike's tone was pressing.

'I don't know, as I chose not to look in detail at the orders I signed off. The intermediary has the details,' said Dacre with an air of finality.

Mike could see that he and Libby had gone full circle and were back to the mysterious intermediary again. He could understand why Thomson and Dacre had had second thoughts about the success of Woodville's plan. There was no way that the rank and file were going to be persuaded to deliver a *coup d'état* even if a group of military and social elite wanted one. He had to find out more – and that meant getting hold of the middleman.

'What do you know about this intermediary?' asked Mike.

'No more than that he exists,' was the unhelpful reply.

Mike knew there was nothing more to be gained from the general. Dacre had no further part to play and the only other man who could help them was dead. He thanked the general for being so candid and said that he and Libby were leaving. The general crossed the room and undid the bolt before lifting the heavy trapdoor for them.

'What are you going to do now?' Libby asked Dacre.

'Pray, seeing as time is short,' he replied.

Dacre followed Mike and Libby outside into the sunshine and breathed in the fresh air. It was his last breath.

Mike knew the crack and thump sounds a high-velocity bullet made after being fired. Dacre's head blew apart like an exploding watermelon and he dropped like a stone to the ground. Mike also dropped to the ground, dragging Libby down with him.

'Stay down! And if anyone you don't know approaches, shoot them,' he said urgently before rolling away from her and crawling towards the remains of the ancient ditch defence.

Libby rolled to her side and pulled out her pistol. She looked across to Mike. He motioned for her to crawl towards him and into cover. He had his pistol ready to give her covering fire if she needed it. He knew there was no point in trying to shoot back at the gunman, who would be too far away. Once Libby was safe, they crawled along the shallow ditch a short distance from where they had taken cover.

'Cover me if anyone comes too close. Pity we didn't bring a rifle,' he said as he retrieved his binoculars and crawled away to find some heather for cover. The shot had come from the south, so the sun was in Mike's eyes. Spotting a probable sniper was going to be difficult. He guessed from the crack and thump that his adversary was no closer than three hundred yards and began scanning the ground from that point.

Nothing moved – not even the sheep resting nearby. *Patience*, he thought to himself. He guessed rightly that the sniper had slipped back into dead ground. He needed to know if the man was preparing for a second shot or if his mission was complete.

Unnoticed before and to the south was a dip by the road, where a lone car had parked. Mike estimated the distance at five hundred yards. He gambled that the sniper was heading for the car, and not waiting for them to break cover.

Mike got up and dashed forward a few yards before dropping to the ground again. There was no shot, so he repeated the short dashes until he was off the plateau and into dead ground himself. Keeping low, he advanced quickly towards the parked car. Suddenly he picked up movement – the retreating figure of a man carrying a Lee Enfield sniper rifle. The man was only seconds ahead of Mike as he opened the back door of the car and hurriedly placed his rifle on the back seat. After another second, the man was in the driving seat and starting the car.

Mike was close enough to shoot. He took a two-handed grip of his Smith & Wesson and let off two shots into the car. The double-tap smashed the back windscreen and Mike calmly took another two shots. He was sure he had hit the man, but the car sped forward on to the road and away. Its acceleration increased as it gained momentum on the downhill slope towards a sharp bend where a bridge cut across the ravine made by the river. Mike could see it was going too fast to make the bend, so with a last burst of energy he ran towards the bridge. The car took off from the road and smashed on to the rocky bank of the river with a metallic crunch.

Pistol held ready to fire, Mike cautiously approached. He could now see the car was a Humber. He could hear the angry hissing of hot water escaping as steam from what was left of the car's front end. The lone gunman's chest had been caved in by the steering wheel. Two bloody holes in his back told Mike he hadn't missed when he'd opened fire.

As Mike got closer he could smell petrol vapour and suddenly the crumpled car became a petrol-fuelled fireball, forcing him to back away. There was nothing more to be done. The immediate threat to himself and Libby was fast becoming a set of charred remains for the local police to pick over. Small explosions of igniting ammunition forced Mike to turn and run back up the hill to find Libby. He immediately bumped into her, far closer to the bridge than she should have been.

'I told you to stay where you were,' he said angrily.

'You also trained me to use this,' she retorted equally angrily, holding up her pistol, 'and staying in that ditch was not going let me help.'

Mike smiled and kissed her firmly on the lips. She smiled back, elated that he was unharmed and running on the adrenaline of the encounter.

'What are you going to say to Wesley?' she asked.

15
IN THE GARDEN

Wesley had left his office, having taken the phone call from Mike Armstrong. As soon as he arrived home he made himself a large gin and tonic before wandering out into the back garden.

His garden was well established, stretching away from the house and allowing the mature trees to provide gentle shade and leafy privacy. The high-hedged privet borders were edged with overflowing bright-coloured bedding flowers that were testament to the skills of the gardener Wesley and Evelyn employed. The hedges also raised the level of privacy to a secrecy that suited Wesley, even meant isolating Evelyn. An oak bench stood halfway down the garden in the shade of a horse chestnut tree. The bench faced on to the perfectly mown lawn that stretched back up to the wall of the house.

Exiting through a set of tall French windows, Wesley stepped straight out on to a level carpet of grass. There had been no need for a patio, since no guests were ever going to be entertained in the garden. Wesley noticed that he enjoyed the peace and quiet, and he began to ask himself why he had never made more use of the space before.

The grass was gratifyingly manicured to provide a springy carpetlike experience when walked over. It was trimmed to perfection, ending in straight edges that provided uncannily precise delineations between the crowd of multi-coloured blooms and the green monoculture of the lawn. As Wesley walked towards the bench he loosened his tie and undid the collar button on his shirt. He placed his drink on the arm of the bench and stretched out to make himself comfortable. With his eyes closed, he picked up on the sound of birdsong, then the soporific buzz of bees steadily working their way about the flowers. He decided that if the hot summer weather kept up, he might repeat the exercise over the short time he now had left in Welwyn. Wesley also felt he needed to give himself some time to mull over final events as they unfolded.

He felt agreeably pleased with himself at getting Armstrong and the Kembrey woman involved. They were proving useful in probing into the activities of Charles Woodville. The pair remained deniable, regardless of the events due to be taking place in just over a week's time, so in the short term they provided little threat to him.

Armstrong, however, had been unable to get Thomson or Dacre to disclose the identity of the intermediary between Woodville and Mazarin. At the present time, Armstrong did not have any more leads to follow. This suited Wesley's purpose, as he did not actually want them to find out who that person was. Armstrong was easier to control when he was under pressure and lacking vital information.

Currently, Wesley had Armstrong linked to five killings, making it a simple matter to exert pressure on him if needed. Regardless of the outcome of Woodville's planned coup, these links remained useful. That meant that, in the event of the coup failing, Armstrong could be forced into silence or would face arrest by Special Branch. If the coup was a success, however, Armstrong would no longer be needed and could melt away into his shadowy fugitive life once more. He would have nothing to gain by going to the authorities to expose Wesley, because those who had forcefully put themselves in power would be the beneficiaries of Wesley's secret activities.

Wesley then realised that he needed Armstrong to stay alive for at least another week. Until the regime change in Whitehall – or the failure of the coup – there was the risk that if Armstrong was killed, his death might trigger the dissemination of documents exposing Wesley's illegal activities. He was unsettled by this detail: one he had not properly considered before.

Wesley then came around to the idea that he was worrying too much. Armstrong's death could be concealed for a long enough period to lose its importance as events took their course. In any case, he mused, news of Armstrong's death reaching those in possession of the documents that incriminated him would easily take more than a week. That was enough time to render them useless, as the world would have moved on in one way or another. He smiled to himself and took a sip of his drink.

Armstrong's mention of collateral damage was another matter that Wesley mulled over. The whole telephone conversation had been made in veiled speech so that anyone monitoring the conversation would be unable to grasp its full meaning. As no names were mentioned, a listener would be unaware of the subject of the conversation. Briefly, Armstrong had relayed the message to Wesley that their friend had died intestate. Wesley knew this meant that Dacre was dead and had provided no new information to Armstrong.

The mention of the unexpected death of another man in a car crash that afternoon had caused some initial alarm for Wesley. It soon became clear, however, that Armstrong had no idea who the sniper was or who had sent him, and in fact, Armstrong assumed that the sniper was acting on Woodville's orders. From Wesley's point of view the sniper was dead and therefore another investigative avenue was closed to Armstrong. He took another sip from his drink.

As Wesley had arrived home earlier than usual, Evelyn, who had not been expecting him, had been taking a bath. After briefly looking around downstairs, Wesley had called out her name to see if she was even at home. She had called back down, telling him she was bathing and would be down shortly. That was when he had decided to make himself a drink before sitting out in the garden, half expecting her to come out and join him.

It occurred to him now that she was taking rather longer than necessary. His eyes lingered on the rear of the house and he glimpsed movement in the upstairs master bedroom. He saw Evelyn moving to and fro across the window. She was retrieving items of clothing from a chest of drawers and taking them in the direction of their bed. Although she knew he was home, she seemed unaware of his presence in the garden.

What surprised him most was that she was not dressed and had not bothered to close the curtains. He had not seen such a lapse of propriety in her before and it intrigued him. He downed the remains of his gin and tonic then sat and watched her as she went about her business. The bedroom windows at the rear of the house were full length with low sills, allowing him to see her pulling on her underwear then her stockings. She faced directly towards the window with her breasts in full view as she put on her bra, and it was then that she saw him.

Their eyes met. There was the tiniest hesitation from her before she carried on as if nothing had happened. Finally, a hint of irritation crossed her face as she turned away from the window and disappeared out of his sight. Moments later, she reappeared through the French windows to join Wesley. She was wearing a pale pink charmeuse satin nightgown, tied tightly at the waist. The slippers on her feet matched. He vaguely remembered it being a wedding gift to Evelyn from her mother.

'Isn't that a bit careless, getting dressed without closing the curtains?' he asked, trying not to sound irritated.

'Apart from you, Wesley, who else could possibly see?' she replied as she took her place next to him on the bench. She noted the uncharacteristic loosened collar and tie but said nothing. Her gown slipped open as she crossed her legs, making her hold on to the trim to stop it happening again. He knew she had a point as he glanced in the direction of the neighbouring houses and gardens. The screen of tree foliage provided all the privacy they needed. *Except in the wintertime*, he thought to himself.

'Suppose old man Greening was here, mowing the lawn. You would have given him quite a surprise,' he challenged.

In a way that irritated Wesley further. Evelyn laughed, appearing to be amused by the idea that their elderly gardener might have seen her naked.

'Nonsense, Wesley! He's too short-sighted. Besides, he was only here yesterday so I knew no one was about,' she said.

Wesley felt somehow stupid and a bit prudish. He realised he was getting jealous about a wife he was about to abandon. Evelyn, on the other hand, kept the fact to herself that the old man now sent his youngest son to work in the garden.

'So, why are you home earlier than usual?' she asked.

'Just relaxing a bit and thinking about my future,' he half lied.

Evelyn gave him a sideways glance. 'Well, well, well. What's got into you? I barely see you because of work and suddenly you are home early and worried about your future.'

'Not worried. Just considering my options,' he responded.

'Now you have options? Whatever next? You can tell me if you are having problems at work – or are they a secret too?' she needled.

Wesley sensed an uncharacteristic argument brewing.

'I'm thinking about early retirement, Evelyn,' he said, trying to move the discussion to safer ground.

'Were you going to talk about this if I hadn't been home?' she asked, sounding as though she only half believed him.

'Of course. That is why I am home early,' he lied, trying to sound as convincing as possible and knowing he hadn't given her any thought at all. Wesley knew she could catch him out when he told her lies, and he waited for her to carry on with more questions.

'Well, when you have some firm ideas we can talk about this again,' she said soothingly.

Wesley was surprised by her tone and response. Her apparent acceptance was implied in the fact that she did not wish to pursue the matter further. He decided that not discussing his supposed thoughts about retirement would reduce his chances of being caught lying to her and readily changed the subject.

'What were you doing in the bedroom, anyway?' he asked.

'I was packing a suitcase. I haven't been to see my sister in a while, so she is due a visit from me. I expect I will be staying with her for at least a week, perhaps longer. The taxi will be here to pick me up in half an hour,' she replied.

'I can get the car out and run you down to the station if you would like?' offered Wesley, pretending to be helpful.

'No thank you. I have made the booking and it would be bad form to cancel with so little notice. Besides, you have had a drink,' she said insistently, before getting up to go back inside the house.

A disconcerting feeling went through him when Evelyn appeared to look at him as if evaluating what he might say. Wesley watched her go whilst considering the exchange that had just taken place between them. For a few moments she had taken some interest in him and his future regarding retirement. They had never discussed his work like this since the very early days of their marriage. They were now emotionally different people who had slowly, irrevocably drifted apart. He began to wonder if she had any suspicions that another woman held a special place in his heart.

Wesley decided that Evelyn choosing this time to visit her sister was a happy convenience. The next seven days were now clear for him to focus fully on Woodville's progress with the *coup d'état*. He needed to make a final decision on whether to get behind it or expose it.

The man who was key to him making this decision was Armstrong. Wesley was annoyed that, despite the chinks in Woodville's security, Thomson and Dacre had not provided an opportunity for Armstrong to get his hands on the overall plans for the coup. The only information he would get first-hand would be the orders given to Armstrong. As these were only specific to the role of Victor Mazarin and his men, he would have no knowledge of the overall plans for the rest of the conspirators.

Wesley sat for a while longer then, when he had finished his drink, he went back inside to get himself another. A silence had fallen over the house and he realised that Evelyn had already gone, leaving him alone with his thoughts.

The house was morguelike. It was cold inside despite the time of year – silent, lifeless and mirroring his marriage to Evelyn. He moved from room to room as if looking for something that could be found to evidence their time together. It felt like he was looking around a neat guesthouse where all the contents expected in a home were present yet remained impersonal. The meaningless pictures on the walls, the empty vases that should have contained flowers, beds waiting to be made up and wardrobes waiting to have clothes put in them. The environment was so sterile that Wesley felt the urge to leave there and then.

Like Evelyn, he found himself a suitcase and packed. Wesley decided that he would return to London that night and book himself into a hotel with the intention of never returning to Welwyn again. Once he had finished packing, however, he changed his mind. The prospect of sitting around in a featureless hotel room was worse than spending another night in the house he only loosely thought of as his home. He went downstairs and made himself another large gin and tonic before returning to the wooden bench.

It was getting dark when Wesley resurfaced from his reverie and took himself inside. After another large drink, he went upstairs. He undressed, leaving his clothes in a pile on the floor, and fell into bed.

* * *

The following morning, Wesley woke up early. The light of the new day shone through the window as he had forgotten to close the curtains. There was a dryness in his throat from all the alcohol of the night before. He also had a headache.

He stumbled out of bed and completed his morning ritual in preparation for going to work. His breakfast consisted of tea laced with aspirin, and some toast and marmalade. He switched on the radio in time to hear the news, then promptly switched it off again once the bulletin was over. The major news story continued to focus on the revelations regarding the spy Kim Philby and other communist spies.

Wesley had a wry smile on his face, knowing that the news in a week's time would contain an even greater revelation. He was pleased that, for now, the high-profile spy stories were providing red-under-the bed scares that were an extremely useful distraction from the political upheaval being planned.

He took his usual seat on the train that morning. The usual thoughts about his fellow passengers ran through his mind and he did all his usual things. He masked the growing excitement within him in expectation of the arrival of the orders for Mazarin. He travelled by tube to Tottenham Court Road and headed south-east before turning left and north-east by way of Shaftesbury Avenue. As part of a largely circular route, he took the next major left and walked along to arrive at St Giles-in-the-Field churchyard. During his walk he constantly checked he was not being followed before walking into the churchyard. Near to the graves was a dead letter drop he had used occasionally. At the drop, hidden in the undergrowth, was a canvas bag that he deftly withdrew before exiting the churchyard by a different gate.

Without stopping to check the contents of the bag, he walked along and headed south-west in the direction of Seven Dials. From there he made his way to a busy café on the edge of Covent Garden. He ordered a coffee then took a seat tucked away at the back. By the time he had finished the coffee, Wesley had transferred the document protected by the canvas bag into his briefcase. He left, the canvas bag lying empty and abandoned underneath the café table.

Wesley unconsciously upped his pace as he walked to his new secure offices. He and his team had recently been relocated to the bowels of Somerset House by the River Thames. It was a convenient walk that allowed him to double check that he was not being followed.

The excitement he once felt on operations with the partisans in Yugoslavia seeped back through his body like a drug. Thanks to the Mazarin affair, he had realised how comparatively humdrum his secret working life had become. Once he had read and digested the orders destined for Mazarin, he would be able to brief Armstrong on what was going to happen next. The briefing was scheduled for that evening and, as he had not heard otherwise, he assumed that Mike was returning to London. To save time and complications, Wesley had reluctantly decided to meet with Mike and Libby at their hotel suite.

* * *

Mike and Libby had wasted no time on making their return to London. They had taken turns driving south during the remains of the previous afternoon and through part of the night. Both wanted to get as much rest in London as they could before they met with Wesley once more. There was no doubt in their minds that his intention was to not let them rest until they were finally of no further use to him.

Mike had niggling questions that troubled him throughout the long journey from the fortified house at Blindburn. He hoped to confront Wesley with them, and he also hoped that some of the answers were going to come to light once they knew about the mission Woodville wanted them to undertake.

16
QUESTIONS AND LIES

Mike and Libby sat together on the large sofa in their hotel suite, each content with the silence of the other. Libby had draped her legs over Mike's lap as she scanned the pages of a newspaper. Mike sipped on a coffee as he mulled over the events since the pair had arrived back from Canada.

Central to his thoughts was Wesley. So far, the man had been one step ahead of them and maintaining full control. From the start Mike had suspected that whatever Wesley was up to must have some element of illegality. He also sensed there was something different about him. The man was displaying an edginess that underlined his inherent sense of superiority and disdain. Though he would never have admitted it, Wesley needed Mike and Libby, and Mike knew this would only last for so long. He needed to be alert to the change: when they would no longer be an asset to Wesley.

The telephone in their suite rang and brought Mike's thought process to a halt. Libby folded the newspaper and placed it on the coffee table.

'Wesley?' she asked.

'I guess so, but he usually wants to meet at some random location, like a museum or some other remote place. Now he's not being so careful. We need to watch and listen to him very closely in case he slips up,' said Mike, before picking up the receiver.

'You have a visitor, sir – a Mr Brown. Shall I send him up to your suite?' asked the concierge.

Mike gave his permission.

Libby sat up and straightened her dress then slipped on her shoes. The pair waited in silence for a knock at the door. When it came, Mike went to the door and opened it. Without a word, Wesley breezed straight past him and into the suite. Without the need for directions, he made his way through to the living area, where Libby sat.

Mike and Libby looked at each other. Wesley was fully familiar with the layout of the suite.

'Been here before?' asked Mike, with a mix of humour and curiosity.

'As soon as you left for the continent I had this place turned over in case of any stupidity on your part,' Wesley replied.

'Stupidity?' asked Libby.

'Such as leaving two hunting rifles in the closet, for example,' said Wesley, with an air of exasperation.

'The hotel armoury was full. I also took the precaution of taking the rifle bolts with me,' Mike said sarcastically, attempting to puncture Wesley's bluster.

'Indeed,' said the other man, indignant with Mike's continued disrespect for him. He was also annoyed that he had not managed to fully establish himself as the man in charge.

'You searched our suite?' asked Libby angrily.

'Of course. He is a criminal,' Wesley said, pointing at Mike, 'and you are an accessory to his crimes. Not to mention a wife on the run,' he added, with a venomous and judgmental edge.

'I don't think anyone in this room is whiter than white, Wesley. Your hands are far dirtier than ours,' said Mike, attacking what he saw as Wesley's hypocrisy.

Wesley looked at them coldly. Anger coursed through his veins; this man was nothing more than a common villain. He burned inside, trying to suppress his anger at Mike and his frustration with his own life.

'So why didn't you have the guns removed if you were so bothered about seeing if they were here?' snapped Mike, who had checked the weapons were still in place when he and Libby arrived back in their suite the night before.

Wesley said nothing. He refused to justify himself or his actions to an upstart criminal. Both men knew that the risk of leaving the rifles had been minimal. Wesley had simply used the search as an excuse to try and put Mike in his place.

Mike knew that for some reason Wesley had ignored his own security precautions by coming to the hotel. Time was short – or perhaps he was under some other kind of pressure. He certainly appeared uncomfortable and edgy. Mike had no way of knowing why.

Wesley took out a folded envelope from his inside jacket pocket and threw it on the coffee table. 'You had better read this.'

Mike sat down next to Libby and took out the contents of the envelope. Without a word, he read each page of the document, removing the paperclip holding the sheets of paper together and passing each one on to Libby as he finished it.

Wesley sat in a nearby armchair and observed the pair. During those quiet minutes he fixed his eyes on Mike. He looked forward to personally killing him. Not only that, but Wesley planned to kill the Kembrey woman in front of Mike immediately beforehand. He wanted Armstrong to suffer as much as possible during his last minutes alive, and Wesley knew the woman had to be the most – probably the only – precious thing in the man's life. Destroy her and he would destroy Armstrong. As far as Wesley was concerned, there was no justice in a crook like him finding real love and keeping hold of it. Wesley had chosen to walk away from the love of his life and had regretted it ever since. He wanted Armstrong to feel the same pain and loss, even if only for a few brief agonising minutes.

Wesley watched Mike and Libby's reactions as they read through the papers, and noted with satisfaction the worried looks passing between them. Their discomfort was his pleasure. The lifestyle they led had everything he coveted. Frustratingly for Wesley, he remained no further forward in uncovering how they had achieved it. Armstrong was a common criminal and Kembrey seemingly a love cheat married to a penniless farmer. Wesley comforted himself with the thought that Kembrey was only staying with Armstrong until his money ran out. The injustice, as he saw it, of the pair having such a comfortable lifestyle that was neither deserved nor earned frustrated Wesley to the core.

Mike and Libby finished reading through the orders for the dead Mazarin and stacked the papers neatly on the coffee table in front of them. Wesley expected myriad questions from them about what they were expected to do, and he looked forward to explaining the contingency plan he had for them. To show how he had everything under control, to emphasise how much they needed him.

'I have a few concerns,' said Mike.

'I can imagine,' replied Wesley, feeling smug.

'No, not about that madness,' said Mike, waving his hand dismissively at the papers.

Wesley bristled once more but managed to catch himself before giving away his reaction. 'Go on,' he said, trying not to sound suspicious.

'I go to talk to Thomson and find him dead. Libby and I talk with Dacre and he's shot dead. Each time we get a chance to exploit a chink in Woodville's armour, the gap is violently plugged. Someone is always one step ahead of us and the only person I can think of is you,' said Mike accusingly.

'You are a fool, Armstrong. Of course I am always one step ahead of you. If I weren't, you would probably be dead by now, and you are of no use to me dead. Incidentally, how could I benefit from the death of Thomson and Dacre?'

'I don't know the answer to that, Wesley, but I do know that Libby and I are expendable pawns in this game of yours,' responded Mike.

Wesley could almost taste the distrust in his words. Things were not going the way he had planned. Mike's question had to be answered carefully. Say too little and he would possibly alienate Armstrong, while saying too much might expose the double game he was playing. He decided on mixing a little truth with his lies.

'I knew Woodville wanted Thomson and Dacre dead because he had found out they were a security threat. Discovering what the two men had to offer was your job, and that was a race against time. You were too late with Thomson, who knew too much, and you only got to Dacre to find out he actually knew very little. My job is to identify and verify the security leaks,' said Wesley.

'And to do that effectively I guess you are the mysterious intermediary between your people and Woodville,' said Mike.

Wesley looked at him sharply. Once more, this man was forcing him to play his hand. Once more, Wesley decided to provide a mix of lies and truth.

'We have got to where we are today *because* I acted as the intermediary. Woodville's plans must not be leaked because we need to catch him holding the smoking gun,' he said, trying to sound exasperated at Mike's tardiness in realising this.

Mike and Libby looked at him suspiciously and said nothing.

'The whole idea is to keep Woodville reassured that the security services have no idea of his plans,' he added, sounding a little more desperate than he wanted to.

Mike and Libby maintained their silence for a while longer. The pair seemed to be evaluating what he had said.

'So, a week from today, Woodville plans to depose the government by force so that he and his co-conspirators can put the world to rights? You know this is madness, Wesley,' said Mike flatly.

'Yes, you are right.' He nodded. 'It *is* madness, but we need the man to play his hand. We also need to see his supporters break cover, so they can be arrested. The aim is to preserve the government's security and stability,' he said, trying to convince them.

Mike and Libby simply couldn't decide if Wesley was lying to them or not, and they couldn't figure out whether he was trying to prevent or facilitate the coup. It had not occurred to Libby that Wesley might be so involved with Woodville, so she followed Mike's lead. He was pretending to appear satisfied with what Wesley had said and now he changed focus and began asking about the orders.

'Obviously Mazarin's military force has all gone, so what are we going to do? Woodville is bound to check we have the means to deliver what he needs. What happens when he finds out we have been lying to him?' asked Mike.

Wesley began to feel he was on safer ground and was more than happy to respond to the question. He gave himself a congratulatory smile.

'Mazarin had a substantial stockpile of weapons, ammunition and vehicles hidden on the old airbase where he made his headquarters. He even had a store of uniforms left over. They are still in place and the airfield is still secure. From a casual observer's point of view, nothing much has changed. There are still security patrols going on to keep out the locals – and any other snoopers, for that matter.'

'You have men masquerading as Mazarin's attack force?' asked Mike, trying not to sound surprised.

'Of course, we need the continuity of security.' Wesley allowed himself another small grin.

'Who the hell are they, then?' asked Mike incredulously.

'The world is full of mercenaries,' said Wesley. 'When the army withdrew from the base, a skeleton force of troops remained as a perimeter guard until I completed the recruitment of a replacement force. Within a month I had the base sealed.'

'Where did you get the men?' Mike asked, as his curiosity increased further.

'They are a mix of Rhodesians, South Africans and Belgians. All sourced from Africa. Led by British ex-army officers, of course,' Wesley replied, trying not to look smug.

'Of course,' Mike repeated sardonically. 'That's all very impressive, Wesley, but aren't you forgetting one thing?'

'I doubt it,' he snapped, irritated by Mike and his questioning attitude.

'Mazarin's helicopters have all gone, so how will you get the men to the target? You can't make an airborne assault using lorries,' challenged Mike.

'Do you really think I would miss the obvious?' Wesley replied testily. 'I have a flight of Royal Air Force Belvedere helicopters put on standby to transport the assault force.'

'Now I know you are mad. The RAF aren't going to help you deliver a *coup d'état*!'

'The brief is they are carrying out an exercise for a highly prestigious national security plan in conjunction with NATO. The fools jumped at the chance when I told them the Navy would get the job if they were not interested,' said Wesley.

'Do they know the intended target yet?' asked Mike.

'Of course not.'

'So, there is still a chance there may be resistance once they are told,' ventured Mike.

'They won't know until they are in the air and, if necessary, the crew will be forced at gunpoint to comply with the mercenaries' orders.'

'Perhaps, but I wouldn't bet on it,' replied Mike, searching Wesley's face for a glimmer of doubt. There was none.

'Even when the crews find out they are to land troops at Buckingham Palace?' asked an astounded Libby.

'They will know something is wrong, Wesley,' said Mike, challenging Wesley once more. 'The palace is of no military value and they will know that before asking why they have to insert troops there.'

Wesley's patience was at an end. 'Get packing. You are driving up to Norfolk today!' he said in a loud voice.

Mike and Libby looked at each other in disbelief.

'But it sounds as though we have done our job, Wesley. No more investigating Woodville means you are either up to your neck in the coup or you're playing a dangerous game by allowing the plans to advance. Which is it?' said Mike in anger.

Wesley could feel a blind rage enveloping him as he drew his pistol.

'You two are going to Norfolk. Either drive there, or you get driven. My men are outside waiting so you have no choice. As far as Woodville is concerned, Mazarin is very much alive, thanks to you and your trip to Germany. I aim to keep him thinking that,' he said, before picking up the orders and returning them to the envelope.

He stood up, keeping the pistol trained on Mike and Libby. He then walked to the door and opened it. A team of six grim-faced men stepped into the room. The team leader casually opened his jacket to show he was armed.

'Get on with it – and don't try anything stupid,' said Wesley before he left.

The heavies stood around looking bored or stared at Libby's legs, so Mike and Libby went into the bedroom to pack their suitcases. There was no attempt by the men to follow or supervise them.

'I don't think that lot are from the security services and I think Wesley has forgotten to tell them we have weapons. His own men would have checked our belongings as we packed. He must have assumed these ones will do the same,' said Mike quietly.

'Are you sure?' asked Libby.

'Yes. They are not really keeping an eye on us and the man in charge has an accent that sounds South African.'

'Do we take our pistols and rifles, then?'

'We'd be stupid if we didn't. The pistols will be easy to conceal in the cases and if we strip the rifles down they will fit in there too,' Mike replied.

'Are we really going to back to Norfolk? We could always make a break for it once we are on the road,' said Libby, beginning to sound desperate.

'Wesley would have us picked up by the police and whisked away before we could do any real damage. It's better we go to Norfolk where we have a good chance of escaping and stopping Woodville,' Mike replied.

Libby desperately wanted to avoid a return to Norfolk. Fate seemed to be dragging her back to the world she was so sure she had escaped from. She shuddered at the thought of encountering her husband. She thought things could not get any more difficult.

Mike knew what she was thinking and took hold of her. 'Don't worry,' he said, trying to reassure her. 'The chances of an accidental meeting with anyone from Little Stratton are zero.'

'What about Canute?' she asked.

'He is the one man I do intend to meet,' said Mike.

The pair quickly finished packing and closed their suitcases, both of which went unchecked by Wesley's men. Just as well, because their weapons and ammunition were contained inside, hidden in towels. Both Mike and Libby firmly held on to their suitcases as they took the lift to the underground car park. Mike's gamble that the men would give no attention to the suitcases paid off.

Once in the underground car park, the group headed towards the Jensen. Two of the men split off, each of them returning in green Rover saloons. The engine burble from both cars was noisier than usual, making Mike think that specially tuned engines had been fitted. He placed their suitcases in the boot of the Jensen before turning to face the team leader.

'How do we do this? Are we driving in the lead or do we follow you?' he asked.

The man smirked and let out a cruel laugh. 'You lead. We follow, but the princess stays with us. We don't want you doing anything stupid, do we?' the man replied, grinning.

Mike looked at Libby. A flash of panic crossed her face.

'Touch her and I'll kill you,' he said to the team leader.

'You misbehave, and Wesley has said that she becomes our fringe benefit,' replied the man. Mike could see he meant what he said.

He turned towards Libby. 'You'll be fine. I'll see you in Norfolk,' he said to her, trying to sound as reassuring as he could.

'She will be in the car following right behind you, so you can blow kisses in the rear-view mirror,' said the team leader with a cold laugh.

Libby gave Mike a weak smile before taking her seat in the back of the nearest Rover. She was pushed into the middle, with one man sitting on either side of her.

Mike looked at the man in charge. 'I meant what I said,' he muttered coldly.

'I know. Just get to Norfolk with no funny business and she will be fine.'

Mike looked over to the Rover as the doors slammed shut. One of the men gave Mike a leery smirk through the side window. Mike made a note of his features and resolved that he would kill him regardless of what happened next.

17
HEADING SOUTH

A huge pair of curtains hung from the ornate moulded ceiling down to the thick carpeted floor. They were so large they could easily rival those being used in a small cinema. They were moss green in colour and covered almost all the internal wall in the long corridor-like room that made up most of one side of Alston Hall, which stood in the South Tynedale valley, west of Newcastle upon Tyne. The external wall opposite to the curtains consisted of shuttered windows. There were four large chandeliers at equidistant points, hung midway down from the high ceiling and providing ample light to the room. Even at that level the chandeliers were well above the height of a tall person such as Woodville.

At either end of the room were two sets of Victorian oak double doors. Charles Woodville always kept the keys to these doors in his possession. His staff had no access to duplicate keys and were only allowed into the room after he had personally checked that the curtains were closed. He trusted his staff in almost all things except for the room with the huge curtains, and always remained in the room, allowing his staff to work around him. If he was needed elsewhere he ordered the staff to leave the room before locking the doors behind him. On his return, the staff then continued with their duties.

That particular morning the cleaners had vacuumed and dusted under his watchful eyes before leaving to carry on working elsewhere in the house. Woodville locked the end doors after them and returned to the huge pedestal desk where he had sat earlier, patiently waiting for his staff to complete their tasks.

The large oak desk and the chair Woodville sat on were the only two items of furniture in the room. It had previously been cluttered with smaller operational map boards, usually hidden under dustsheets to prevent staff seeing them. Other desks, chairs and various ancillary items had recently been sent south and put in his new command centre. A small highly polished wooden box with a set of switches set into its top surface lay on the desk's ornate green tooled-leather writing insert. Otherwise, it lay bare.

Whilst supervising his staff, Woodville sat on a mahogany Hepplewhite dining chair with a shaped back and splayed back legs. He found this the most comfortable chair for working at the desk because of an old injury to his back. Early in the war against the Nazis, he had been badly injured in a naval encounter with the Kriegsmarine. Shrapnel from a naval artillery round was left embedded close to his spine and sometimes caused him great pain. When he was posted to the Admiralty for the rest of the war, the chair went with him to London.

Instead sitting down on the chair, Woodville leaned against the front of the desk and picked up the box with the switches on it. Electrical cables ran out of it to a connecting point set into the wall opposite the desk. Nothing beyond the cables could be seen until the curtains opened. He flicked one of the switches. It allowed power to be sent to the electric motors used for opening and closing the curtains. With a low humming noise, the huge curtains moved apart at a majestic pace until he could see a large wall-mounted map. Woodville flicked some of the other switches on the box to power up the spotlights that illuminated the map, complementing the light from the chandeliers. He then placed the switch box back on the desk.

Now that the map was fully illuminated, he began to scrutinise it in detail. His concentration was evident from the way he crossed his legs and used his left hand to hold his right elbow. His right hand and thumb supported his chin. If he had been sitting down, Woodville could have easily adopted the same pose to play a game of chess. Instead of a chessboard, however, his eyes flicked over the map displaying the area of Greater London and small parts of the Home Counties. Military symbols and acronyms printed on labels indicated the types of army units and where they were going to be deployed in six days' time. Key locations such as Parliament, Whitehall, Heathrow Airport, and television and radio stations were all covered. Woodville and his generals even had a unit assigned to monitor and control the movement of traffic on the M1 motorway.

The only element of doubt in Woodville's mind concerned Mazarin and his helicopter force. Mazarin was an outsider and came from a background that was alien to the military men who had come together to plan the overthrow of Parliament. Charles Woodville, a bemedalled naval veteran, was the sixth Viscount Woodville and Baron Tynedale. The portraits hanging on the uncovered parts of the walls in the room where he stood were of his aristocratic forebears; some of them depicted men from centuries ago. All the major participants in the *coup d'état* were his personal friends and had an aristocratic heritage in common with him. Woodville knew them all either from school or university, but he did not know Mazarin.

That was another reason why he had decided to keep feeding Wesley MacDonald limited amounts of information. MacDonald, like Mazarin, was also an outsider – he provided a useful link into the security services but nothing more. Woodville believed that letting MacDonald know his full plans created too great a security risk. Despite the man's inroads into MI5 and 6, it frustrated Woodville that he had been unable to gain any useful support from the security services themselves.

He had no idea that both departments loathed MacDonald's team and looked forward to the day the man was gone. There was not even a hint of how the departments might be disposed to a regime change when it came. He assumed, perhaps optimistically, that they might simply wait to see how events played out. The current revelations resulting from the uncovering of communist spies in the security services provided a small measure of comfort to him. The national focus on activity to uncover the enemy within had left Woodville more freedom to prepare his forces unhindered.

As Wesley had predicted, Woodville took the precaution of sending an observation team to Norfolk to report on Mazarin's airfield base. The reports had proven positive. A large force of men had been observed providing physical security for the base, though Woodville's men had not seen Mazarin's helicopters.

They assumed the aircraft were further secured inside one of the massive hangars. What Woodville didn't know was that Wesley had given orders for fuel bowsers to be parked in full view so they could be seen by anyone spying on the base. The ruse had worked with Woodville's men, who had assumed – as planned – that the bowsers were there to refuel the helicopters. Woodville was reassured enough by this report about the base to allow the release of his orders to MacDonald, who would then pass them on to Mazarin.

Woodville believed Mazarin's largely foreign force had no qualms about occupying Buckingham Palace and confining members of the Royal Family there until the interim government was put in place. Despite this, Woodville wanted Mazarin and his force replaced at the earliest opportunity by an army unit he could fully trust. Annoyingly for him, he had no idea how long that might take. It all depended upon how much resistance his other army units encountered.

He continued to mull over the likely outcomes until he was as satisfied as he could be that nothing had been missed in his preparations.

In less than a week, as the head of an interim government, he would march into the House of Commons to tell the forcibly assembled MPs they were surplus to requirement and must return to their defunct constituencies. He would then make his way to the House of Lords and ask them to vote to support his regime. Those who did not would be summarily dismissed from the House and barred entry whilst they hastily reconsidered their position. His actions of political theatre would be filmed in their entirety, then broadcast to the nation that same evening. He was sure his actions would portray him as a loyal patriot and a man of action seeking to save his country from economic and political disaster – this would be overwhelmingly accepted by the nation. He relished the idea of being at the centre of a world stage and proving his worth as a true leader. Regardless of what happened in the Houses of Parliament, he meant to retain an iron grip on the country until the rest of the armed forces and the police fell into line to preserve peace for the nation.

Finally, he switched off the spotlights and closed the curtains using the switch box. The room darkened as, one by one, the lights were switched off before Woodville let himself out through the double doors and locked them behind him.

Waiting on the other side were the men that formed his personal bodyguard. As a phalanx, the men strode purposefully behind him, fully confident in their rightness and purpose.

As he walked along, it occurred to Woodville that he might wear his naval uniform on the day he entered the Houses of Parliament. His uniform and medals would provide an appropriate picture of patriotism as he dismissed the MPs, and when he stood before the House of Lords he would be the very image of a man born to lead. He thought it ironic that, whilst the coup was to be executed by the army, it was himself – a navy man, an admiral – who was the supreme commander and soon-to-be self-styled First Lord of the Admiralty. He glowed with pleasure as he gave orders to have his naval uniform packed and sent down to his temporary headquarters.

For the last few days leading up to the coup, Woodville had decided to relocate his headquarters to his cousin's Palladian mansion in Surrey. The proximity to London and the anonymity of the estate were ideal for allowing him to prepare in secrecy. Woodville thought his cousin was a terrible bore but, by chance, the man had decided to take himself down to Monaco for the month. The grand privacy of the mansion would also allow him to enjoy some time with his mistress.

Woodville felt almost childish in his optimism. His forces were being put into the final stages of readiness to allow him to take his place at the head of the nation – a nation he believed was being destabilised by the Americans and the Russians in their relentless downward spiral of nuclear brinksmanship and eventual destruction.

He wore his favourite Savile Row wool suit that day, a classic navy three-piece with a white shirt made of heavy cotton. His silk tie was dark blue with tiny white polka dots. An equally crisp white handkerchief rose from the top of the outside breast pocket of the suit.

He thought it best to say goodbye to his wife before leaving, even though he was reluctant to do so. At that time of the day she was either out riding her horse or somewhere in the stable yard. Both options meant getting his highly polished shoes dirty, so he sent one of his men to try and find her. He fidgeted irritably whilst waiting alone in a large drawing room for the man to return with his wife, but the man returned alone. In lowered tones he passed on a verbatim message to Woodville from the viscountess: 'he should not send monkeys to do his dirty work'. He scowled and made his way out of the house to the car, thanking his lucky stars that Parliament would not be as intransigent as the viscountess.

Wearing his favourite suit was as superstitious as Woodville chose to be. He generally regarded flying as a dangerous mode of transport, and yet that day he had to fly down to Surrey. The tedious options of a long car or rail journey appealed even less. He wore the suit to try and put himself more at ease.

A midnight-blue Bentley S3 saloon sat parked outside on the gravelled drive at the front of the hall, waiting for its owner to appear. A uniformed chauffeur stood by the vehicle, ready to open the door for Woodville. His instructions were to drive to Newcastle Airport. Once Woodville was airborne, the chauffeur then had to drive south to an address given to him by his employer. There he had been instructed to collect a female guest who would be accompanying Woodville during his stay in Surrey. The next day the chauffeur had to have the Bentley cleaned and ready for driving in and around the London area.

A team of men that made up Woodville's headquarters staff had travelled ahead of him. They had taken over an estate manager's house in the grounds of Hindhead House, which belonged to his cousin, Lord Edward Clarence. The original grand house had existed on the Hindhead estate since the sixteenth century and had been added to over the centuries. That was, until 1932, when Clarence's father decided to have the house demolished and replaced by a twelve-bedroomed modern building in the William-and-Mary style. The house also had a walled garden and an indoor swimming pool that Woodville intended to make full use of in the company of his mistress.

He intended to use Hindhead solely as his residence, while the smaller estate manager's house, tucked away among the trees on the estate, would act as his command centre. The estate manager had already been turfed out and rehoused at a smaller property well away from the command centre. Military pantechnicons were then parked around the house. The vehicles were loaded with radio equipment to be used to direct and monitor the delivery of the *coup d'état*. Painted matt green and further disguised with NATO camouflage netting, the vehicles melded well into the rural landscape. Tall radio antennae had sprouted up above the trees that surrounded the house, whilst large generators were started up to provide electricity to the powerful transmitters hidden nearby.

A mix of military vehicle and foot patrols provided an impenetrable inner and outer cordon to secure the area of the house. The local military commander had driven around to check the site was secure in preparation for briefing Woodville when he arrived. Guard posts were strategically placed around the environs of the estate, manned by more armed soldiers. The men had been briefed to tell local people and estate workers that a military exercise would be taking place over the next few days, simulating a state of national emergency, and that there was nothing to fear.

Woodville's flight to a private airfield in Surrey had been uneventful, but he was glad to get his feet back on solid ground after the aircraft finally landed. The de Havilland Dove's pilot had struggled to deliver a perfectly smooth landing on the first try, and this had unnerved Woodville. Despite the sunny day, a strong crosswind had sprung up from nowhere and the pilot had aborted his initial attempt at landing. Second time around, the pilot was better able to allow for the crosswind.

A white Rolls-Royce belonging to his absent cousin, Edward, was waiting for Woodville at the edge of the runway with its engine running. As he walked over to it, he winced. The colour was inappropriate to the stature of the Rolls, but typical of his cousin's odd tastes. In contrast to the Rolls-Royce, two black Ford Zephyrs were parked nearby for transporting his personal guards.

Minutes after landing, the three vehicles set off for the grounds of Hindhead House. Rather than waste time up at the main house, he directed his cousin's chauffeur to take him directly to the command centre. Woodville wanted to meet his local commander and make a joint inspection of the security arrangements that had been put in place to keep the estate and command centre secure.

Despite Woodville's sharp eye for detail, he was unable to fault the security of the estate. Back at the command centre, he was pleased to find that his orders had been followed in their entirety. The battle plan was plain to see, along with his maps, which perfectly replicated the details shown on the large-scale map hidden behind the curtains at Alston Hall.

Woodville ordered the local commander to give him all the updates on the deployment and readiness of military units as they occurred. There was little he could do now except monitor the final preparatory actions being undertaken by the army units. A small VHF radio receiver had been set up at the main house to allow him to listen to high-level radio traffic and be given transcripts of messages that needed passing directly to him, and Woodville had given the order that telephones should be banned from being used to pass on information as the coup reached its final preparatory stages – after that, all radio transmissions had to be encoded to prevent unwanted interception from third parties. The last thing he needed was for a bunch of radio enthusiasts to pick up on the increased use of the airwaves and go to the police.

Woodville finally began to relax as his plans came ever closer to fruition. Instead of using the Rolls-Royce, he decided to enjoy the afternoon sun by walking back to the main house. Once there he could take a late lunch before being reunited with his lover. He expected her to be at Hindhead by evening and was eagerly anticipating her company at dinner.

Standing outside the estate manager's house, Woodville took in the stillness before the storm. The only noise was the subdued drone of the large diesel generators under the camouflage nets that fluttered gently in the warm breeze. Somehow, he felt the sound added to his calmness and reassurance that all would be well. He began his stroll along the smooth road that wound its way through the nearby trees and out into the open. As he continued his walk, the estate opened out on to large fields dotted with horse chestnut trees, with sheep grazing on the short grass. He could hear invisible skylarks somewhere high up into the blue, almost cloudless sky, and felt his time had come at last.

18
CHEAP AFTERSHAVE

Mike drove the Jensen up to the road speed limits and no more. He made sure to accelerate and decelerate at an even pace so that the two Fords following him had no problems keeping up. Throughout the journey he frequently checked his mirrors to reassure himself that the woman he valued most in his life was not far behind. He only overtook slow lorries when he knew the others could easily follow and preferred to wait at traffic lights to prevent the small convoy getting separated. The further away they travelled from London, the slower their progress. Eventually the cars were threading their way along the narrowing roads of Norfolk.

The old airbase they were driving towards was situated on a plateau. Depending on the route of approach, the large aircraft hangars could be glimpsed standing slightly proud of the gently rolling landscape interspersed with woods and islands of trees. Soon Mike was able to make out the large dome Wesley had once sent him to spy on. In summer the base looked slightly mysterious in its remote rural idyll. The block-shaped hangars shimmered gently in the summer heat; very different to the dark and brooding presence they seemed to have during the wintertime.

The village of Little Stratton, where Mike had very briefly lived the previous winter, was situated some miles to the north of the base. This meant Mike did not have to worry about taking a diversion to avoid being seen by a villager who might recognise either himself or Libby. Once he got closer to the airbase the road narrowed to a single track, forcing him to drive even more carefully. The road widened at the final approach to the airbase's main gate and at that point the Ford travelling behind Mike accelerated past. The guards hastily opened the steel gates and the convoy proceeded. Mike shuddered slightly as he watched the gates close behind him. It was not the thought of being trapped on the base once more that worried him. Instead it was the men who wore the same coverall uniforms he had seen when Mazarin was still alive. They were living reminders of death and extreme violence.

Mike was thankful that Libby did not have similar memories of the base. Her appearance there had been a brief, but nonetheless violent episode at the very edge of the base. All she knew about Mike and Simone Powell's battle with Mazarin was what he had told her, and even that had been scant in detail.

In the summer the bleakness of the place had been replaced by the leafy greenness of shrubs and trees. The open areas had been left to run wild, creating islands of long grass and wildflowers overgrowing the kerbstones that set out the matrix of concrete roads laid around the airbase. The sunlight added a touch of cruelty, highlighting the faded and peeling paintwork of neglect. Broken windows were everywhere. Doors to sheds were hanging off their hinges and holes had begun to pock the roofs of the disused buildings. Mazarin's Teutonic orderliness had only worked in the depths of winter, whilst summer exposed how shabby and dilapidated his secret base really was. The place had begun to fall apart as soon as its wartime role ended. The seemingly impenetrable fortress was really a leaky sieve – one he intended to escape from with Libby.

The cars drove the short distance to the officer's married quarters. The encroaching dilapidation included these houses and their immediate surroundings. Long grass extended over the tops of walls and gardens as bramble bushes made their thorny takeover. The cars stopped outside what Mike knew had been Mazarin's house, which now seemed pathetic as its menace had evaporated with the death of the man. Now it was just a large house, soon to be abandoned to dampness and deterioration. Mike looked forward to getting away from the base more than ever.

The men in the lead Ford got out and signalled to Mike to do the same. He stepped out into the warm summer air and looked back towards the other Ford parked directly behind him. The men had got out of it, along with Libby.

'You and the woman will stay here for the next few days,' said the team leader. 'Wesley wants us to keep up appearances, and that means making sure that anybody keeping surveillance on this place gets to see you two.'

'How can anyone see us tucked away in here?' asked Mike. The South African smirked. 'We have an old Mercedes like Mazarin's and you are going to take rides in it around the base and its perimeter. You will be both high profile and under guard all at the same time,' said the team leader, maintaining his confident smirk.

'Then she'll need to be with me as well. Mazarin was never without Carla Mancuso nearby,' replied Mike, motioning to Libby.
It was obvious the team leader was unsure about Mike's comment. Was he being helpful or was he up to something?

'Anyone who knows Mazarin will wonder why she isn't with him. Or do you have to get permission from Wesley?' Mike needled, trying to get the man to think his authority was being challenged.

'I don't need to bother him with little things like you,' said the man, trying to imply that Mike and Libby were of no consequence any more.

Mike knew he had duped the man into a mistake. He smiled and walked over to join Libby. 'Are you all right?' he asked her, whilst looking directly into the eyes of the man who had leered back at him from the car window earlier.

'I'm fine. Is this where we are staying?' she replied, sounding as business-like as she could.

'Yes, this is Mazarin's old place. Bit of a mess outside but much nicer inside – unless these clowns have messed it up,' said Mike, referring to the men around them.

The comment earned him a punch in the kidneys that almost felled him. Libby rushed forward and held him close, her eyes flashing hatred at the team leader.

The man smirked even more. 'Don't forget – we are in charge here, you prick,' he said, with a quiet menace that accentuated his South African accent.

Mike caught his breath then went to the Jensen to collect the suitcases. The men watched him carefully, their hands hovering over their pistols.

'You are going to regret that,' said Mike, facing up to the team leader.

'Oh, sure I am. Get your arses inside!' the man barked in response.

Mike carried the suitcases inside, Libby following right behind him. They went straight upstairs. Libby looked around and, to her pleasant surprise, the interior of the house was luxuriously fitted out to be as comfortable as possible for its occupants. All the doors bar one that led off the upstairs landing and corridors were closed.

The team leader headed for the open door that led to the master bedroom. 'This is your little love nest for now,' he said. The men then withdrew from the room and the door closed with a final click of a key in the lock. The bedroom was ornately decorated, including chairs and a coffee table. Heavy Italianate wallpaper made the room seem smaller than it was. Similarly, large radiators mounted around the room seemed to intrude even further.

'Someone must have felt the cold,' said Libby.

'Yes, Carla Mancuso was Italian, so I guess she didn't like the cold and damp of a British winter. How was the drive up?' asked Mike, changing the subject.

'Sandwiched between those apes?' She arched an eyebrow.

'Did they touch you?' he asked directly.

'The creepy one wanted to but was warned off by one of the others.'

'The one on your right?'

'Yes, the one wearing cheap aftershave. I even asked him what it was called. I told him I wanted to avoid buying you a bottle. The creep didn't like that,' said Libby.

'Good, I will look forward to seeing him later,' Mike replied.

'What do you mean?'

'He will volunteer to babysit you while we get driven around the base. He'll be distracted by you and therefore off guard,' said Mike with a smile.

Libby looked alarmed as her eyes scanned the room. 'They might be listening, Mike,' she whispered.

'No, they are overconfident. They think it is game over for us. Look at the window, it's had bars fitted on the outside. The bathroom will be the same, if it has a window. The door is locked and there will be a guard sat outside,' said Mike.

Libby had not noticed the bars, and nor had she realised the room had an en-suite bathroom. She went in and opened the heavily patterned privacy glass window. It opened only so far before hitting vertical metal bars. She swore.

'What are we going to do? There is no way out of here and time is running out.'

'The longer we are kept here, the harder it will be for us to escape. We have to escape today, and I think I know how we'll do it,' replied Mike, opening the suitcases and taking out the concealed Smith & Wessons to check them over.

* * *

Wesley had ordered Mike and Libby's captors to ensure that whilst pretending to be Mazarin, Mike must have a visible presence on the airbase. He hoped to establish the idea that Mazarin regularly inspected the security arrangements around the base using his Mercedes as transport.

By early evening, the time had come for the first of these inspections. Mike and Libby had armed themselves with their pistols and had concealed as many spare magazines of ammunition as they dared to without being obvious about it. The wait had been uncomfortable, with the bulk of the weaponry pressing against them, but they wanted to be ready the moment the bedroom door opened.

The room had become hot as the sun tracked across the large window, and even with the opening as wide as possible, the room was stifling. A sheen of perspiration clung to Mike's forehead as he sat waiting. Libby lay on the large bed, feeling sticky with the heat.

A few minutes before six o'clock, the bedroom door opened. The South African, flanked by two other men, entered the room and eyed Mike and Libby suspiciously.

'Get up, you two are going for a ride,' he said gruffly.

Libby had sat up when the door opened and now stood by the bed. Mike casually stood up too. He noticed that one of the other men was the man who at leered at him from the back seat.

'You will sit in the front of the car and you will be in the back,' said the team leader, looking firstly at Mike and then at Libby.

Mike could already smell the cheap aftershave coming from the thug who would sit with Libby. Without a word, they followed the men downstairs and out through the front door to the Mercedes. Mike took his place in the front seat and Libby climbed into the back. The leering man sat next to Libby, took out his pistol and held it in his lap. The muzzle pointed directly at her. In his other hand was a small VHF mobile transceiver for keeping in radio contact as the car proceeded around the base.

'You try anything stupid and my colleague will shoot her,' said the driver to Mike.

'Understood,' said Mike.

The team leader remained at Mazarin's house, watching from the drive as the car pulled away. Mike was feeling confident now that the numbers had evened up. It was two against two and the men had no idea that both he and Libby were armed.

The man who was driving took a circular route of the airbase, making sure the car and its occupants could be seen from outside. They lingered at the main gate and at various convenient points near to the perimeter fence, where sentry posts were in place. Mike said nothing whilst Libby turned away and stared out of her window to avoid eye contact with the thug sat next to her. Her right hand, masked by the open jacket she wore, concealed her pistol. As the circular journey progressed, the Mercedes was driven further out on to the airfield and away from the main site where the hangars and buildings were located. This was exactly where Mike had planned to make his move.

'What we are doing is no good. You do realise this charade is not going to convince anyone who might be keeping surveillance on the base?' he said.

The driver glanced at him suspiciously. 'Oh yeah, and what would you know about that?'

'Victor Mazarin served in the military long before he arrived here. This is not how he would carry out his routine inspections,' Mike continued.

The man gave him a sideways glance. 'Go on,' he said.

'He'd never stay in the car and just be driven around. He would speak to the guards to check they knew their orders and responsibilities. He would inspect weapons and physically test the gates. You know the sort of thing I mean, don't you? What we are doing isn't fooling anyone,' he said, hoping the man would take the bait.

'Yeah, that kind of makes sense,' said the driver, though he still sounded slightly unconvinced.

'Your team leader should have known that. I bet your officers won't be too happy with you if they see you just driving around like this,' Mike persisted.

The driver looked at Mike again. This time he appeared to be appraising him.

'OK, we stop at the next crash gate up ahead,' he said.
The man in the back with Libby spoke up. 'Shall I let HQ know what we are doing?'

'No. What are these two going to do, run away while we point guns at their backs?' the driver responded confidently. He pulled up next to the locked emergency access gate and turned to Mike.

'You and I get out slowly – and together, so don't try anything stupid,' he said, with a menacing edge to his voice.

Mike simply nodded. In case they were being observed from the other side of the perimeter fence, the man had to keep his pistol holstered to maintain the pretence that Mazarin was not under duress.

As Mike and the driver got out of the car, Libby slipped her pistol out from its holster. The flap of her open jacket masked the small movement because the man sat next to her was momentarily distracted by the others.

This was the moment Mike had told her to open fire.

Libby did not hesitate and fired twice at point-blank range. The force of the bullets threw the man back against the door. His face was a rictus of surprise and pain as he tried to make sense of what had just happened. He glanced down at the bloody mess that used to be his belly, and then back at Libby. He knew this was the end but he still moved his hand towards his own dropped pistol. Libby gave him a cruel and victorious smile, then levelled her pistol at him before firing once more. The bullet smashed through the man's sternum and tore apart his heart. Life vanished from his eyes and his hand fell limp. The radio he was holding dropped to the floor. The smell of his cheap aftershave, mixed with the coppery scent of blood, filled her flaring nostrils.

As the driver had been exiting the car, he turned around in total surprise upon hearing the shots. He reached for his pistol, but it was all too late. Mike had already outstretched his arm and used the roof of the Mercedes to steady his aim. He fired a single shot and one side of the man's head exploded into a crimson spray of blood and viscera. His body crumpled and dropped to the ground, his now-redundant pistol clattering across the concrete.

Mike flung open the rear passenger door and the body of the man Libby had shot fell out on to the ground, leaving just the lower portion of his legs and feet caught in the foot well of the car. He hurriedly dragged the inert body clear of the Mercedes before checking inside. The passenger window had remained intact. A large amount of blood was on the back seat and the lower half of the door, but miraculously none had splattered up the windows. Mike hoped that meant the car would not attract attention as they made their escape along the roads outside the airbase. He grabbed the small radio out of the foot well and slammed the door shut.

Libby had already got out of the car and, with her pistol at the ready, kept watch for anyone approaching. Everything was quiet except the skylarks singing high above them.

'What do we do now?' she asked.

'We have plenty of time. We are on the opposite side of the airfield to the main site, and even assuming anyone heard the shots, we still have a few minutes. There is no chatter on the radio, so I think we are going to be fine,' he said.

'You seem pretty sure, Mike,' replied Libby, scanning the expanse of the airfield.

'The man you shot kept in contact with base using his walkie-talkie every ten minutes. The last communication was four minutes ago. Get in,' he said, with reassurance.

Libby holstered her pistol and dropped into the front passenger seat of the car. Mike ran over to the nearby gates and shot at the rusty padlock that was securing a chain until it disintegrated. He flung open the gates, then holstered his pistol as he dashed back to the car. Mike started the Mercedes and accelerated down a moss-covered concrete track. Overhanging brambles slashed and tore at the paintwork of the car as it sped the few hundred yards downhill to where it met a country lane. Mike veered to the right as they approached the lane, then accelerated smoothly away.

'Turn up the volume on the walkie-talkie so we can hear what is happening on the base,' he said.

'Where are we going?' Libby was starting to sound edgy as she did as he asked.

'To Canute's house, where else?' replied Mike, looking over to her with a large smile.

19
IN THE WOODS

The handset of the telephone bounced off its cradle when Wesley threw it back in place. He reached down by the side of his desk and picked up the instrument before putting it back with a careful but firm slam. His hand rested on it for a second as he recovered his composure.

He was beginning to get tired of being spoken to by Woodville as if he were a hired help. The man's arrogance irritated him enough to confirm Wesley's view that remaining in a country ran by men like that was not a good idea. Once his payment from Woodville, or more probably his secret backers, was received, he was leaving for France.

He patted his forehead with a handkerchief to mop up the perspiration and let out a sigh. Now the telephone call had concluded, Wesley went across to the window and opened it as wide as he could. His office faced south and was stifling hot with the summer sun streaming through the glass. Despite his discomfort, he had not allowed himself to have the window open when using the telephone. He preferred not to risk even the tiniest chance of his words being overheard.

Wesley had spent the morning working through a tedious backlog of files and papers. The boring nature of the work had put him in a foul mood well before the irritating telephone call had come from Woodville. As he was alone and expected no visitors, Wesley slackened off his tie and undid the top button on his shirt. The collar was damp with his sweat and he detected the slight smell of body odour.

His eyes returned to his overfull in-tray. The thought of using the afternoon to clear it was too much, and he flicked through the files with a growing sense of disinterest and boredom. Having found that most documents were for his information rather than needing progression, once signed he picked up the tray and placed it in his steel-grey security cabinet. He shut the doors and turned the combination lock half a dozen times to clear the settings before leaving the office to have a walk and enjoy some fresh air.

As he walked through Green Park and on to Hyde Park, he relaxed. In a few days he would be gone, so he decided to leave the files for some other unfortunate to deal with.

Minutes after Wesley had left the office, his phone rang and rang until the caller gave up on him answering.

* * *

Mike floored the Mercedes' accelerator pedal to make sure he put as much space between themselves and the airbase in the quickest possible time. He headed straight towards Little Stratton, and Libby soon worked out where they were going. Adrenaline continued to course through her veins from the fear and excitement of the shooting.

'Why are we heading to Little Stratton, of all places?' she asked. Her voice was pitched a little higher than normal and she looked at Mike with wide eyes.

'We're not going into the village proper. Just to Canute's house,' Mike replied.

He sounded too determined to be argued with, so she held back from any further discussion. He concentrated on driving as the Mercedes flashed across junctions and barely kept to the road as he manhandled it through bends, pushing the tyres to the limits of their adhesion.

He knew their lives depended on not wasting a second of time. There was a good chance that Canute would not be at the rectory, but Mike had run out of choices about where to go. He was sure that once the alarm was raised at the airbase, Wesley would be contacted. Men would be sent to check on Canute soon afterwards, as Wesley knew he was the only person Mike could turn to. Libby tried to listen in to the handheld radio but they were soon out of range to hear anything useful.

Precious minutes passed as the Mercedes tore along the narrow country lanes. The closer they got to Little Stratton, the more Libby scanned around her to see if anyone was taking notice of the car. Finally, Mike braked heavily to slow down and turn into Canute's drive. Seconds later, they were outside the house. They were relieved to find no other cars parked there, so hopefully Canute had no visitors that evening. Mike sharply accelerated the car around the side of the house to try and hide it from view and left the engine running.

'Libby, go around the front and keep watch while I look for Canute,' he said urgently.

Without a word, she drew her pistol and made her way to the front of the house. Mike tried the kitchen door and found it to be unlocked, so he rushed inside. He called out Canute's name but there was no reply. A few seconds later he dashed outside and nearly collided with the rector himself.

'Canute, Libby and I need somewhere safe to hide but we need to go now! Can you help?' asked Mike desperately.

The huge man seemed to hesitate, but this was only while he thought of a place to hide Mike and Libby.

'Of course, my boy, of course. I know just the place. Can I drive you there?' Canute asked as he looked around for Libby.

'I can't leave the Mercedes here. I'll explain later. You take your car and we'll follow,' said Mike.

Canute raced inside to collect the keys to his Austin Cambridge while Mike opened the wooden garage doors then went back to the Mercedes. Canute pulled around the Mercedes and headed up the drive, waiting for Mike to follow. After stopping so Libby could jump back in the car, Mike caught up with Canute and both cars headed away.

The leafy expanse of Bacton Wood came into view and Mike wondered if this was where Canute was heading. The Austin continued to circumnavigate the massive wood, following roads that were barely discernible from tracks, then promptly disappeared from their view when Canute braked and took a sharp left into the wood itself. Mike followed and found he was driving along a bumpy track that gently rose and fell with the contours of the land. A minute after entering the wood, they were in dead ground and out of sight. Canute came to a gentle halt and Mike pulled up behind him.

'Follow me,' said Canute, and they climbed out of the Mercedes.

In silence they walked hastily along a track for a few more minutes before entering a small clearing. The lengthening evening shadows partially obscured a wooden hut situated at the western end. Canute shambled up to the hut before bending down in front of the door. He pulled at a short wooden plank that formed a step and lifted out a small metal cash box. He opened it and took out a key, then unlocked the door before replacing the box. He motioned for Mike and Libby to go inside the hut, then glanced around the locale. Sensing all was well, he too entered the hut.

Mike began to speak but Canute raised his hand to stop him.

'You can tell me all about your adventures in a moment. We are quite safe here and no one will be coming to the hut as it is church property. I look after the place, letting the scouts, girl guides and local youth groups use it for their activity weekends. Now then, priorities – do you want the Mercedes disposed of?' he asked.

'Yes, we escaped from Mazarin's base in it,' said Mike.

'He is dead and yet it is still "his" base?' queried Canute.

'It's a long story. Can we get the Mercedes hidden first?' asked Mike, wanting to have the only link to their whereabouts kept out of sight.

Canute heard the urgency in Mike's voice and told them to wait in the hut until he returned. Mike and Libby heard the Mercedes being slowly driven past the hut and further into the wood. As the windows on the hut still had their removable shutters in place, they sat in the warm semi-darkness, infused with the faint scent of wood smoke coming from the fireplace.

Canute's large frame filled the doorway as he re-entered the hut a few minutes later.

'I backed the car into a large patch of rhododendrons to screen it from view. There is enough tree cover to prevent anyone seeing it from the air,' he said, before opening a cupboard and taking out two Tilly lamps.

He passed one of the lamps to Mike for lighting whilst he lit the other. Minutes later the hut was illuminated by the white-hot glowing mantles, placed on a table surrounded by tubular chairs. Canute told Mike and Libby to sit down whilst he made the hut more habitable.

He filled a kettle with water from the single tap set over a square stainless-steel sink. The kettle was then placed on a gas-ring burner connected to a large gas bottle outside the rear of the hut.

While they waited for the ring of tiny dancing blue flames to bring the kettle to the boil, Canute pointed out the bunk beds Mike and Libby could sleep in. He then rooted around in a cutlery drawer, looking for a small key. He used it to open a large padlocked metal box and pulled out two cardboard boxes. Mike recognised them straightaway as army ration packs.

'The food is a bit basic, but I am sure you will manage,' said Canute.

Mike nodded back with the knowing smile of one ex-military man to another. The kettle came to the boil and the whistle began to squeal, making Mike and Libby jump. Canute made tea using large teabags taken from the ration packs.

'There is powdered milk in there, or I can open a tin of evaporated milk,' said Canute. Mike and Libby opted for the evaporated milk.

The dark of night was brought on early by the shade of the trees, whilst the hissing lamps exaggerated the contrast of light and dark. Canute closed the door to the hut to prevent moths fluttering in to an untimely death. With the world shut outside, Mike and Libby recounted the story of how they came to need Canute's help once more.

Canute nodded as he listened, seeking clarity here and there on different matters until they had told him everything up until the point they had arrived at his house. He also noted the gaps left deliberately by Mike to prevent any interrogator extracting information from Canute about their wider travels and how they had been able to live so freely. Canute knew he was working on a need-to-know basis and did not press Mike for information unless it linked to Wesley.

'With so little time left, why don't you go to the security services?' he asked.

'They won't believe me, and the next thing I know it will be Libby and I in the spotlight. We need to stop Woodville and still remain free somehow,' Mike replied.

Canute rubbed his chin as he worked his mind around the problem. 'I can contact some old friends and be your indirect link. If Woodville has a mole in the security services who might catch me, I'm sure I can hold out until you get your hands on his overall plan. That would massively tip the balance in your favour.'

'You don't think Wesley is working as Woodville's man on the inside?' asked Mike.

'No, Wesley does not have the same background, socially or politically. It is very unlikely that a man like Woodville would trust him enough. I'm afraid we will have to leave a question mark over Woodville's potential inroads, if any, to the security services,' Canute replied.

'But we don't even know where Woodville is, so how can we find out his overall plan?' asked Libby.

'We need to stir things up a bit and see what happens,' Canute replied. 'I will make the necessary phone call tonight and get back to you as soon as I can. Make sure you get something to eat and plenty of sleep, as you may be very busy for the next few days. No one will find you here, so just relax,' he added reassuringly as he disappeared into the warm darkness of the night.

Mike opened the ration packs and emptied their contents on to the table. He examined the contents labels printed on the tins and smiled.

'These will taste pretty good by the time I'm finished with them,' he said.

Libby smiled briefly. 'I hope so, I'm starving. Do you think Canute will be able to keep us out of trouble?' she asked, sounding worried.

'I can't guarantee that, but if you mean not getting arrested, then yes. Why don't you try one of those bunks for size while I make dinner?' he said, trying to sound as positive as he could.

Libby nodded, kicked off her shoes, and lay down on the nearest bunk. She stared up at the cobwebbed roof of the hut. Her pistol lay across her stomach, her hand resting upon it.

* * *

Wesley returned to his office in a more positive frame of mind. The walk and a late lunch had given him time to think through his minor frustrations concerning Woodville. With his black mood lifted, he climbed the steps to his office two at a time. He then filled in the last hours of the day signing off the tedious files he had abandoned earlier. Before leaving, he made a routine call to Norfolk to be updated by the senior officer who was now in charge of the airbase. The news was bad for Wesley, and was made worse by knowing that, while he had been enjoying his temporary freedom from the tyranny of paperwork, Mike Armstrong had gained his freedom from the airbase.

Wesley guessed that Mike Armstrong must have put distance between himself and the base. The discovery of the two dead bodies on the base had been made soon enough, and there had been a prompt attempt to contact him by the officer in command at the base. The fundamental delay had been caused by himself, so he had no one to blame for that. He berated the officer anyway, as the men chosen to guard Mike and Libby had failed miserably in their simple task.

Wesley tried to suppress the panic that was clouding his mind and preventing him from making clear decisions. Unless Armstrong had been exceptionally stupid or unlucky, Wesley knew he was merely closing the stable gate after the horse had bolted.

The commander at the base was ordered to have the surrounding area searched. The operation had to be as low-key as possible to avoid arousing local interest or giving anything away to Woodville's observers. Wesley also directed the officer to have the base searched in case Armstrong was trying to dupe them by circling back. Before ending the telephone call, Wesley testily gave orders to be updated on the situation every hour or immediately if the local police turned up after someone had reported seeing what had happened,

His panic subsided a little now that he had accepted the situation was dire and that he must come up with a plan to resolve it. The answer came to him like a light switching on in his head. He swore to himself for not seeing it straight away. The only help Armstrong could reasonably expect would be from Canute Simpson.

Wesley called the airbase commander, gave him Canute's address and told him to have the house put under immediate covert surveillance.

An hour later, the phone rang again. Wesley picked up the receiver and listened to the situation report given to him by the officer at the airbase. The Mercedes and its passengers had vanished into thin air. The officer was sure the car was off-base, as his men had found tyre tracks on the moss-covered track that led off the far side of the base and on to a local road. The search had been stopped once it became dark and was to resume at first light. Wesley gave orders for more men to be used for the surveillance of Canute's house. He also ordered a search team to be sent in during the small hours of the night to see if the Mercedes was hidden in the grounds of the rectory. Wesley was sure that focusing on Canute was the answer to locating Mike and Libby.

* * *

The following morning delivered not a single crumb of comfort to Wesley. Neither the Mercedes nor the two fugitives had been found. As ordered, the immediate vicinity of the rectory had been stealthily searched during the night. When it had proved unsuccessful, it was widened still further until daylight and eventually the search parties were forced to withdraw in order to avoid suspicion from the general public. Even more worrying for Wesley was the news that there was no sign of life at the rectory. The surveillance team's reports contained no reference to any movement either inside or going to and from the house. The garage had been checked and all that was found inside was a motorcycle. The space next to it looked as though it was usually filled by a car, but it was now empty. Wesley guessed that Mike, Libby and Canute had not wasted the few hours he had inadvertently gifted them. They were well hidden in Norfolk, or far away from it.

Wesley was faced with the crucial decision of what to do next. He could take no action and hope that the few days left gave no time for Mike Armstrong to do anything to endanger the *coup d'état*. Woodville would be none the wiser and once the coup was over, their whereabouts no longer mattered. For Wesley, this was a massively risky strategy. Both Mike and Canute could act in ways that would seriously impact on Woodville's plans, and if Wesley did not warn the man then there would be a price to pay. He did not want to find out what that price may be.

There was no way he could solve the problem other than to warn Woodville. That would mean revealing the truth about Mike and Libby masquerading as Mazarin and Mancuso, and it also meant he would face serious consequences when Woodville realised he had been duped.

If Mike and Libby had been standing in the room now, Wesley would have shot them both. That was not an option, though, so the lesser of the two evils was to get a meeting with Woodville as soon as possible.

20
DM

Canute Simpson drove straight back to the rectory after ensuring that Mike and Libby were safely hidden in Bacton Wood. By the end of the short drive, he determined that Mike had no other choice but to speak to someone from the security services.

As he had not seen anything unusual happening in or around the rectory, Canute left his Austin on the drive outside the front door. He casually entered his home, keeping all his senses at high alert for any covert surveillance. He enjoyed the returning thrill of danger, just as he had done when fighting alongside Balkan partisans against the Nazis. Once he was sure there were no intruders in the house, he hastily packed an overnight bag then went around securing all the windows and doors. He couldn't stop someone breaking in, but they would be forced to leave tell-tale signs from the resulting damage. Canute knew there was nothing to be found in the house that would endanger Mike and Libby, but that did not stop him from wanting to make life difficult for any would-be intruders.

He left the rectory, driving at a steady pace into the summer darkness and frequently checking he was not being followed by another car. After half an hour, he stopped to remove his ecclesiastical white collar and put on a heavyweight cotton shirt from his overnight bag. He then carried on driving as far as Cambridge and parked in the yard of St Barnabas' church, near to the railway station. He left a carefully worded note in the windscreen for the vicar of St Barnabas to find in the morning. That would ensure that Canute's car would be left alone and would still be there when he returned the following day. Taking his bag from the passenger seat, he walked around to the station and took the last train to King's Cross.

Canute made his way across London to Oxford Circus, feeling relaxed and confident that he had not been followed. He took a room in a comfortable hotel just off Oxford Street before finding a public telephone box. There was no point trying to get in touch with his old colleagues at MI6, because he was sure the main exchange number had changed years ago. Even if he had got through, he did not expect anyone he knew to be working past nine o'clock at night.

Instead, he called a private Kensington telephone number and waited. The delay in answering was considerable, but Canute knew the man he was calling never rushed to the telephone and, if possible, always had someone else take the call. That night was no different.

'Yes?' questioned a woman with an imperious-sounding voice.

'Please can you tell David that Canute would like to meet with him tomorrow at the usual place and time,' he said, then waited for a reply.

'I shall,' said the woman, before Canute heard the click of the receiver being replaced.

He reflected on the unknown voice and wondered if the woman was another of David's flings – or had he finally met someone who could put up with him? Anyone else would have asked more questions or called David to the phone, but not this lady. Canute could only conclude that she must have an idea of what David did for a living. Now all he could do was wait until the following morning to see if she had deigned to pass his message on. He knew a second call would simply go unanswered, so Canute walked back down the street to his hotel.

Once back in his room, he got ready for bed. He drank a slug of Laphroaig whisky from a large hip flask he kept in his overnight bag before falling into a deep sleep.

* * *

The sun shone down upon London from the light-blue cloudless sky as Canute emerged from London Bridge underground station. Taking the Tooley Street exit, he headed east until he reached the top of Bermondsey Street and then turned south. He felt confident enough by then to drop the precaution of checking to see if he was being followed. Earlier, he had taken a circular route back to the Oxford Circus tube that would have foxed anyone trying to keep him under surveillance and that was enough for him.

The morning heat took its toll on Canute as he walked along, so he took off his tweed jacket and neatly folded it over his arm. His country clothing was of a heavier weight than the fashion city dwellers wore, however, having to make a no-notice journey to London had left him no choice in choosing what to wear. His slight discomfort was nothing compared to what he endured during the war, so he largely ignored it.

The usual time that Canute spoke of over the telephone was nine o'clock in the morning, and the usual place was a limestone and pink-granite drinking fountain in the grounds of the St Mary Magdalen churchyard situated at the junction of Bermondsey Street and Abbey Street. He gratefully drank the cool water emerging from the fountain then checked his watch. He was a minute early, but he knew the man he had come to meet would have been waiting somewhere nearby, watching.

'What brings you out of hiding after so long, Canute? Something important, I'm sure?' asked a quiet and cultured voice.

Canute turned towards it. He had not heard the man approach across the grass before stopping at the edge of the fine-gravel path.

'I am in retirement, DM, not hiding,' Canute said, smiling and holding his hand out.

The man shook his hand warmly even though the features on his face remained neutral. David Martin Styles had been known by his initials since his first days in the army. By asking for DM using his proper first name the night before, Canute had indicated that he was calling on a business matter and not making a social call.

DM had once asked Canute to join him in the post-war MI6 set-up but he had been had politely refused. Canute had let the opportunity go, saying he needed to recover his soul after the years of blood-letting across Europe during the war. His old comrade-in-arms now looked and dressed like a city accountant, appearing to be the very opposite of the shambling hulk of a country gentleman standing in front of him.

'The churchyard makes an appropriate place to meet now that you are a man of the cloth,' said DM.

'That was not my intention when we first agreed on a place to rendezvous.'

'Yes, but even all those years ago we pretended to be something other than who we really were,' said DM, scrutinising him.

'Indeed, doesn't everybody? Scrape away the shiny gold paint and all you will find underneath is base metal,' replied Canute.

DM gave a little laugh then gestured to a nearby wooden bench. 'You know I moved on from working in the field, Canute. I am manacled to a desk and involved with things that situate myself far and above anything you might have gotten involved with. However, I may be able to help, so do tell me more.'

DM crossed his legs and adopted a pose that indicated Canute had his full attention. Canute got the impression that DM thought he was going to be asked some small favour for old times' sake. Instead, he set out to rattle his friend's sensibilities.

'Four days from now a *coup d'état* is going to take place here in the UK. Charles Woodville is the man behind it, and you know how visible he is in British affairs. Wesley MacDonald is up to his neck in this and I don't know who else in 5 or 6 he might have got involved with him. That is why I am speaking to you now, as the only man I can trust. I am protecting the man who can probably stop all this from happening, but he can't do it by himself,' said Canute as plainly as he could.

'Woodville? MacDonald? Are you sure?' repeated DM. 'They are the last candidates I would have suspected of committing treason. Surely someone is trying to make a fool of you, Canute,' he said, with a smile that came close to mocking.

Canute gave DM another name. 'Victor Mazarin. My man has impersonated him at a meeting of conspirators where Woodville outlined his plans to oust the government. This happened only days ago,' he said, trying to further convince his friend.

DM's face became attentive and his indulgent smile disappeared. He knew of Mazarin's criminal adventures from his regular intelligence meetings with the government's Foreign Secretary. He understood that the brief, though catastrophic, threat from Mazarin and his paramilitary force had been neutralised and the matter was closed.

'This is a matter for 5 and Special Branch, Canute, not me' he said.

'I understand that, but who can I trust?'

'Certainly not a man like Wesley. Do I know your man?'

'You won't have heard of him and I will only make the introductions when you meet. He isn't working alone, either. He has a female companion,' said Canute.

'Interesting. Does your man know Woodville's plan?' asked DM, sounding a little more convinced.

'Only his part of it. Woodville has already had men killed to prevent information leaks, so my man is now in hiding.'

'I have to be honest, Canute, this sounds so incredible that I have no choice but to believe you. If your timeline is correct I need to meet your man as soon as possible.'

'I will be in touch,' said Canute, getting up to go.

'Here, use this number to contact me early tomorrow morning.' DM passed over a piece of neatly folded paper. 'I prefer to keep my wife away from this sort of thing.'

'You are married?' asked Canute in disbelief, looking at the most sophisticated womaniser he had ever met.

'I am human, Canute. You must come to supper once this is over,' replied DM, smiling once more.

Canute nodded and smiled back. The two men set off from the churchyard in different directions with different plans on how to spend the rest of their day.

* * *

With hindsight, DM was not entirely surprised upon hearing that Woodville was planning something. The man had been a vociferous critic of British foreign policy and political leadership in general for some years. His rants had made the newspapers and continually embarrassed the political establishment. Woodville had also been interviewed on television, where he had openly criticised British affairs of state. Now DM understood why Woodville had been seen less and less in public recently. With Canute appearing from nowhere, claiming he had a witness who could expose Woodville and his treasonous plan, it seemed that the threat of a coup could be very real. DM was also very conscious of the fact that he should pass on what he had been told to MI5, but was wary of doing so – keeping such sensitive information from Wesley MacDonald would be impossible.

* * *

Canute flagged down the first taxi he saw and was driven to Oxford Street. He alighted outside Selfridges and entered the department store. After ensuring he was not being followed, he exited via a side entrance and returned to his hotel. Minutes after his arrival, Canute had packed his bag and settled his bill. Satisfied that he had still not been followed, he had the hotel call a taxi that took him to King's Cross to catch the first train back to Cambridge.

Instead of driving straight back to Little Stratton or Bacton Wood, Canute left his car parked at the railway station in King's Lynn. He assumed that Wesley might have the station checked and finding Canute's car there might create the impression he had gone away for some reason. He then went into town to find a car to rent. He chose a pale-blue Vauxhall Victor saloon that provided enough space inside for himself, two passengers, and their luggage.

It was late afternoon when Canute arrived back at the hut, having taken a circuitous route to Bacton Woods.

Canute told Mike and Libby about his meeting with DM. They would need to stay another night in the hut, so he told them they had better make the best of it. As returning to the rectory was not an option, Canute said he would also stay that night. With time getting short, he suggested they get as much rest as possible.

'Why the delay?' asked Mike.

'DM is calling the shots. He is a careful man and I'm sure he is going to try and find any shred of intelligence that might substantiate everything I have told him,' replied Canute.

'I hope he is very careful and will not do anything that might compromise us,' Libby replied.

'Don't worry. He works in a different part of the security services to Wesley and has always kept him at arm's length from his own departmental business,' said Canute, trying to reassure her.

'Can't DM simply raise the alarm, so it can all be over?' she countered.

'It is a little too late for that. Woodville has maintained such a high level of security that no one knows anything about his plans. Yes, we can stop the Mazarin part of the operation, but that will not prevent the *coup d'état* going ahead without it. We need enough time to work out how to counter Woodville's plans, and raising the alarm might simply force him to bring it all forward before we are ready,' explained Canute.

'How sure are you that we can even trust DM? He might be involved,' challenged Mike.

'If that were so, we would all be under lock and key or dead by now,' Canute replied.

Mike reflected on his friend's response. Canute had not been asked to reveal anything of their whereabouts. Nor had any promises been made that sounded too good to be true. If Canute had been followed back to Norfolk, he supposed there was no point in waiting to have Libby and himself recaptured. It would have been simple enough to give Wesley details of their whereabouts and have him send a team of men to the hut to either kill or capture them. None of this had happened.

'Supposing your man is able to pinpoint where Woodville is – will he have him arrested?' asked Mike.

'I don't believe that would prevent a *coup d'état* either. Woodville will have secret backers ready to step in and ensure the plans go ahead. There has to be another way to cut off the head of the snake and at the same time paralyse the plot,' said Canute.

'Why can't DM mobilise the army?' suggested Mike.

'That will be a massive signal to Woodville that his security had been compromised. Besides, there is always the danger that any army units sent to counter the *coup d'état* might very well be part of the conspiracy itself. We just don't know,' said Canute wearily.

'It seems to me that the only way to move quickly against Woodville is by using people who are outsiders, to keep him unaware of what is happening,' said Mike, glancing towards Libby.

Canute had already reached that conclusion by himself.

'Will your man let us do that?' asked Libby.

'That depends entirely on what he can find out by tomorrow morning,' said Canute.

Mike and Libby prepared to stay the extra night at the hut. Canute dared not return to the rectory, as he was sure that the house and grounds would be under surveillance by Wesley's mercenaries. He knew that a search of the place would provide no information, however, Canute's timely disappearance would have implicated him as being involved with Mike and Libby's escape.

Thankfully, Wesley would have to avoid using the resources of the police and Special Branch to mount a search-and-arrest operation against Canute. To do so might raise awkward questions, especially if they did arrest Canute and he started making allegations about a *coup d'état*. Instead, all Wesley could do was focus on the rectory and the local area using his team of mercenaries. He would have no idea that Canute had changed cars so finding the Austin at the railway station would not provide any information on his whereabouts.

Canute relaxed, knowing that the three of them were safe for now. He took out his large hip flask from his bag and passed it to a grateful Mike and Libby.

The three ate an evening meal made from the army ration packs. Afterwards, they retired to the bunk beds to try and get some sleep. They all anticipated a difficult few days ahead of them. Mike and Libby had trouble sleeping, whilst Canute slept soundly despite squeezing his large frame into the limited space provided by his bunk bed.

All three woke early the next morning, knowing they had only three days left before the *coup d'état*. They had a breakfast of army tea with no milk and some dry biscuits. Canute insisted on tidying up the hut and made sure that everything was left as they had found it on arrival. He did not like the idea of leaving any clues about their movements, even though the chance of Wesley's men finding the hut was remote.

After securing the front door and returning the hut key to its hiding place under the step, Canute joined Mike and Libby, who were already sitting in the Vauxhall rental car. Although confident they would not be seen by any of Wesley's mercenaries, Canute headed north to the coast to avoid Little Stratton and the nearby airbase.

As the day was so bright and sunny, the windows of the car were wound down to allow a cool breeze to flow into the car.

The feeling of the fresh air reminded all three that they had not washed or changed clothes for two days.

On reaching the coast, Canute turned the car west along the coast road to head towards King's Lynn. He stopped at the first telephone box they happened upon and made his telephone call to DM. It was brief. Canute returned to the car and drove away with a sense of urgency.

'What did he say?' asked Mike, trying not to sound too eager.

'We must return to London by the quickest means possible,' replie d Canute.

'That's it?' chimed Mike and Libby.

'Not quite. Don't underestimate the importance of being summoned to meet with DM.'

21
SKY HIGH

Mike groaned inwardly on hearing Canute say they were going to meet DM. As far as he was concerned, the man sounded exactly like Wesley. That meant the meeting would waste precious time with travelling to a seemingly unnecessary and obscure rendezvous, then more time would be wasted with elaborate security precautions.

'You said "not quite", Canute. What did you mean by that?' asked Mike.

'We are going to drive to a pickup point not far from here. There we will meet up with DM and you both can travel with him. I think everything will become clear then,' he replied.

'Does that mean he believes us?' asked Libby.

'Yes, you can be sure of that. He must have found out something that he prefers to discuss face to face.'

Following a route that kept them well away from Mazarin's former base, Canute drove for a short while in a south-easterly direction then headed due east. After another twenty minutes, they arrived at their destination.

'What are we doing here?' asked Mike, as Canute drove into a small airfield with a single grass landing strip.

'DM is waiting to meet you here,' replied Canute with a smile.

Mike and Libby looked at each other in bewilderment. All they could see was an old-fashioned-looking light aircraft parked in the distance near to an orange windsock that was hanging vertically in the still air. The sun was strong, and even with their windows wound down no cooling breeze entered the car as Canute continued to drive towards the aircraft.

The high-winged single-engine monoplane was finished in bright yellow and rested on a small tail wheel that tilted the airframe slightly upwards. The design was not one that Mike recognised. A slim and elegant-looking man in a light-grey flying suit emerged from beneath the shade of the wing and stood with his hands on his hips, facing the car as it approached. He wore a service issue aircrew holster, holding a Colt .45 pistol on the outside of the flying suit. A pair of green tinted aviator sunglasses covered the man's eyes as he watched the approach of the Vauxhall saloon.

Canute stopped the car a short distance away from the aircraft and stepped out on to the grass. Mike and Libby followed him. The man strode nonchalantly towards them and removed his sunglasses before he shook hands with Canute. Canute introduced the man as DM.

DM's blue eyes, intensified by the colour of his flying suit, engaged with Mike's before lingering a little while longer on Libby. She felt flattered by his attention as she tucked a piece of unruly hair behind her ear.

'Does it bother you?' DM asked Mike, who wasn't entirely sure whether he meant the pistol he was wearing, or his lingering look at Libby.

'Not in the slightest,' replied Mike, opening his jacket to give DM sight of his Smith & Wesson.

'I have one too,' said Libby, also showing DM she was armed.

'I think we are going to get along very well. We shall talk some more once we get to our destination,' said DM.

Mike looked at the aircraft and noticed there was only space for two passengers. Assuming the seats were for himself and Libby, he wondered what Canute intended to do next.

'Am I right in thinking you are not coming with us, Canute?' he asked.

'Yes, I have to stay behind and act as a time-wasting decoy for your pursuers for just a little longer. I hope to see you again in a day or so,' the rector said cheerfully.

'Indeed, and we really must get going,' said an equally cheerful DM, guiding Libby along by the elbow towards the aircraft.

Mike glanced sharply at Canute.

'Pay no heed. DM has always been very attentive to members of the opposite sex. He has taken a shine to her, that's all,' said Canute.

Mike and Libby squeezed into the aircraft and made themselves as comfortable as possible whilst DM busied himself preparing for take-off. Canute returned to the car and sat inside, watching the aircraft taxi to the end of the grass runway. The sound of the aircraft's engine increased rapidly as DM opened the throttle wide.

Seconds later, the aircraft started to roll forward, quickly gaining speed that allowed it to lift off from the ground. They slowly gained altitude before DM gently banked the aircraft over to fly due south.

Mike rested his hand on Libby's knee and looked back down towards Canute, who was now just a dot in a patchwork carpet of green and yellow fields. He felt her hand rest on his.

* * *

Once the crescendo of the take-off was over, the rippling song of skylarks reached Canute's ears. Although there was little else to do at the airfield, he continued to watch the small aircraft until he could no longer hear the drone of its engine. Eventually it disappeared into the distant expanse of blue haze and Canute started the Vauxhall's engine and drove slowly off the airfield.

Once back on the main road, he headed directly for King's Lynn to return the rental car before picking up his Austin from the railway station. He no longer worried if he was spotted, and instead actually hoped he would be seen by Wesley's men. This meant they could report him being sighted alone, forcing them to maintain their surveillance in the hope that he might lead them to Mike and Libby.

A couple of hours later, Canute arrived home and ran himself a hot bath. He left out a clean set of clothing on his bed ready to be put on afterwards, and as he lowered himself into the hot water, he was careful not to knock over the large hip flask of Laphroaig he had balanced on the side of the tub.

Canute had been correct in anticipating that Wesley would send an order for a mercenary surveillance team to be put in place around the rectory. He was spotted immediately as he drove into the rectory drive, and his return was promptly reported to the commander, who in turn alerted Wesley. He gave the order for a snatch squad to be sent in after dark to abduct Canute. Once captured they were to take him to the airbase for interrogation.

Canute knew that Wesley had to be desperate to discover the whereabouts of Mike and Libby, as this was key to Wesley's survival until at least after the coup d'etat. Canute guessed there would have to be an attempt to kidnap him so that he could be interrogated regarding Mike and Libby's whereabouts. The dilemma for Canute was whether to allow himself to be captured, or to make the lives of his pursuers as difficult as possible in order to distract them from Mike and Libby.

* * *

Mike soon overcame his initial apprehension about flying in the old aircraft. Over the engine noise he asked what type of aircraft they were in. DM told him they were in an Auster Autocrat whilst he piloted the machine smoothly to a cruising altitude. After setting the throttle to maintain a steady and relaxed cruising speed, they gently passed over the verdant Norfolk countryside. Mike glanced down at the compass mounted between himself and DM, noting that their current heading was almost due south.

Looking back over his shoulder, he saw Libby seemingly transfixed by the beautiful views. She smiled back at him momentarily before continuing to watch the slowly approaching, then receding landscape a few thousand feet below. There was little point in having a conversation as the noise of the engine was too intrusive. Mike also thought there seemed little point in asking where they were going. Both he and Libby had to put their trust in the man who was flying them out of immediate danger.

All too soon, DM put the Auster into a gentle descent. The relative peace and tranquility of the flight had provided a welcome interlude for Mike and Libby. The weather and changing landscape had been picture perfect. They had literally been able to leave their care-filled world behind them for a little while and, given the choice, they would have preferred to remain airborne for much longer.

Now, when they looked out from the cabin, the ground was much nearer and passed by at high speed before the climactic rush of the landing. Despite his apparent speed, DM made a precise and gentle landing, almost gliding his aircraft on to the grassed surface of the runway. He then taxied the Auster towards a small grey corrugated metal hangar at the far side of the airfield. The structure was tucked along the side of a large wood and was reached within minutes.

The doors to the hangar were open and DM continued to taxi straight into the hangar before stopping and switching off the engine. The silence was overwhelming, and an unwelcome sign that Mike and Libby had returned to the reality of their current situation.

DM clambered out from the cabin first and nonchalantly wandered over to the hangar doors to pull them closed. Mike and Libby followed, and Mike assisted with the doors after which the three exited through a door at the rear of the small hangar. Once outside, DM locked the door and led them to a silver Lagonda Rapide car that was parked nearby. The twin headlight arrangement reminded Mike of the Jensen, but when he saw that the car had four doors he realised this was a different type of machine.

'We have very little time, so please get in and I will take you to a safe house nearby,' said DM, maintaining his friendly smile as he removed his pistol and pushed his holster under the driver's seat.

Mike and Libby chose to sit in the rear where they could both keep an eye on their driver.

'How safe is your safe house?' asked Mike, looking at DM in the rear-view mirror.

'Safe enough,' was the reply, as DM started the engine.
Mike glanced around the cabin to see if there was any radio equipment fitted but saw none. He hoped this meant the car was DM's private vehicle and did not belong to MI6. DM appeared to read Mike's mind, telling him not to bother looking for any service equipment as the car was his own.

DM drove the car smoothly away, just as expertly as he had flown the Auster out of Norfolk. Both Mike and Libby maintained their vigilance, constantly checking the road behind to see if they were being followed. DM's effortless driving style belied how fast the car sped along the leafy-edged minor roads.

DM turned down yet another lane that was fringed on either side by large deciduous woods. On the right ahead of them could be seen a pair of black wrought-iron gates that opened on to a tarmac drive. The car slowed and entered through the gates, following a drive that wound its way past huge rhododendron bushes and mature oak trees.

The 'safe house' finally came into view and proved to be more hall than house. The large red-brick structure had been built in the Victorian gothic style and looked far from welcoming. DM stopped outside the intricately arched doorway and used two pips of the car horn to alert those inside that they had arrived.

A slim older lady dressed in a matching tweed jacket and skirt came out through the glass-panelled twin doors. As she made her way down the shallow marble steps, her shoes clicked on their smooth surface. Libby involuntarily winced, remembering that this was how she had dressed until she met Mike.

'This is Mrs May, she runs things around here,' explained DM.

Mrs May broke into a beguiling smile that both Mike and Libby could not fail to like.

'Mrs May will show you to your room where you can freshen up. After that, she will show you around our extensive wardrobe facility. We can then have dinner before getting to work,' said DM, leaving Mike and Libby with more questions than answers.

'Please, come with me,' said Mrs May.

Mike and Libby followed her into the house. The interior was as forbidding as the exterior. They entered a large wood-panelled entrance hall devoid of any pictures or decoration. A deep-blue carpeted staircase reached out in front of them and Mrs May led them up to a similarly panelled gallery.

'This part of the house always intimidates our Soviet guests, but we like it that way,' said Mrs May proudly.

Mike and Libby looked at each other but said nothing.

'It seems to be having the same effect upon you two,' added Mrs May, leading the pair down a passageway off the gallery. She unlocked a large forbidding door and motioned for them to enter. She smiled as they walked into a large and unexpectedly light room decorated in a contemporary style.

'Do your Russian guests ever get to stay in here?' asked a surprised Mike.

'No, only DM's special guests have access to the south-wing suite, as we call it. The door self-locks when you close it, but you can open it from the inside. The door is bulletproof, as are the windows. Through that door is your bedroom, and over there is the wardrobe suite where you should be able to find fresh clothes to change into. The bathroom is through another door from your bedroom. Please, do not think you are being held in custody, just respect our need for secrecy,' said Mrs May.

'Just how safe are we?' asked Libby.

Mrs May undid the buttons on her jacket to reveal a Browning 9mm holstered on her waist. Libby began to understand Mrs May's choice of clothing.

'All my staff are similarly armed. That includes kitchen staff and room service. In addition to that, the grounds are patrolled by guard dogs and their armed handlers. No one knows who you are and why you are here except for myself and DM,' replied Mrs May, as if she were describing facilities such as a swimming pool or gymnasium.

Mike noted Mrs May's use of DM's initials in a way that suggested she was not subordinate to him. 'You know DM other than as your superior?' he asked.

He immediately felt he had asked her an impertinent question and apologised, but she brushed his apology aside pleasantly.

'We served together in the Special Operations Executive during the war. Technically, I was his superior only fleetingly during our time in France. DM moved on to greater things after the war,' she replied obliquely.

'Did you work with Canute in those days?' asked Mike, taking a chance and scoring a hit. For a moment Mrs May appeared to reflect on her memories.

'DM went to work with Canute in the final years. You should ask DM about it at dinner. He sometimes likes to talk about his wartime experiences. Dinner will be at six,' said Mrs May, before excusing herself.

The décor and furniture of the suite was modern and differed completely from the Victorian building's overall design. Mike and Libby felt they had arrived in a world within a world that was air-conditioned and spacious. A television set and a radio were installed ready for use in the lounge area, whilst the bathroom included a well-appointed modern shower. There was not an inch of Victorian plumbing to be seen anywhere. After showering, they put on bathrobes that had been left out for them on the large bed. They hunted through the wardrobes and were pleasantly surprised to find clothing that fitted and suited them well. Mike dressed in a dark lounge suit, light blue shirt and matching wool tie. Libby chose a navy-blue trouser suit that could have been bought from Oxford Street the same day.

Respecting the assurance of Mrs May about their safety, Mike and Libby left their pistols in the bedroom when she came to collect them for dinner. She led them back along the gallery and down the large staircase to another door that corresponded with the one she had taken them through on the floor above.

The door led to a dining room that was every bit as modern as their suite. A single large dinner table was set at one end for three guests. DM stood by a set of windows, looking across a large neat lawn. His hands were in the pockets of his trousers and he appeared to be lost in thought. Out of his flying suit and now smartly dressed, he appeared more handsome than ever. Mike looked over to Libby, who was clearly charmed by the man.

'Bit of a culture shock, isn't it? All this modernity in such an old building. I am not quite used to it myself. We need something to contrast with the north wing, which is far more original and austere in its décor,' said DM, without feeling the need to explain further.

Mike had an idea that the house was used somehow as a base to turn agents who had originated from behind the Iron Curtain or similar, but said nothing.

'We found it all a very pleasant surprise,' he said, 'having no idea what to expect.'

'Yes, I hope you are refreshed enough to start work after dinner,' DM replied.

'We'll be fine,' said Libby, joining the conversation and wanting to hear more about the mysterious DM and his time with Canute.

DM waved his hand to indicate they should sit at the dinner table.

'I'm afraid all we have is a set menu, even though it appears we are being accommodated in a hotel. Mrs May had very short notice of our arrival and I expect to be away promptly after breakfast tomorrow,' he said.

Mrs May nodded and smiled before calling the kitchen to tell them dinner could be served. Plates of roast lamb and vegetables were set out before them and the three began their meal. Mrs May and her staff left the room, allowing DM and his guests to speak freely.

'Mrs May mentioned that you worked with her in SOE before going on to work with Canute,' said Libby, trying not to sound too inquisitive.

DM smiled at her as if she was an open book, making her shift in her seat.

'I originally flew Lysanders for the Royal Air Force. I flew her into France on an SOE mission. A collaborator in the French resistance tipped off the Nazis about our landing site and we were ambushed. The Lysander was shot to pieces, forcing me to join Mrs May and the local Résistance members in a shootout against the Nazis. Thankfully we escaped, and we eventually made it back to England a month later. My skills were reported to the SOE by Mrs May and the rest is history.'

'Is that her real name?' asked Libby.

'No, but that is not a concern of yours. Now, I would like to know a little more about yourselves,' said DM.

Mike and Libby looked at each other and wondered what was coming next.

22
FEELING THE HEAT

Wesley felt the cold rot of fear and despair rising within him, acting as a block to prevent him from contacting Woodville. His stomach churned as he mentally surveyed the mire of indecision in which he floundered. He tried to keep his nerve, to find a way to keep out of trouble for the next few days, but the more he thought about things the more intractable the problem seemed to be.

He had forced two outsiders to masquerade as Mazarin and Mancuso and, so far, had managed to deceive Woodville by doing so. Wesley could argue that he did it for the best of reasons, as they had proved useful in weeding out two weak links amongst Woodville's co-conspirators. Their role had contributed to the security and progression of plans for the execution of the *coup d'état*. However, Wesley knew any value in this was now outweighed by the fact that Armstrong and Kembrey had escaped from the base in Norfolk. Not only that, but he had no idea where the pair were. This would be inexcusable to Woodville.

The nagging fear of what the two fugitives might do next induced as much fear in him as that of Woodville's reaction to his subterfuge. The sensible option for Armstrong was to get out of the country as quickly as possible and lie low, Wesley reasoned. In three days, it would not matter what Armstrong did any more. The coup would have gone ahead, leaving Armstrong high and dry and unable to pose any further threat to Woodville.

Wesley supposed that whatever happened to the country next would be of no concern to Armstrong, as he was a fugitive.

However, he knew thinking that was only a delusion. Armstrong had had every chance to escape from Mazarin before and yet he had returned to successfully wreck his plans. He was sure that Armstrong was crazy enough not to walk away. It was simply a matter of time before he would intervene and compromise Wesley's involvement with Woodville.

The other major problem for Wesley was Canute Simpson. The man who had managed to get himself involved in the Mazarin affair was doing the same thing all over again. Wesley was sure that Canute had helped Armstrong escape with the Kembrey woman and had chosen the same time to make himself scarce. Wesley knew this could have not been a coincidence because Armstrong had no one else to turn to. More than ever, Wesley wanted to kill Canute before he tried to inflict damage upon the *coup d'état* and prevent him from beginning his new life on the continent.

The indecision continued to eat away at Wesley. His choices kept coming in the form of greater and lesser evils, all of which left him in a worse position than before. Informing Woodville of the disappearance of 'Mazarin' and 'Mancuso' was essential. He knew that. The only effective resources he had were tied up at the airbase in Norfolk and could only be of use in the immediate area. Wesley was reluctant in the extreme to use his own men from the security services, as too many awkward questions would be asked when it came to be justifying a clandestine search operation. He had no idea where else to mount a search, as the only possible places to look were already covered. The only man who might have the capacity to help in a search was Woodville, the very man he wanted to avoid.

Wesley decided to bite the bullet and go ahead with an attempt to get a meeting behind closed doors with Woodville, but he had no idea where the man was and did not have any means to contact him directly. There had been no further communication of any kind since Wesley had collected the orders for Mazarin's part in the coup.

He left his office and walked along the busy London streets, heading for a public telephone box on Kingsway leading up from the Strand to Holborn underground station. Using one of the call boxes, he was eventually given the telephone number for Alston Hall, Woodville's home, by Directory Enquiries.

'Alston Hall, how may I help?' was the response from an elderly-sounding man.

'My name is Mr Johnson and I have an urgent message for the Viscount. Please let him know I must meet with his representative as soon as possible,' said Wesley. A direct meeting with Woodville could only occur after he had met with the man's intermediary.

'I'm sorry, sir, I don't understand,' came the mystified response.

Wesley tried to maintain an even tone as his frustration began to boil over. 'Please pass the message on to the Viscount word for word, as I have requested,' he said through gritted teeth. Sweat began to drip from his brow under the heat of the sun in the confines of the glazed call box.

'Very well, sir. Where would you like to meet the representative?' asked the man, still sounding unsure about the call.

'The usual place. As soon as possible,' said Wesley slowly, even though he wanted to shout down the phone at the man as he furiously dabbed his brow with his handkerchief to mop up the perspiration.

'Is that everything, sir?' asked the still-mystified voice.

'Yes, as soon as possible, please,' Wesley hissed.

'Very good, sir,' said the man, before putting down the phone.

Wesley, now soaked in sweat, stepped out of the phone box. His heartbeat thrummed. His composure was gone. His plans seemed to be falling apart and he leant against the outside of the call box, feeling sick. There was a taste of fear in his mouth and he could not tell if it was from the thought of confronting Woodville or the end of his dream to live abroad.

Hoping the member of Woodville's staff that answered the telephone did exactly as he was told, Wesley set off after he had regained his composure. He headed straight for Holborn underground station to make the short journey back to the same café in Covent Garden where he had abandoned the canvas bag that had contained the orders from Woodville. The empty bag had been collected and taken away by a watcher as soon as Wesley had left the café. The place also doubled as an emergency rendezvous following the use of the word 'Johnson'. Although Wesley disliked returning to the same place, it was a known location both to himself and to whoever was working for Woodville. There could be no confusion in using an emergency rendezvous.

Wesley's damp shirt continued to cling to his skin, making him feel uncomfortable as he stood on the long escalator descending into the bowels of the station. The atmosphere was unrelentingly stale and hot, adding even more to his sweaty discomfort. He was, however, in no hurry and assumed that even if his message had been passed quickly, there would be a time lag whilst the contact travelled to the rendezvous. Wesley intended to use the delay to prepare himself before making his request to be taken to the lion's den.

Minutes later, Wesley arrived at Covent Garden and emerged to make his way past the chaos and noise of the fruit and vegetable market. The heat of the day continued to stick to him wherever he went, as did the smell of rotting vegetables waiting to be cleaned away. He began to feel slightly sick again.

Fear and paranoia writhed in his stomach like huge worms. Wesley was risking everything. He had gone all-in in life's poker game and had begun to realise that he was not the major player he believed himself to be. He had a minor role to play in comparison to Woodville and his co-conspirators, yet he was about to present himself at the table of the biggest player around. Compared to Armstrong, he was a big shot – but not when it came to Woodville. The power differential made him feel uneasy. Despite all the control he had over other people's lives, it was nothing compared to the power of the political elite he worked for.

Wesley mentally steeled himself for his meeting with the contact. Before entering the café, he walked past it a few times to check for anything or anybody that he judged to be suspicious. A few under-nourished young men were loitering across from the café, smoking and trying to look like hard-men desperadoes, which they clearly were not. The man reading his newspaper on Wesley's first pass was gone. A youth on a small red-painted GPO motorcycle arrived and was gone again within a minute of delivering what must have been, he guessed, a telegram. Wesley was sure that within the short time from making his telephone call to getting to Covent Garden, no one could have got to the café before him. He also felt reasonably sure that there was no surveillance being undertaken by the security services, as he had only used the café rarely.

Although Wesley's shirt had dried out a little, when he sat down in the café an unpleasant dampness pressed against his spine. A girl – still in her teens, he guessed – came over to him and took his order, looking at him in a surly fashion. He ordered a white coffee, one sugar. Shortly afterwards his coffee was dumped on the table as she squeezed by on her way to apparently more important customers. A rush of them had arrived, and she was about to get very busy. The press of bodies raised the temperature in the already hot café, where the espresso machines steamed behind the bar. The increasing fug of smoke from cigarettes added to his discomfort. Wesley wondered why people chose to spend their free time in such a cramped and uncomfortable place.

By his third coffee, the numbers of customers had thinned out again, making him feel a little conspicuous. The surly girl had begun to eye him suspiciously when she set down yet another coffee. He wondered if she had whispered her concerns to the proprietor behind the bar. The man had glanced at him a few times over the past couple of minutes. Maybe they thought he was about to leave without paying, or worse, a pervert waiting for the girl to end her shift.

Wesley resisted the urge to check his watch, unsure how much longer he had to wait in the café. He couldn't leave until he had met with Woodville's man, so he had to sit it out. He sipped the last of his coffee and was resigned to having to order another when a man got up to leave the café. As he passed Wesley's table he dropped his newspaper on to the floor. Bending over to pick it up, he caught Wesley's eye.

'Outside on the left in two minutes,' the man muttered as he picked up the newspaper and left.

Wesley waited for one minute then paid his bill and left the girl a tip. With folded arms and her head dipped down, she watched him leave then went to the table to pocket her tip.

As instructed, Wesley turned left once he was outside and began walking. He had not taken any notice of the man, who must have entered the café after him and observed him for some time before making contact. Wesley was impressed that the man had been able to move invisibly and watch him without being spotted in the process.

From nowhere, a voice – the same voice – quietly instructed him to keep walking. He complied without turning around to see who was talking to him. A black cab drew slowly alongside the pavement and the voice told Wesley to get inside. Wesley opened the door and got in, his contact following closely behind. The door slammed shut behind the man and the cab pulled away.

Wesley noticed that the cab had no clock and the driver displayed nothing that could identify him as being a working cabbie. They followed the throng of traffic and the driver regularly checked his mirrors, but this was not to keep an eye on Wesley. Instead, he was checking to see there was no one tailing the cab.

As his companion spoke freely in front of the driver, Wesley guessed that both men were working for Woodville. He must have access to men and resources that Wesley could only guess at.

'So, what is this all about?' asked the newspaper-dropping man in an even tone.

Wesley looked at him. He had friendly brown eyes and could have walked out of any office in the city. His hair was neatly cut but not too short, and he was clean-shaven. His tie was knitted and sported a popular red and green tartan pattern, worn with a half Windsor knot. The man's jacket and trousers were separates and appeared to be off the peg but fitted him well. Looking a little more closely, Wesley got the impression the man might be ex-military.

'I need to speak Woodville urgently,' replied Wesley.

'Why don't you tell me what it is? Then I can decide whether what you have to say is urgent,' said the man, continuing in the same friendly tone of voice.

'No, this has to come from me only,' said Wesley, looking directly into the man's eyes.

'Well, he isn't going to like this, so it had better be damn important.' The man returned his gaze, sounding a little impatient.

'Don't worry, this is important,' Wesley replied insistently.

The man shrugged. 'Very well, but this is on your own head.'

He told the driver to pull over at the next convenient point. Before getting out of the cab, he asked where Wesley was staying in London and if he was using the name Johnson.

Wesley gave him details of the hotel and said that, yes, he had registered under the name of Johnson.

The driver was told to continue to the vicinity of Wesley's hotel and let him out there. Wesley would be contacted at teatime or early evening. The next second, the man had gone.

The remainder of the journey continued with neither Wesley nor the driver speaking. He was let out at the Aldwych and left to walk along the Strand back to his hotel above Charing Cross station. The hotel was not his usual choice. This had been deliberate on his part, as he wanted to avoid running into anyone he knew; personally, or professionally.

As Wesley had no idea how long he had to wait to be contacted, he showered as soon as he got back to his room. His shirt collar and cuffs were slightly grubby from sweat and had the distinct smell of body odour. He also decided to have a shave to remove the five o'clock shadow that was beginning to show on his face. He wanted to feel as smart and confident as he could when he met with Woodville.

He put out a fresh suit, clean shirt and tie on the bed then cleaned his shoes. He reflected that these were the actions of a subordinate preparing to meet with someone very much his superior, and this was not something he had felt the need to do for many years. *That damned Armstrong*, he thought to himself.

Wesley ordered a fillet steak from room service as he was in no mood to eat alone in the busy hotel dining room. A further treat was a half-bottle of dry red Burgundy to accompany the meal. Once he had eaten he relaxed on the hotel bed, feeling much more confident than he had earlier in the day. The contact at the café had left his newspaper, the *Financial Times*, in the taxi and Wesley had taken it with him when he left. Although folded, the newspaper had not been read so Wesley flicked though its pages whilst waiting to be summoned.

As the soporific effects of the wine began to ebb away, Wesley's room telephone rang. He picked up the receiver and listened. A man spoke clearly, giving Wesley his instructions. The voice was new to him and spoke with the authority of a man who was used to giving orders.

Without a word, Wesley replaced the receiver and got ready to go out. His confidence deserted him once more as he fumbled while tying his shoelaces. Woodville's fearsome reputation had put Wesley on the back foot once more and he knew it. He was not about to bring the man good news, and all of this was Armstrong's fault. Once more he recalled the power differential between them and knew he had nowhere to hide. Everything depended upon what he told Woodville.

With a deep breath, Wesley left his room and made his way down to the front entrance of the hotel. The evening air had lost its heat, yet it felt unrefreshing as Wesley walked towards Trafalgar Square. The chaos and noise of the rush-hour remained in full swing. He crossed Northumberland Street and turned south on to Whitehall. Keeping on the left and with the traffic behind him, he continued towards Horse Guards. He kept a watch on every passing black taxi, checking each one for its registration number. Soon enough, the same taxi he had travelled in earlier that day passed by him and pulled in to the kerb. Wesley walked up to the cab and got inside. He noted he had the same driver as before.

The taxi driver set off, maintaining the same routine of checking his mirrors and not engaging in conversation with his passenger. They headed south, upriver, and crossed over into Vauxhall before continuing to Brixton. The taxi pulled up outside a public house called the Prince of Wales. Wesley assumed this was where he was to meet Woodville's man.

He was surprised to be told not to enter the pub, but to wait outside until he was contacted by another driver. This was unknown territory to Wesley and he felt exposed as he waited to be contacted. His discomfort lasted all of three minutes before a Land Rover pulled up in front of him. The driver reached across and opened the passenger door.

'Jump in!' he shouted in a friendly manner.

Wesley took his seat, slamming the door a few times before it finally shut.

'Be careful not to lean too much against the door. It tends to fly open and you might fall out,' said the man.

Wesley began to wonder if he had done the right thing.

23
GOING UNDERGROUND

Following dinner, DM led Mike and Libby to another room that had been refurbished and set up as a comfortable lounge. The room's décor and furniture were modern, matching the contemporary style of their bedroom as well as the dining room. Mrs May had anticipated her temporary guests by ensuring that tea and coffee was available for them in the lounge. Mike and Libby sat together on a low-back sofa, whilst DM sat opposite on a similar one.

'Help yourselves,' said DM, gesturing towards the tea and coffee.

Mike and Libby thanked him politely and poured some coffee. The conversation had become stilted and there was an air of mistrust in the room. Mike glanced around, searching for anything that might give away the presence of hidden cameras and microphones. The pair had realised they had dropped their guard slightly during dinner. Libby abstractly avoided DM's gaze as she sipped on her coffee.

'You are right to think there are recording devices concealed all around us,' said DM, 'but they are all switched off. I can assure you of that.'

'We don't know that, though, and it is unsettling,' replied Mike.

Libby's eyes engaged with DM's in an attempt to gauge his reaction.

'The whole place is dripping with concealed cameras and microphones. Even if we went for a walk in the grounds you wouldn't be able to escape them,' DM continued.

'You understand why we are reticent then,' she said, holding his gaze as she put down her coffee cup.

'Keeping our conversations private is as important to me as it is to you. I am not here to investigate you, nor am I intending to have you put under lock and key. You come highly recommended from Canute Simpson and, believe me, that is worth more than rubies. Another plus point is that you appear to be acting against your will for Wesley MacDonald – though that, perhaps, is not so unusual.'

'How can working against our will be a positive?' asked Mike.

DM sat forward and poured himself a coffee. 'It means that if you are not in league with Wesley, then you are against him. I don't have to persuade you of anything, nor do I need to turn you against him either,' was the candid reply.

'That assumes we are going to be working for you, though, doesn't it?' said Mike.

'Of course. The difference being that you are willing volunteers seeking a positive outcome for yourselves.' DM took a sip of his coffee.

'And "positive outcome" means what?' asked Mike.

'First, the successful prevention of Woodville's *coup d'état.* Second, your return to the anonymous lives you were leading prior to Wesley finding you,' said DM, glancing between them.

'One can't happen without the other, I suppose,' said Mike.

'Exactly,' replied DM.

Mike and Libby looked at each other. They had been in this same situation before with Wesley and learnt the man could not be trusted.

DM noted the exchange of glances but was unperturbed. He knew, as with Wesley, that they had little choice but to go along with him. The difference was, he meant what he said when he had told Mike and Libby they were free to return to their lives once they had brought Woodville's plan to an end.

Mike and Libby, meanwhile, were not completely convinced by DM's assurances that they would be left alone once the Woodville affair was over. The only certainty was that not putting their trust in DM meant they were going nowhere.

Mike spoke first. 'How can we help you when we don't even know where Woodville is, or what he is doing?'

'I have my people working on the problem right now,' DM replied. 'You need not worry about any leaks getting back to Woodville. The information being gathered has a general focus that will hopefully catch him in our net.'

'How will you do that?' asked Libby.

'The machinery of state has its epicentre in London, as do the national television and radio broadcast services. That means Woodville must be in or around the capital so he can closely orchestrate events. His house is in the far north of England and that is too remote for him to maintain adequate control of a *coup d'état*. He will have travelled south in the past twenty-four to forty-eight hours and will probably have left a trail for us to pick up on,' DM explained.

'He could have travelled to London anonymously,' countered Mike.

'The man is a victim of his celebrity-like desire to project himself into the public eye. He cannot risk being seen using public transport and will be unable to travel the distance by car,' responded DM.

'You don't know that,' said Libby.

'Ah, but I do. He has a back problem caused by wartime injuries. He has often been interviewed on the television just before or after a flight in a private aircraft, a de Havilland Dove. The man has often argued that his apparent extravagance in choosing to fly everywhere is because other forms of transport take too long and become too painful for him,' said DM.

'Do you believe that?' asked Mike.

'I do, and that is why I have my people collating a list of all logged flight plans covering the United Kingdom for the past two days. They believe I want the information in connection with the transport of Soviet agents by air from the continent before being flown to a destination within this country. In amongst that list will be Woodville's flight,' explained DM.

'That's a massive leap of faith,' said Mike.

'At the moment it is a calculated guess that prevents Woodville being alerted that we are on to him. The best part is, this information will coincidentally link to something else I have been informed about,' said DM, flashing his wide charismatic smile.

Mike and Libby looked at each other and then back to DM in expectation.

'A wartime colleague who now works for the French *Deuxième Bureau* contacted me. He asked if I knew about the bursts of radio transmission activity across the south-east of England during the past week. The report given to him had initially expected the radio traffic to be British military because of the frequency bands being used, but the Bureau's cryptographers soon realised the codes being used did not equate to those normally used by the British Army. The Bureau was intrigued by this and contacted me,' said DM.

'The French intelligence service monitors British radio traffic?' asked Mike.

'Indeed – and the rest of Europe, including all emanations from behind the Iron Curtain. NATO countries share much of the radio intelligence gained by France; when it suits both sides, of course.'

'How was that information helpful?' asked Mike.

'Our first assumption was that the transmissions were being made to ships in the North Sea or the English Channel. Nothing made sense as the transmissions could not be linked to Soviet naval movements in the North Sea, the Baltic or the Atlantic. Equally, Soviet airforce activity was minimal during the same period. The only conclusion to draw was that the radio transmissions were intended for UK-based formations,' continued DM.

'Were you able to identify the military units involved?' asked Mike.

'That's the problem. The source of the transmissions has been located but the whereabouts of the outlying stations remain a mystery. If I go poking around the Ministry of Defence to find out what is happening, someone is bound to tell Woodville. The important thing is, we know where the transmissions are being sent from.'

'Where is this radio base?' asked Libby.

'Somewhere on the estate of Hindhead House, a mansion not far from here. The house and estate belong to Lord Edward Clarence, who is currently out of the country. Another thing to be aware of is that Clarence is a cousin of Woodville's. I do not believe this is a curious coincidence,' said DM.

'So that's why you flew us down here. You think Woodville's control base is on the estate of Hindhead House. You want us to confirm that it's the base and have it shut down before the *coup d'état* can go ahead. That leaves us only two nights,' replied Mike, looking dismayed.

DM stood up. 'I need to show you what I have so far,' he said, motioning with his hand towards the door.

Mike and Libby returned their cups and saucers to the table and got up to follow. They retraced their steps to the main staircase and then entered a door set at the back of the lobby. The door opened on to a stone staircase that led down to what Mike and Libby guessed was a basement.

At the base of the stairs the light began to fade. DM reached into the darkness to operate a light switch. Overhead strip lights plinked into life, illuminating a long corridor that stretched out before them. The air was cool compared to the upstairs rooms and the sound of their footsteps was subdued as they walked. They passed a few doors situated on their left until they reached the end of the subterranean corridor. At the end were two steel doors that faced each other. DM took out a key and turned the heavy-duty lock in the left-hand door. Once more he reached into the darkness and another strip light plinked into life. He then closed the door behind them once they were all three inside the room.

Around the room were wooden trestle tables covered with green army blankets. A map was pinned to a board set up on an easel that stood between two of the trestle tables. Mike recognised straight away that two of the tables were basic models, like those made by officers or NCOs to use as aids for a mission briefing.

DM noted Mike's interest in the models. 'We use the tables as props for agents we have turned to provide information about locations and layouts of facilities or military units that are of interest to us. Sometimes we already have the information. The models allow us to check the accuracy of what we are being told or shown.'

'I suppose this table provides us with the general layout of the Hindhead estate, while the other is a layout of the house itself?' asked Mike.

'Yes, but as you can see, we do not have much to go on,' said DM.

'Is there somewhere to land an aircraft?' asked Libby.

'Plenty of space for a Lysander, but nowhere for a modern aircraft. The yellow pins on the map show the nearest airfields able to accommodate the landing of a de Havilland Dove. The other red pins are for the more distant airfields that the de Havilland might use,' replied DM.

Mike and Libby moved over to the map to take in the detail it provided. A large blue plastic-covered drawing pin sat almost centrally in relation to the array of yellow and red pins. Next to the drawing pin was a label displaying the word 'Hindhead'.

'Where are we on the map in relation to the estate?' asked Mike.

DM pointed to the location of the safe house.

Mike looked at him sharply. 'We can't be more than a ten-minute drive from there.'

'The irony is not lost on me, Mike,' said DM.

'No wonder you were happy enough to personally fly us down from Norfolk.'

DM smiled but made no comment.

'You must be very confident that this is the place Woodville is using as his base,' said Libby.

'I am, and once I get confirmation of the flight plan, the last piece of the jigsaw puzzle will be in place,' DM replied.

Mike turned his attention away from the map and went to look at the table representing the estate. 'All we have is an upscaled simple representation of the map,' he said, noting the location of woods, roads and the mansion itself. 'You have no precise idea of where the command centre is, or how it is protected.'

'That is where you come in, Mike. You need to find this out for yourself,' DM replied.

Mike smiled. In some ways this man was no different to Wesley. He wanted to use Mike and Libby as expendable, and at the same time deniable, assets in a game where the stakes could not be higher. The price of success – if DM was to be believed – was their freedom, whilst the price of failure was certain death.

'When do you want a recce to be carried out?' asked Mike.

'Time is of the essence, so you would have to make your reconnaissance tonight,' said DM.

Mike and Libby looked at him in surprise.

'What if you've got it wrong and the estate is not Woodville's base?' asked Libby.

'Then Mike has a quiet evening stroll and the *coup d'état* proceeds to its inevitable conclusion,' DM replied.

Mike looked towards the model of the mansion house and its immediate surroundings. 'This doesn't tell me a lot. Are you *sure* that this will be Woodville's operation headquarters?' he asked.

'You can see now why an immediate night reconnaissance of the estate is crucial,' said DM.

Mike knew it was pointless going in to the mansion blind on a seek-and-destroy mission. Apart from being a wild-goose chase, he could be tripped up at any point without being able to ensure a safe point of entry or exit. Mike anticipated that Woodville's commanders would have defence screens in place and he had to be able to evade these without detection. He was also not entirely convinced that Woodville had chosen to set up his headquarters within the confines of the mansion. To do so made his location an obvious and easy target that could be attacked. Mike made no mention of this to DM, deciding to wait until he was able to see for himself what was going on in the grounds of the estate.

'Do you have a map showing more detail of the estate?' asked Mike. The Ordnance Survey one on display did not show the level of topographical information he needed to see. 'I want to get a better understanding of the ground to try and cover my route of approach.'

DM nodded and went over to a wall-mounted telephone. There was a brief conversation over the receiver and minutes later Mrs May entered the room carrying a cardboard tube. She handed it to DM and then left. DM extracted a map and pinned it on top of the existing one. It provided all the extra detail Mike was looking for.

Looking at the map, it was easy for Mike to understand the rise and fall of the land. He put himself in the shoes of the local defence commander, who would identify the likely routes of approach to the mansion and then work out how they could be guarded to provide the maximum protection for the headquarters at Hindhead. He also looked for routes that might provide cover for himself as an intruder, areas where he could slip through, likely places where guard posts and sentries might be positioned.

It also occurred to Mike that if the deployment of troops around Hindhead was being passed off as a defence exercise, then the soldiers forming the outer ring of defence may not have been issued with live ammunition. Instead, only the armed men were likely to be posted around the core operations area. This possibility might make his night reconnaissance safer, as he did not have to get inside the headquarters. He only needed to know its location and how it was being protected. His follow-up incursion would be when he needed to get inside the heart of Woodville's operation.

'What do you think?' asked DM.

Mike smiled. 'I reckon the outer defence cordon will be regular or territorial troops who will not have been issued live ammunition because they think they are on an exercise. There will then be an inner cordon of troops who are armed and possibly in on the *coup d'état*. These men will be far fewer in number and working low-key so as not to spook the other non-involved troops. This makes me think Woodville's headquarters may not be as secure as we first supposed.'

DM nodded, thinking. 'Woodville might order his commander to raise the alert state and get ammunition issued to his men.'

'That will only happen if I am unlucky enough to be spotted,' countered Mike. 'I'm sure there will be no other reason to make him do such a thing.' He looked over to Libby, who appeared to be less convinced.

'You can't be sure that those soldiers are not fully armed, Mike,' she said in a quiet voice.

'I will be using the cover of darkness. Even if they are live-armed, the men must catch sight of me first and, at best, will be shooting at shadows,' he said, trying to allay her fears.

'Even if you do get away, they'll suspect you might return later and will be waiting for you next time,' she replied.

'This worst-case scenario is only a possibility, Libby,' said DM. 'The more likely possibility is that Mike gets past the outer cordon, identifies the HQ and extracts himself safely without the alarm being raised.'

'No, the worst-case scenario, DM, is that Mike is captured or killed by Woodville's men,' she responded in a louder voice.

'That's just a risk, Libby,' Mike interjected. 'I'm sure making a night recce is not going to be a bad as I first thought.'

'But you have no back-up,' she said. 'Once you melt into the darkness, how can I give you covering fire?'

Libby had correctly assumed that she would accompany Mike to provide him with cover, should he need it.

'I need you to watch my entry and exit point to the estate. That will be where your support will be most effective,' he replied, continuing to try to reassure her.

'Where will we get the firepower to do that?' she asked.

'I'm sure that small problem can be remedied,' said DM. 'Now, Mike – have you seen enough to work out where you will need to be dropped off to enter the estate?'

Mike nodded. Taking Libby's hand, he squeezed it gently. Her look of concern remained but she knew there was no other way they were going to stop Woodville.

'Good,' said DM. 'Now, follow me. I can't let you go up against Woodville without some final preparation.'

24
TARGET PRACTICE

Mike wondered what DM meant by 'final preparation'. That same night he was going to try to infiltrate Woodville's headquarters, and that meant he had only a few hours left before going in. Libby was as perplexed as he was. There was little left to do, except the reconnaissance itself.

The pair followed DM through the metal door and out across the underground corridor to the door opposite. DM was fiddling with the keys he was carrying. This door had two locks fitted and he had to unlock them both before they could enter. Another set of strip lights came on to illuminate racks of weapons.

DM showed Mike and Libby around his subterranean arsenal. The wall-mounted racks held row after row of small arms. Mike could scarcely believe his eyes. The number and variety of weapons on display was unlike any military armoury he had seen before. Rifles, pistols, machine guns, and shotguns from around the world filled one wall under the stark lighting. Opposite to these racks were benches, under which were metal boxes containing thousands of rounds of ammunition. Small yellow lettering, painted on using a stencil, indicated the contents of each box. Mike noted there were even boxes of Soviet and Chinese ammunition as well as those from NATO. On top of one bench were open boxes, inside of which were grenades waiting to be primed with detonators.

'There are a lot of standard-issue NATO weapons here, along with those we have acquired from the Soviets and the Chinese. There are also pistols purchased on the civilian market; primarily American, Swiss, German and Italian. Some weapons are customised items and might be of interest to you,' said DM.

Mike had already spotted a rifle with a dull black finish and a bipod fitted to the barrel that sported a silencer. The rifle also a large and unusual cigar-shaped telescopic sight that Mike had not seen before.

'That looks like a SIG SG 510, but what has happened to the rear-sight and fore-sight?' asked an incredulous Mike.

'I see you know your weapons. I had our armourer remove the sights, along with the bayonet mount. They became superfluous once the night sight was fitted. The silencer has reduced the effective range of the weapon, but this piece of Swiss ingenuity is a very effective night-time sniper rifle,' said DM, resting his hand on the barrel of the weapon.

'What type of sight have you had fitted?' asked Libby, who stepped between Mike and DM before lifting the rifle up to gauge its weight.

'A telescopic one. It enhances the available light even in apparent total darkness,' replied a surprised DM.

'It's a bit heavy, but I could use it,' said Libby.

DM looked at her and then Mike with another look of surprise.

'Libby knows her way around a rifle as well as she does a pistol,' explained Mike.

'Can you show me how the sight works?' asked Libby.

A smile formed on DM's face. He went out into the corridor and switched off the strip lights. He then came back inside and opened a box that contained an identical sight. He took it out and flicked a small switch fitted with protective guards on either side. A tiny hum could be heard coming from within the body of the sight.

'Let's go into the corridor, and make sure you pull the door closed behind you,' said DM.

Only the tiniest chink of light found its way through the crack left by the unsealed door, but otherwise, the corridor was pitch black. Unseen, DM pulled the cap off the front of the sight before handing it to Libby.

'Put the sight gently to your eye and look through,' he said.

She gingerly placed her eye against the rubberised eyepiece that opened like a tiny clamshell. To her surprise, she could see down the length of the corridor. The view she had was an eerie green glittery glow, and she could make out every detail of DM as he carefully walked through the darkness, heading away down the corridor. An illuminated reticle allowed her to zero on to him and make an easy target. She passed the sight to Mike to allow him to see how well it worked. DM stopped at the end of corridor and turned back towards them.

'This is fantastic, where did you get it?' asked Mike.

'It's still on the secret list so you don't need to know,' DM replied, walking slowly back down the corridor.

He took the sight back from Mike and switched off the device before putting the corridor lights back on. They returned to the armoury and DM carefully placed the sight back in its box.

'The damn thing is very sensitive and blows if it is exposed to natural light; even when the cap is fitted. Remember to switch it off and avoid pointing it at a very strong source of light,' he said, with a note of caution.

Mike was confident that Libby would have the perfect weapon to provide cover for him when he entered and exited the Hindhead estate. 'Do you want to use it?' he asked her.

She nodded with enthusiasm. 'I'll need to get the sight zeroed first. Is there anywhere we can do that before heading out?' she asked DM.

'Of course, but what about you, Mike?'

'I don't intend to get into a firefight. That is much more likely tomorrow night, so I want something light, just for protection. There is no way I would want anything like the SIG. An automatic pistol would be perfect for the job. I can use my Smith and Wesson as back-up,' he replied, scanning the collection of automatic pistols arrayed in front of him.

'I expect you will want something with a silencer,' said DM.

Mike began looking at the pistols that were threaded to take a silencer. He soon spotted a Smith & Wesson Model 39 that had been suitably modified.

'That one will be perfect. Do you have a modified holster for it?' he asked.

DM turned and crossed the room. Against the opposite wall stood a metal two-door cabinet. He took a holster out from one of its shelves and handed it to Mike. He also gave him spare magazines and boxes of ammunition.

He then unboxed some spare magazines for the SIG, as well as boxes of ammunition for Libby. They started filling their respective magazines, with DM choosing to help Libby.

'Where will I be able to zero the SIG?' she asked again.

'There is an underground shooting range within the grounds of the house. I had the army come and build it. That way, its existence could be kept secret. Now, before we go to the range you need to change into more appropriate clothing,' said DM.

The weapons were left behind and the three returned upstairs to the house. When Mike and Libby went back into their room they found two sets of camouflage clothing laid out on the bed. Mike had never seen the patterns and colours of the material before.

'These are the latest developments of the new Disruptive Pattern Material combat clothing for issue to the army,' explained DM. 'Your civilian clothes aren't going to be much use to you tonight or tomorrow.'

Mike looked at the mix of brown, green, black and dark sand-coloured patterns on the clothing. The camouflage was of a more advanced design than his old Denison paratrooper smock.

'You will find the clothes will fit you quite well, and over there are some lightweight rubber-soled combat boots that should be in your sizes,' said DM, pointing to two pairs of boots that were set out on the floor beside the bed.

'No expense spared,' said Mike.

'What is the point of a budget if you cannot spend it?' replied DM. 'When you are ready, meet me back in the armoury.'

Once Mike and Libby had changed into the army uniforms, they did as they were asked. Libby continued to holster her pistol under the combat jacket.

'I doubt if you have realised it, but this corridor extends outside the footprint of the house. Through that door is the shooting range,' explained DM.

Mike and Libby picked up their weapons and followed him through yet another door at the end of the armoury. Mike let out a low whistle as they emerged on to a rifle range, fully lit and extending way into the distance. At the far end were targets that seemed tiny from where they were standing.

'This is incredible. What else have you got hidden away around here?' exclaimed Mike.

DM simply smiled and did not reply.

Unfazed by events and her new surroundings, Libby straight away began to ready her rifle for firing. DM produced a small torch and an adjustment tool for her to use to zero the weapon. He then switched on the extractor fans above them to keep the air fresh within the range and turned off the lights. A tiny click was heard, then the zing of the night sight began. Mike and DM stood in the darkness, unable to see Libby as she continued zeroing the rifle. The silencer was so effective that neither of them needed to wear any ear protection. What seemed like only minutes later she stopped firing. The subdued zing of the night sight ceased.

'All done,' she said, sounding satisfied.

Mike was pleased that her training in Canada had been put to good use. DM switched the lights back on and checked the distant targets with a pair of powerful binoculars. One of the targets had the bullseye completely missing. Libby unloaded the SIG and stood up.

'Very impressive, Libby. Let's see how Mike does,' said DM as he flicked switches on a small console behind the firing point.

Libby's distant targets silently descended out of sight, then a whirring sound could be heard that was much closer to where they stood. Just ahead, three full-size targets depicting a man standing and aiming a pistol emerged from the floor of the range. DM dimmed the lights until the targets were barely discernible, then they were rotated ninety degrees until they were virtually invisible.

'Your turn, Mike. When the targets flick round towards you, open fire,' said DM.

Mike readied himself and his pistol. For what seemed like an age, nothing happened. Then, unseen, DM pressed a button and the targets flew round towards them. Mike quickly fired twice at each one, then DM returned the lights back to full intensity. From where they stood it was easy to see the pairs of bullet holes in the chest area of each target.

'I don't think either of you need to spend any more time down here,' DM remarked as he turned off the extractor fans.

Mike placed his pistol back into its modified holster and Libby picked up the rifle then they both followed DM out of the range. They stopped only to put the spare magazines of ammunition in their jacket pockets before going upstairs into the house.

Mrs May stood waiting in the hall. 'One last thing you should do,' she said, holding out a small green plastic tub towards Mike. He nodded and took it, pushed off the lid and began applying the brown camouflage cream to Libby's face and hands. Once he had finished, Libby did the same to him. Just as they had prophetically practiced in Canada.

Inexplicably, they both felt for a moment as if they stood as strangers to each other. That moment of truth: so familiar to Mike, yet so new to Libby. The point of no return, where something really begins and has an outcome that is far from certain. Both DM and Mrs May recognised the tension between Mike and Libby, but the moment was soon over. The pair faced the threshold of danger and chose not to turn away. From then on, words would be sparse, assuming any were uttered at all.

The front doors to the house were open and all that could be seen through them was the summer darkness that had finally fallen. DM led the way outside to a Land Rover that was parked in the drive. Unbidden, Libby clambered over the tailgate and sat on a rudimentary seat under the canvas canopy. Mike passed the SIG rifle to her and then also climbed in and took his place. DM turned around to check his passengers were aboard before starting the engine and driving off.

Mike was just able to make out Libby's face in the darkness. He was glad to see her looking calm and resolute. The Land Rover bumped along the back roads for nearly fifteen minutes before DM pulled over and switched off the lights. Mike and Libby got out and moved into the shadows of some nearby oak trees. They silently knelt, watching and listening to everything around them.

Another fifteen minutes passed. Mike and Libby had let their eyes get more accustomed to the darkness before moving off.

They also orientated themselves to the surroundings. They needed to easily recognise this spot when they returned.

Mike stood up and tapped Libby on the shoulder. She, too, stood without a word and the pair moved off into the darkness. DM had waited by the Land Rover, watching and listening for danger. When he saw Mike and Libby move off into the darkness, he waited a further fifteen minutes before driving off. He too had memorised the spot where he had dropped them off and would return there in four hours' time.

Libby kept her distance from Mike. He was only just visible to her as they threaded their way through the woodland. They avoided going through open fields to avoid curious livestock alerting anyone to their presence. Their progress was slow, as Mike stopped frequently, looking and listening to check there was no danger ahead.

Using his memory of the map back at the safe house, Mike rehearsed in his head the route they would need to take to get to the edge of the Hindhead estate. That meant walking across countryside for nearly a mile from where DM had dropped them off. Mike had no idea what might be waiting for them and was taking no chances. He also wanted to use the woodland as cover on their return if something went wrong, mainly because of its inaccessibility to any vehicles that might be pursuing them.

Above the canopy of the trees, the moon and stars shone brightly. Mike hoped the moonlight would not be a problem once he broke cover and made his way into the grounds of the mansion. The warmth of the day had not completely gone, making Mike and Libby feel hot in the combat clothing and boots they had been given. Perspiration mingled with the camouflage cream and created an unpleasant clammy sensation as it soaked into Mike's clothing. He was aware that the rifle Libby was carrying was much heavier from having the night sight fitted. Thankfully, his frequent stops to look and listen for danger were providing useful respite. Finally, they reached the point where he would leave Libby behind and enter the estate proper.

Mike had picked the promontory of a wood as the spot where Libby would remain until he returned. From this position they overlooked a small and shallow valley running north to south. In the bottom of the valley ran a small river that formed the border of the Hindhead estate. Mike intended to head due east across the river and climb to the other side of the valley. From there it was a few hundred yards to the mansion house, where he hoped to find Woodville's headquarters.

Mike tapped Libby on the shoulder and indicated the left-hand edge, then the right-hand edge of her arc of fire. She understood the significance of the shoulder tap, as they had rehearsed this before in Canada.

His route forward would roughly follow the centre of her arc of fire. Libby moved forward silently and found herself a position from which she could easily provide covering fire for Mike. The backdrop of the dark wood provided a shadow, masking her outline and preventing any observers looking from the east from seeing her. Once Mike saw that she was in position, he moved forward and down the gentle slope into the valley.

Moving across grassland made Mike feel vulnerable in such open country. He hoped his gamble that the outer security cordon was manned by troops thinking they were on an exercise was correct. With luck, these troops would be less alert, allowing him to easily slip through the outer cordon and on to the mansion.

Within minutes he had reached the river and found it to be only knee-deep where he chose to cross. The coldness of the water contrasted with the warmth of the night as he waded forward, expecting to hear the call of an alarm at any moment. Once across to the other side, he moved into the cover of some thorn bushes. From there he looked up the ridge that rose gently away from him and listened. Over the sound of the running water behind him, and as if on cue, he heard the unmistakable engine noise of an approaching Land Rover.

It was following a farm track that ran just below the ridge. The canvas canopy had been removed from the vehicle and, with the help of the moonlight, Mike saw four men sitting in the back. The headlights were on, illuminating the valley directly ahead. Mike could hear the men talking and laughing. They were on a mobile patrol but did not appear to be taking the exercise too seriously. Mike relaxed – this made his job easier until he got close to the mansion, where he expected security to be tighter.

Libby had followed Mike's progress using the night sight. It seemed she was looking into another world. The light from the moon was massively enhanced by the device, making it appear as though Mike was walking in mysterious green daylight. He had disturbed a fox, which had watched him with eyes resembling the palest of emeralds before slinking away across the fields. She also heard the approach of the Land Rover, which caused her heart to hammer and sent her breathing out of control. Her finger curled around the rifle's trigger and she was thankful that the bipod steadied the weapon. The vehicle's headlights momentarily created a wash of light, forcing her to take her eye away from the sight. Then, seconds later, it was gone letting her heart rate slowly return to normal. It was like Tantallon Castle all over again and she had never felt so isolated in her life.

25
EVELYN

The chauffeur drove Woodville's midnight-blue Bentley at a majestic pace across the highways of England. He avoided any unseemly rush as the vehicle cut its swathe along the oil-stained asphalt usually driven over by commoners in their diesel trucks and small proletarian cars. Looking neither right nor left unless necessary, the chauffeur seemed oblivious to all other road users. He piloted the motor car of the elite and had none of the concerns or anxieties of the ordinary motorist. Despite the hot weather, he was cool and relaxed in the frigid luxury of the Bentley's air-conditioned interior. The fact that he did not own the Bentley and was simply a paid employee seemed not to matter whilst he was in the driving seat.

Woodville had provided the chauffeur with elegant handwritten details of where he was to collect the passenger before driving down to Surrey. Although being a professional driver, the man had never been to Hertfordshire, let alone the Crown Hotel that was set in the countryside just outside Welwyn Garden City. The former country house, reworked into a neo-Palladian-style mansion, complemented the collection of expensive cars parked along its gravelled front. Short fence posts dazzling in their fresh white paint, linked by heavy spiked white chains, demarcated the boundaries of the bowling-green lawns.

Evelyn MacDonald sat waiting inside the lounge of the hotel where she had stayed the night after being dropped off by the taxi driver. She revelled in the luxury of her surroundings, delighting in the foretaste of her new life. The suite where she had stayed so briefly was the most opulent set of rooms she had ever slept in. She knew that a man like Charles Woodville could afford such luxury without a second thought, and she felt equally privileged. Wesley would never take her to such a hotel – he could not afford to. Even though her new life as Charles' mistress meant she would never be officially recognised in her own right, her life was about to change forever. *That was enough*, she thought.

Evelyn glanced out of the hotel's full-length windows into the gravelled car park and wondered who would be arriving to collect her. She had no idea what to expect, and although she registered the arrival of the Bentley, she had no idea whether it was for her. Her anticipatory excitement felt almost juvenile, but the idea of sharing her body with Woodville once more was intoxicating.

She had woken early that morning and luxuriated in the suite's huge bathtub. Afterwards, she ate breakfast in bed before getting herself ready for her final journey to join her lover. As she sipped on her morning coffee, she had fantasised about the night to come.

Just as Evelyn began to pour herself another coffee, one of the hotel staff walked across to her and quietly let her know that her transport had arrived. He also asked if her stay had been satisfactory. She confirmed that yes, indeed she had found her stay most satisfactory, and asked for her suitcase to be brought out. The man nodded and told her the case had already been taken. She glanced out of the window, trying to hide her surprise and pleasure. It seemed that Charles was out to spoil her, and she looked forward to spoiling him in return.

Evelyn wore a crisp sleeveless two-piece cotton suit in pale lemon with matching high heels. She carried with her a small patent-leather handbag to complement the outfit and had spent more time than she cared to admit drawing her hair back into an elegant chignon. Her perfume was Chanel.

Walking slowly through the huge hotel lobby, she enjoyed the interested looks from men as she passed by. Her two-piece was tailored to exaggerate the curves of her body. She pretended not to notice her admirers as she continued outside into the bright sunshine. The chauffeur had left the Bentley's engine running whilst he opened the rear door on the passenger side.

He said good morning before introducing himself, and he finished every sentence with 'madam', following his strict instructions from Woodville not to mention her name.

Once Evelyn had seated herself he closed the door behind her before making his way around the front of the car to the driving seat.

Before they moved off the chauffeur asked his passenger if she preferred the built-in privacy screen up or down. She said she preferred it up and he pointed out where the microphone switch for the intercom was in case she needed to speak to him.

There was a mutual sense of relief as the screen glided silently into position. Evelyn did not want to share her space with a member of staff, whilst the chauffeur preferred to drive unencumbered by his passenger. Sat comfortably on the perfectly sprung grey leather seat, Evelyn watched the world pass silently by through a green glass sunshade. She had not realised how private the customised rear compartment was, with its tiny curtains that could be opened or closed at the touch of a switch. She found the idea a little more exciting than she might have expected.

Within two hours the Bentley had crossed the western fringes of London and now approached the gates of a country estate. A black metal sign with white lettering indicated they were at Hindhead House. The journey had been relaxing for Evelyn, even if her anticipation of joining her lover had had the opposite effect. She had discovered the drinks cabinet and allowed herself an early gin and tonic during the journey.

The Bentley followed a long drive flanked by huge elm trees, with wide densely interwoven canopies that provided a shaded end to her journey through the bright English countryside. She knew that Charles' estate was set in the far north of England and had wondered where she would be reunited with him. Not that it mattered too importantly to her, because she would soon be fêted like royalty on country estates along with Charles as he toured his inner circle of supporters over the coming weeks.

Evelyn felt a frisson of excitement as the Bentley approached the checkpoints that were set out along the drive to the mansion. It was clear the soldiers had been briefed not to stop the car and the men, full of curiosity, craned their necks to get a glimpse of her as she was driven by. She gave the impression that she was not at all interested in them and their obvious curiosity. Her seeming disdain hid how thrilled she really was with the attention she was getting, taking it as another foretaste of what was to come.

Once inside the inner cordon of troops, the Bentley picked up speed as it completed its journey along the final stretch of driveway to the front of the mansion. Just ahead of it was a much slower vehicle, a Land Rover.

The chauffeur sounded the horn at the Land Rover as a signal for it to move out of the way. The other driver complied and slowed down to pull off the drive and allow the Bentley to pass.

Evelyn glanced to her left in mild curiosity. She did not recognise the driver, but when she saw the passenger, a thunderbolt of shock and surprise passed through her. There was no mistake: it was Wesley.

The very man she believed she had escaped from had arrived right where she intended to rendezvous with her lover. She looked back at him as the Land Rover receded in the distance. He had not seen her, and nor had he even bothered to look in the direction of the Bentley. In his thoughts, he appeared to be far from Hindhead.

As the Bentley continued up to the front of the mansion she lost sight of Wesley and second-guessed herself into thinking that perhaps she had just seen someone who looked very much like him. The ploy did not work. She knew that Wesley, for whatever reason, was at Hindhead.

Evelyn was unable to put together a sequence of events that had brought herself and Wesley together once more, and in such a disastrous fashion. The Bentley stopped. She could feel her heart racing and she looked down at her shaking hands. To get out of the car now and be seen by Wesley would be a cataclysm.

Her anger grew as she realised he had ruined her reunion with Charles. She decided there was to be no embarrassing confrontation with her husband outside of the mansion. In her heart, she was completely resolved never to see him again. Instead, when she saw Charles she would ask him why Wesley was here. She also wanted to know what Charles was going to do about it.

She spoke calmly into the Bentley's intercom and told the chauffeur to stay put in the car. The man looked over his shoulder towards her and nodded. He knew better than to ask why. It was clear to Evelyn that the chauffeur had made no connection between her and the occupants of the Land Rover.

She waited until the Land Rover passed around the side of the house and was out of sight, then using the intercom once more, Evelyn told the chauffeur she was ready to get out of the car.

A member of the Hindhead household staff had emerged from the mansion as soon as the Bentley had come to a halt. The man, in a butler's uniform, was followed out by a younger man and woman. Both were dressed in servants' uniforms. On the instruction of the butler, the young man opened the boot to the Bentley and took out Evelyn's suitcase.

Now that she had regained her composure, Evelyn stepped out of the car. Her mood darkened with the realisation that Charles had not come out to greet her personally. The glorious start to her new life had fallen at the first fence and at that moment all she could think of was how to rid herself of her husband.

The man that Evelyn assumed was the butler introduced himself, along with the young woman standing slightly back and to his left. She would be Evelyn's maid during her stay at Hindhead. He also told Evelyn that the Viscount was most apologetic that he had been unable to greet her himself, and that they would meet at dinner.

The maid led Evelyn to the rooms that had been prepared for her stay. They were on the first floor and gave Evelyn an expansive view of the estate. She found that her suitcase had already been brought up and set to one side, ready for unpacking. When the maid had completed this task, Evelyn said she could go.

Before leaving, the maid asked Evelyn if she wanted something to eat. Evelyn declined, as any appetite she may have had was now gone. The maid thanked her, pointed out the bell-pull that could be used to call her, then left.

Evelyn flounced into an adjoining sitting room and dropped into an overstuffed chair. Still feeling devastated that she had been unable to escape from Wesley, she sat brooding over her misfortune.

* * *

Charles Woodville's face was darker than a winter thunderstorm. His long experience working in the military had given him a nose for impending bad news. He had the ability to read between the lines of the briefest of messages and sniff out the sender's desperation, and his nose told him that the message from Wesley MacDonald had more than a taint of fear about it.

The timing of the message was very bad, with his plan for the *coup d'état* reaching its climax only the day after next. He was about to propel himself into a position of power that was second to none, and suddenly an urgent meeting with Wesley MacDonald had come from nowhere.

Even though he had not heard a single word of what the man was going to say, he already knew it had to be bad news. Wesley's fate was entirely dependent upon what he was about to say and being the husband of the woman Woodville now possessed placed him in the greatest of danger. If Wesley could not resolve whatever disaster had overcome him, then Woodville believed his usefulness had come to an end.

Woodville's headquarters staff tried to keep away from him and not get caught in his gaze. This was proving difficult, as the control room was housed in a cramped military communications caravan. The big man hovered hawk-like behind worried-looking radio operators, who sat pretending to study the handwritten notes they had made in their radio logs. The junior watch officer felt trapped and tried to look busy or find a reason to absent himself from the control room. Some senior officers exhibited their maliciousness by remaining to watch the upcoming spectacle.

The Land Rover that had brought Wesley from London pulled into a designated parking area beneath the huge camouflage nets that concealed Woodville's command centre. The journey had been uncomfortable, leaving Wesley feeling stiff as he stepped out on to the ground.

A complex of military caravans formed a huge crucifix from where the *coup d'état* would be directed over the next few days. Metal grilles formed elevated walkways between caravans and there were metal steps dotted around to allow access to and from the walkways. The acrid smell of exhaust gases coming from generators used to power the complex entered Wesley's nose. The immediate area also felt hot, as there was no breeze to take away the heat of the generators and the radio equipment in the caravans. Wesley thanked his lucky stars that he'd never had to work in such a place.

The driver of the Land Rover had chain-smoked cigarettes throughout the journey from London and after stepping out of the vehicle, he lit another one.

'You'll find him in that one. Good luck,' he said sarcastically, pointing to the nearest caravan in the complex.

Wesley did not bother to thank him. He walked across the well-trodden grass to the nearest set of metal steps and climbed up on to the walkway. He stood outside a large hatchlike door and took a deep breath, then entered by pressing on a lever that acted as a door handle. The door swung open and a gentle wave of over-pressured air passed over him. The warm air smelt stale, tinged with the just-discernible aromas of sweat and farts. Feeling slightly disgusted Wesley confidently stepped through the door before closing it behind him. He stood in an upright and assertive manner, looking straight back at the men inside who were staring him down.

This sort of situation was not new to Wesley. The petty politics of the types of personalities that filled security-service meeting rooms were no different to where he now found himself at Hindhead. He knew the stern-looking men in their uniforms felt safer now, with the luxury of having another in their midst to draw Woodville's fire.

He had undertaken many successful battles to save his small department from the grandees of both MI5 and 6. Often he had come through a crisis by calling the other person's bluff, but he was not so sure this time as his eyes locked with Woodville's. This was not inter-departmental power politics he was dealing with. He knew this was possibly a matter of life or death – *his* life or death.

Wesley was unprepared for the unexpected level of Woodville's personal enmity. He had anticipated the man's wrath by calling the unprecedented meeting, and he also understood the expectation that he was bringing bad news, but he sensed Woodville's deeper antipathy as the man spoke slowly in a tone that was lower than usual.

'What is so important that it needs to be discussed in a face-to-face meeting?' he asked.

Wesley felt the words drip with menace and he could almost sense the salivation in the senior officers' mouths as they watched. Their fear of the great man was transferred on to Wesley as the spotlight was, for now, pointing away from them.

In an instant, Wesley could see the man ruled only through fear. The leadership and charisma he displayed via a television camera lens was nothing more than a front. Wesley knew now that all he had to do was lie, just as he had planned to do all along.

'Something you do not want these people to hear,' he said, in answer to Woodville's question.

There was an almost imperceptible pause as their eyes locked. Wesley was asserting his importance over everyone but Woodville. Another moment of silence passed.

'Very well,' said Woodville, as he signalled to have the door to the control room opened. Wesley stepped outside into the relatively fresh air, closely followed by Woodville himself.

'You have a lot of nerve,' the man said angrily once the door had closed behind them.

'That is why I am good at my job,' replied Wesley. He was feeling more confident now and reinforced this by continuing to talk to Woodville as an equal. It was something he grudgingly acknowledged that Mike Armstrong would have done.

'Get to the point,' snapped Woodville.

'It's Mazarin. He has been playing a double game and is working for MI5 or 6. Both he and his sidekick Mancuso have disappeared from the airbase in Norfolk. I believe 5 or 6 extracted him when he called time on his involvement in the plan,' lied Wesley.

His gamble to demand a private meeting had paid off. Woodville would not want anyone to know that his organisation had been successfully infiltrated by the security services. He needed to avoid senior army officers losing their nerve and pulling out of the coup at the very last minute.

'What do you suggest?' asked Woodville, sounding cautious.

Wesley could see he had bought himself time, if not a reprieve.

'Mazarin can't derail the coup, as his subordinates can easily complete the Buckingham Palace mission with or without him. As Mazarin only knows his own part in the proceedings, the rest of your operations are safe. I would suggest that all you need do is strengthen local security at Hindhead,' said Wesley, trying to sound as reassuring as possible.

'How certain are you about him?' asked Woodville.

'I am completely sure. He knows we will want him killed, so he will lie low before getting out of the country. The security services are going to stand to one side because they still lack the full picture,' Wesley responded, continuing with his subterfuge.

'Speak of this to no one. I will make arrangements for you to stay here at Hindhead until after the coup,' said Woodville.

Wesley had expected be sent on his way rather than be forced to spend even more time in the lion's den. He was caught off guard and felt sure there was something Woodville had not told him.

26
UNDER THE MOONLIGHT

Mike lay perfectly still until he was sure the patrolling Land Rover was not going to stop or turn back towards him. His heart rate slowly sank back to normal and everything around him became quiet once more. He looked back across the valley towards the impenetrable darkness, where his invisible sentinel kept watch. He knew that she lay there, somewhere, in the shadow of the wood. He wondered if she could see him through the incredible night sight that was fitted to her rifle.

He slowly raised himself from the ground to continue in the direction of the mansion, expecting to find the house nestled on the far side of the ridge. Although he was treading very carefully and keeping his movements as fluid as possible, he hoped there were no boobytraps ahead of him. The country was now just open fields and a trip flare would easily leave him exposed in its light.

Within minutes Mike had reached the top of the ridge on the eastern side of the river valley. He crouched down once more to avoid creating a silhouette against the moonlit sky. Once he was below the skyline, he relaxed a little and began his descent of the hill towards the mansion. It was easy to pick out the house, as its ghostly white outline contrasted with the darkened landscape that was dotted with oak trees planted centuries before.

The scene was peaceful, warm and idyllic. This was worrying Mike, as no military vehicles, motorcycles or sentries could be seen. If it had not been for the mobile patrol he had encountered earlier, he would have thought he'd made a huge mistake.

Mike pressed on regardless across the moonlit landscape as carefully and quickly as he dared. Every so often he was forced to stop, observe and listen. Everything was still annoyingly quiet. The closer he got to the mansion, the surer he became that Woodville's command centre had to be located elsewhere. He stopped a hundred yards short of the house, trying to pick out the inevitable radio masts of a military headquarters, but there were none visible. Mike swore under his breath – this was confirmation that the mansion at Hindhead did not contain Woodville's headquarters after all.

The big house had a few lights showing here and there through the windows. Looking at them for several minutes, Mike saw no movement. He knew there was no point sitting in the dark looking at windows all night for clues as to what was going on, so he decided to focus back on finding Woodville. The trouble was, he had no idea where to start. He had not come across the inner security cordon he had expected to be in place, so he knew he had some way to go yet.

Afraid that floodlights could come on at any moment, he skirted the immediate area of the house. He kept just outside the edge of where the manicured lawns and gardens butted up to the fields of the estate, walking in an anti-clockwise circle around the house and hoping to come across any clue as to where the headquarters was based.

He soon crossed the driveway where, unbeknownst to him, Wesley and Evelyn had arrived earlier that evening. Everything was still annoyingly quiet.

As Mike continued to circumnavigate the house, he began to pick up on the dull rumble and hum of concealed generators. Listening carefully, he sensed they were to the right of the house and some way off in the distance. The stone of the house had masked the sounds before this, as it had stood directly between him and the headquarters. Now he had reached the other side, he was able to pick up on the sounds much better. His mood lightened as he continued towards them, putting the house behind him. He stopped once more for his eyes to get accustomed to the darkness after looking at the lights of the house and saw a copse in the middle distance. There the shadows of the trees concealed unseen generators in the same way Libby was using the gloom of the night-time trees to stay hidden.

Mike could tell the site had been set up by professionals. There was nothing to be seen that gave the headquarters away. It was only the sound of the generators that could not be completely suppressed from someone who might get close enough to the site. He was sure that even in the light of day, locating the headquarters would be difficult. In the darkness, however, there was a total absence of life and movement that could easily fool the unwary into thinking that no one was there to keep watch.

Somewhere hidden in the darkness, though, were pairs of invisible eyes scanning the night for intruders such as himself. There was no doubt in his mind that the hidden eyes belonged to men who were armed and ready to kill. Woodville would not have been stupid and overconfident enough to leave the nerve centre of his *coup d'état* vulnerable to intrusion – or worse, an attack. Mike knew his job was still far from over. He needed to precisely identify the key parts of the headquarters, so they could be destroyed in twenty-four hours' time.

Mike was forced to move much more slowly and carefully as he approached through the darkness. The moonlight bathed the fields around the copse with a gentle silver aura that was impossible to walk through without being spotted. Men looking out across the fields would easily see his outline as if it were daytime.

From where he lay, Mike could see the gentle undulations of the fields that lay between him and the headquarters. He cursed, knowing that the only way across the fields was to crawl all the way using the dead ground created by the undulations. There was no doubt in his mind that the force of men protecting the headquarters had already anticipated that this was the only way to approach unseen. They would have set out boobytraps across the field. Getting past them would take extra time. Mike silently swore again.

After checking his Smith & Wesson was secure, Mike slipped under a barbed-wire fence that was normally used to separate livestock into their own fields. As far as he could see, the field was empty of animals. Crawling forward and along the shallow dips in the ground, he began to pick up on the smell of sheep urine and droppings. He cursed even more when he realised the foul-smelling dampness would impregnate his clothes and adhere to his skin. The smell might alert sentries, or it could help to mask his presence. Mike had no idea which way the path of events would unfold, and he had no choice but to carry on despite the risk. Gritting his teeth and trying to ignore the close-up stench of sheep urine, he continued to crawl towards the headquarters.

The effort began to make Mike sweat. Drops of liquid began to drip off his nose. The sweat made his eyes sting, and even though he wiped his eyes constantly, the maddening irritation continued. Despite his distractions, Mike did not fail to notice the touch of an invisible metal strand as it gently collided with his forehead. He froze and waited, his heart hammering as if it were trying to burst through his ribcage. The next thing he expected to hear was the 'pop' and fizzing sound of a parachute flare high above him.

But the sound never came, nor the white circulating light of a flare as it slowly returned to earth. There was no eruption of orange light from a trip flare, either. Both types of light would have been precursors to his capture and interrogation – or a burst of machine-gun fire to finish him off. The few seconds he lay there felt like a lifetime to Mike. The night remained placid and warm. Nothing moved.

Mike was relieved and resisted the urge to pop his head up to look around him, thereby giving away his presence. He had been lucky and had somehow avoided activating the tripwire. Slowly raising his hand, he probed the darkness, feeling for the wire strand to work out in which direction it ran. He was able to use the moonlight in his favour as he scanned left and right along the length of the wire. Sure enough, he saw the silhouette of a flare pot mounted on a stake off to his right. He carefully crawled around the pot before resuming his original route to the trees.

As Mike got ever closer, he began to pick up on other sounds around him. The whispers of apparently bored soldiers reached his ears. It was obvious the men had no idea he was just feet away from them. The smell of a cigarette being smoked mingled with the aroma of freshly dug earth. Someone was taking a break at the bottom of a freshly dug fire trench. Whoever it was had taken the precaution to keep undercover and keep the light from the cigarette concealed. The red glow was hidden, but the smoke still permeated the night air.

Mike hoped he had reached the inner ring of sentries and trenches that formed a defensive ring around Woodville's headquarters, and he had his heart rate and breathing back under control as he crawled into the darkness of the trees. Once he felt sure no one had seen him, he moved safely past the trenches and knelt beside a fallen tree trunk. He waited to allow his eyes to re-acclimatise to the darkness under the trees.

Being so close to the diesel generators meant that his fear of being heard receded; their rumbling hum hid most other sounds. All he had to do now was avoid being seen.

All the operating lights of the generators were concealed under panels. Mike risked standing up with his back against a tree and took in his surroundings. Soon his eyes were picking up on the straight lines of the caravans set up a short distance away from the huge generators. He looked up and could see where the camouflage nets stretched across the openings in the tree canopy, allowing the twinkle of stars to be seen. By day or night, anyone looking from the opposite direction would be unlikely to make out what the copse concealed. There was no doubt in his mind that this was the place to be.

Mike walked slowly forward, trying not to break any fallen branches that might be waiting to snap loudly beneath his feet and give him away to an alert sentry. His senses were in overdrive as he tried to take in more of his surroundings. He soon noticed the cruciform of large darkened military caravan. Suddenly a door to the nearest caravan was opened, then just as quickly closed as a figure made his way along the steel walkways and down some steps. Thankfully, the red lighting from within the caravan had not pierced the night, and it failed to illuminate Mike standing nearby. During the seconds in which the door was open, Mike heard the hushed tone of talking inside the caravan. It sounded as though someone in authority was briefing others.

Mike climbed the metal steps and stood outside the door. His heart was hammering again as he pressed his ear against the small painted-out window. He could hear only muffled speech, so he quickly moved away from where he was vulnerable to discovery and settled back into the safety of the darkness.

There he found himself standing next to a small vertical ladder that went up on to the roof of the caravan. Seconds later, he was on the roof and carefully searching for an air vent through which he could listen to the occupants. He was surprised to find he had a choice of several. The temperature of the operations room below had obviously become intolerable in the summer heat and had failed to cool down in the night. Mike crawled over to the vent that was open the widest, giving him the opportunity to look down inside.

Woodville was standing centre stage and briefing a small group of officers. Behind him were maps that he was using as part of his briefing. Mike knew he had hit the jackpot and found the epicentre of the *coup d'état*.

Mike carefully retraced his steps to the ladder to climb back down on to the metal walkway. All he had to do now was get back to Libby and DM.

'What do you think you are doing, laddie?' came a voice out of nowhere. 'Get down here and explain yourself.'

Mike froze for an instant. The voice, with a Scottish brogue, had the air of authority but seemed largely unconcerned at Mike's presence on the ladder. As he was wearing military clothing, Mike guessed the man thought he had caught a soldier who had gotten too curious for his own good.

Mike slid down the ladder and jumped the last few feet on to the walkway. At the same time, he twisted to face the man and pushed him backwards into the darkness. There was a thump as the man hit the ground and then an attempt to speak, but he had been badly winded, so no words came out. Mike jumped down on to the man, landing with his full weight on the man's chest. There was a sickening crack of bones as the man's ribcage collapsed inwards on his heart, then silence.

There was no time for Mike to ponder on his actions. He hurriedly rolled the dead man into the darkness beneath the caravan before checking that no one had seen what had happened. There were no shouts of alarm or any sign at all of somebody witnessing him kill the man.

Mike knew he had to keep the body concealed for as long as possible to give him the best chance of escape. He noticed some spare camouflage nets stacked under the walkway, so he grabbed one and unrolled it. He then dragged the dead man on to the net before rolling him up in it. Mike then dragged the net containing the body out of sight and pushed it as far under the caravan as it would go. Although the man's absence would be noticed soon enough, Mike hoped he had built in enough time to allow him to make his escape.

Now that he had all the information he needed about the location of Woodville's headquarters, Mike was desperate to get back to Libby and DM. After checking his watch, he realised that time was running out well before he had expected. He needed a faster way to get back to where Libby was waiting for him.

He moved through the shadows, glancing around for some sort of car park. As the headquarters site was not extensive, Mike knew there had to be one somewhere. He was rewarded with a neat row of a few parked Land Rovers and what looked like some army staff cars. All the vehicles were backed in to allow a fast exit in case of a fire or some other emergency. Mike hoped that meant the vehicle keys had all been left in place.

He quietly approached the nearest Land Rover and pressed down gently on the driver's-side door handle. It opened with a quiet clunk and he pulled open the door. Mike felt around in the darkness, checking to see if a key remained in the ignition. Once more, his luck held.

Just as Mike was about to climb into the driver's seat, he felt the muzzle of a gun press against his neck.

'Move away from the vehicle so I can get a good look at you,' said a man with a gruff voice.

Mike slowly turned around to face the man. He was taller and held a Sterling sub-machine gun with one hand. The muzzle of the weapon was inches from Mike's face. In the other hand he held a small two-way radio. He turned his head slightly as if he was going to talk into it, and that was the moment Mike chose to make a vicious upward punch into the man's throat.

The soldier stiffened for a second, and the radio fell out of his hand and down to the ground. The man closely followed as he toppled over. With time running out, Mike left the man where he lay but picked up the small radio and stuffed it into his jacket pocket. He then clambered in to the Land Rover and started up the engine.

With the vehicle headlights off, Mike slowly pulled forward and drove at a steady pace. He followed the track made by other vehicles that led towards and then past the mansion. He maintained a steady speed, trying not to attract attention and hoping that any soldiers watching would not pay much heed to a military Land Rover cruising past. The plan seemed to work and, using the moonlight to his advantage, he carried on driving past the front of mansion. Mike then turned on to the estate's drive, which he had crossed earlier that night, to drive a short distance before turning up towards the crest of the hill. He stopped the vehicle short of the crest and got out. Moving swiftly, he descended into the small valley, heading towards the river and out of the estate.

Just as Mike neared the river, headlights from a patrol Land Rover flashed on, illuminating him on the exposed slope. There were challenging shouts from the direction of the headlights, but Mike ignored them and bolted towards the river and freedom. Shots were fired in his direction, but none connected. All that mattered was to keep going and then some more.

The adrenaline made his downward path easier as he careered towards the river somewhere in the darkness. Mike did not have time to think about why the men had now switched off the vehicle's headlights, nor did he give any thought as to what happened to them. He splashed across the river and started up the gentle slope towards where he had left Libby earlier. By the time he reached the edge of the copse his breath was heavy from the exertion.

Mike instinctively dropped down into cover to look back across the valley. No one had pursued him across the river, and no other shots were heard. Someone was moving carefully towards him.

'Mike, are you OK?' whispered Libby anxiously.

'Yes, I'm fine. What about you?'

'I was terrified they were going to shoot you. I could only get off a couple of aimed shots before the headlights swamped the night sight,' she replied.

'You must have reacted quickly. I had no idea what was happening after the men opened fire,' said Mike.

'You smell of something horrible. Let's get out of here and back to DM. They may send a search party to get us.'

Without another word they began making their way back through the wood to find DM. As they approached the rendezvous point, they slowed their pace and looked for any hint of danger.

'You two took your time. I've been here for an hour,' said a cheery voice out of the darkness. 'A spot of bother?' asked DM.

27
FINAL ENCOUNTERS

Charles Woodville studied Wesley's face throughout their short meeting. He had been unable to pierce the inscrutable exterior of the man, leaving him unable to tell if he had been lied to.

With less than a day to go before his ascent to power, he was not about to take any chances with a man like Wesley, and so he gave orders for him to be handcuffed and secured in the cellars of Hindhead House. Wesley's fate became dependent upon the events of the next few days. Woodville even considered the idea of getting Evelyn to choose her husband's fate. He had never liked the man and only dealt with him out of necessity. As far as he was concerned, the disposal of his supposed love rival could come at any time. Wesley could never be a serious contender because of the way he had treated Evelyn during their marriage. He reflected for a moment on the similarity of his own marriage, then dismissed the thought just as quickly.

Woodville had tired of Wesley, and of the distractions of the day. His concentration began to lapse as thoughts of Evelyn entered his mind. He wanted to join her and enjoy the temporary solace of her company before returning, rejuvenated, to complete his task. Despite the pleasure Evelyn could offer him, he knew he had to return to the headquarters and personally oversee the remainder of the preparations for the *coup d'état*.

Woodville had a driver called to take him back to the mansion in one of the waiting staff cars. Not a word was spoken during the short journey. Only as he stepped out of the drab olive Ford Zephyr did he dismiss the driver with a word of thanks. With his thoughts fixed on Evelyn, he strode across to the mansion entrance. At that moment his desire to see her was fuelled more by his sexual tension than any romantic thought. He could expiate his guilt over his animal desires another day, if at all.

Only Evelyn seemed to be capable of reaching inside his ruthless façade to soothe his cruel soul. He knew he had the cruelty of a malcontent that could only be tamed temporarily. To try to quench it was impossible, as his wife had discovered soon after they married. She chose to live a separate life, being his wife in name only.

Knowing his lover's husband was incarcerated at Hindhead excited him. He wondered if Evelyn knowing about Wesley might add a frisson to her lovemaking. His pace quickened as he made his way through the big house and the rooms that had been set aside for Evelyn and himself. The weight of his responsibilities seemed to drop away as he got closer to her. Each step became lighter in his expectation of being with her to experience a few hours of solace.

Woodville entered the sitting room and closed the door behind him. The sight of Evelyn looking small and tense took him aback. His hope that he would find her excited and radiant vanished. Her night of relaxed luxury at the hotel followed by her trip in the Bentley to join him for their final reunion had come to nothing.

Her eyes met his. There was no sparkle. Instead they looked dull and burdened.

'Whatever is the matter?' he asked.

'Why is Wesley here?' She sounded tired and angry.

'How did you know?' he asked, instead of answering her question.

'I saw him when I arrived. Someone had driven him to Hindhead and the only person he would want to see is you. He is the very man I never wanted to see again, yet here he is!'

Woodville had been wrongfooted. His fantasy of a grand romantic reunion with Evelyn evaporated as he tried to come up with a way to overcome her smouldering anger. He was desperate to rebuild the confidence and trust that Wesley's presence had so quickly demolished. He was also surprised by the thought that he felt he needed to do this and had to admit to himself that Evelyn was more important to him than he cared to admit.

'Evelyn, it was Wesley who insisted he spoke to me in person. Tiresome as it must be for you, he came of his own free will.'

Now he felt anger and resentment at Wesley for putting him in a position of having to explain himself. The man only brought strife and division into his life. Not only had he allowed the escape of suspected secret-service agents, he had also driven a wedge between himself and Evelyn. Both his public and private lives were in disarray, all caused by a man he had never liked and trusted even less. His instincts had proven to be correct.

'What was so important that you agreed to meet him here?' she asked. Her voice had begun to break, though there were no tears in her eyes.

Woodville decided to be direct in his answer. 'The fool has allowed two agents to escape. It seems they may have been working for the security services,' he said.

Evelyn looked back at him in shock. 'Can they do anything to stop the coup?'

'Oh, I doubt that. It's far too late for them to do anything now,' he replied, trying to sound more assured than he felt.

The *coup d'état* was not a foregone conclusion, despite the confidence he had in himself and his officers. Woodville began to see Wesley as someone who attracted misfortune like a magnet. This made him wonder if he had made the right decision to have Wesley secured so close to the epicentre of his operations in the first place.

'I gave orders for him to be taken and secured in the mansion cellars. I suppose his fate is in your hands, Evelyn,' said Woodville, waiting to see her reaction.

Her mood change was instant. Wesley's reversal of fortune appeared to excite her with its possibilities. Woodville was intrigued by her reaction and how easily her cruel nature appeared from beneath the surface of her apparently placid exterior. She stood up and moved closer to him.

'Can I see him?' she asked, as her hand gently brushed against his groin. Her voice dripped with sexual tension as the two lovers made a subliminal reconnection.

'Why don't we go down to the cellars now? We can come back here afterwards,' replied Woodville.

A cruel and triumphant smile formed on Evelyn's lips.

Woodville led her down to the cellars, where Wesley had been taken. They followed a stone-flagged corridor that took them to a wrought-iron gate in the form of a trellis. The padlocked gate formed a secure barrier to the house wine cellar to keep out unwanted visitors. The corridor was lit by old-fashioned light bulbs that only provided minimal light by which to see. A slight smell of damp dust was everywhere. As Woodville and Evelyn approached the wine-cellar entrance, they were able to make out the shape of a man sat on the stone floor. One of his arms was hanging from handcuffs secured to the metal trellis. As Woodville and Evelyn approached, he man stood up.

Woodville stood slightly to the right and behind Evelyn, as if presenting her to the prisoner. His hand, unseen, wafted lazily to and fro across her behind. He was unable to see her face, so he watched Wesley's instead.

The first reaction he noted was that of astonishment. At first there came confusion, followed by so many unanswered questions. Then an apparent and wordless realisation as he seemingly found answers to his unspoken questions. Woodville experienced slight disappointment, as Wesley provided no histrionics for Evelyn and himself to gloat over. No demands to be released or pleas for mercy, nothing. Woodville found it surprising that Evelyn had not uttered a word. It appeared that the chasm between husband and wife had become too wide for communication. Wesley's expression said it all: disinterested resignation.

Evelyn turned around and began to walk back down the corridor. Woodville was gratified by the triumphant look on her face. When they reached the steps that led back upstairs, it was Evelyn who reached out to switch off the lights and leave Wesley to the misery of the damp darkness. She then gripped Woodville's hand, almost dragging him along back to their rooms.

After the pair had sated their sexual appetites, they dined together, drinking champagne taken from the cellar where Wesley sat handcuffed. Later, the pair slumped on to a large four-poster bed and fell into a contented sleep.

* * *

A few hours later there was an urgent knocking on the door of Woodville's bedroom. He climbed out of bed, cursing under his breath as he pulled on a dressing gown. He told Evelyn to stay in bed whilst he found out what was going on.

'What the hell do you want? Can't this wait until morning?' he thundered as he thrust the door open.

A colonel, chosen to oversee the defence forces at Hindhead, stood in front of him. 'Sir, I would not have disturbed you unless it was important. One of my majors, a chap called Maybury, has disappeared. He seems to have attacked and killed a sentry before making off in a Land Rover that he then abandoned on the drive a short distance from the mansion. A vehicle patrol encountered him whilst he escaped on foot. The patrol opened fire on him before he disappeared into the night.'

Woodville struggled to make sense of what the colonel had told him. He felt sure there was more to be made of the explanation he had been given.

'Wait downstairs and I will join you there,' he said, shutting the door in the colonel's face. As he quickly dressed, he began to scope out in his mind the events the colonel had related. He hastily embraced Evelyn and told her he would be back as soon as he could, before rushing downstairs.

'Put the men on full alert and double all the patrols until I say otherwise,' he told the colonel as the pair made their way outside. A staff car was waiting with its engine running. Minutes later, Woodville sat in the command caravan listening once more to the accounts of the two men who had tried to stop the intruder.

He remained unconvinced that the major had gone rogue. The man was purportedly the colonel's most trusted and loyal officer, and he remained emphatic that the major was no traitor and not the kind of man to lose his nerve at the last minute.

'Did you see if the intruder wore any rank badges?' Woodville asked the two men.

They hesitated. 'No, sir,' they chorused.

'Did the man return your fire?' he asked.

Again, the men hesitated.

'No, sir. We didn't even hear the shots that put out the headlights,' replied one of the men.

Woodville had heard enough and dismissed them.

'Is it possible that the major is still on site?' he asked the colonel. The man just shook his head.

'I want a search made of the whole headquarters area. Also, the land between where the Land Rover was abandoned and where the intruder was last seen,' he ordered. He was unsurprised to hear that the intruder had worn nothing recognisable, such as rank badges.

'Do really think Maybury is hiding somewhere around the headquarters?' asked the colonel.

'I believe he may still be here somewhere. Either unconscious or dead,' replied Woodville.

'How can you be so sure?' asked the colonel.

'The intruder wore no rank badges and never returned fire on the patrol, yet the vehicle's headlights were shot out. The intruder was not acting alone, because a second person made the shots. Something bad might be about to happen,' said Woodville, more to himself than the colonel.

Woodville was sure the intruder had been sent to spy on the headquarters. His mission had been to collect information because so far there were no reports of equipment being tampered with or destroyed. It was only through chance that they knew an intruder had been there at all. A flash of panic went through him.

'Have all the communications equipment searched for explosive devices or boobytraps and report to me as soon as the checks are complete,' snapped Woodville at his communications officer.

The man rushed off to organise search parties whilst a bemused Woodville sat and waited. In the now-hushed command centre, he began to collect his thoughts. He had no idea who was behind the intrusion of his headquarters, but at least his forces were alert to what had happened and were preparing for an attack, should it come. He assumed a possible attack would take place at dawn at the earliest. If not, he then had to keep a lid on things for the final twenty-four hours leading up to the coup itself.

Finally, news on the whereabouts of the missing major arrived. He had been found dead wrapped up in a camouflage net. This was good news for the colonel, as it proved his man was not a traitor. Woodville had rather hoped that he had been, because now he knew his headquarters had been compromised.

'What do we do now?' asked the colonel.

RA RIDLEY

'Make sure the men are told that an intruder was surprised by the major, forcing the man to make his escape before he could do anything. Tell them our security has not been breached and there is nothing to worry about,' ordered Woodville.

The colonel nodded and left. Woodville knew there was nothing further he could do. Certain that he had anticipated all possible outcomes, his thoughts returned to Evelyn.

'Get a driver to take me back to the house,' he said to the duty officer. 'Have two men sent up there as well. Tell them to wait at the entrance to the cellars. Whilst I am there, if anything – and I mean anything – happens, I must be contacted immediately.'

Once back at the house, Woodville had his chauffeur brought to him. The man was taken into a side room and the door was shut behind them. In anticipation of a need to evacuate Hindhead quickly, he needed to have an evacuation plan in place. The fewer people that knew of it, the better. He wanted as few people as possible to know that he had any doubts about the outcome of the *coup d'état*. The chauffeur was a man he knew he could trust.

'I want you to be able to leave here at very short notice during the next thirty-six hours. If you are required to drive, then myself and Mrs MacDonald will be your passengers,' said Woodville.

'Where will I be driving to, sir?' the man asked.

'I will give you the instructions only if we have to leave at short notice,' replied Woodville.

'Very well, sir.'

Woodville dismissed the chauffeur and made his way to the cellars.

Two men were waiting for him at the entrance. Woodville briefed them quietly to avoid being overheard by any of the house staff. He then led them down the steps and into the cellar. The lights were switched on and the trio headed off down the corridor leading to where Wesley had been secured.

Wesley looked up at the three men. If he was surprised by Woodville's return, he did not show it. The men dragged Wesley to his feet and handcuffed his free arm to the metal latticework of the wine cellar. He now stood with his arms up high and apart. There was no doubt in his mind what was going to happen next.

'We had an uninvited visitor at my headquarters tonight, Wesley. Do you have any idea who that might be?' asked Woodville.

Wesley had no idea and shook his head.

Woodville nodded to one of the men, who stepped forward and punched Wesley hard in the stomach. He gasped from the pain and his legs turned to jelly, forcing him to hang painfully from his handcuffed arms.

'I will ask you again. Who was the intruder?'

'I don't know. How could I? I had no idea about this place until I arrived yesterday,' said Wesley.

Woodville saw the logic in what Wesley had said but remained unconvinced. 'You may have been followed, or you could be carrying a tracking device,' he said, and ordered the men to search Wesley thoroughly.

They found nothing, adding to Woodville's frustration.

'I know you are hiding something from me, Wesley. The sooner you tell me, the sooner all this will end,' said Woodville, in a friendly, almost helpful voice.

Wesley guessed that the 'end' that Woodville spoke of would involve his death. He realised that there was nothing to be gained from speaking to his captors. If he lied, they would eventually catch him out, assuming he could stay alive for long enough. 'I told you everything I know when I arrived here,' he said.

Woodville shook his head. He was sure there was more to know. He gestured to the two men to begin punching Wesley once more. Punch after measured punch turned Wesley's face to a bloody pulp. His ribs broke from the force of the punches and his whole body continued to be wracked with pain from the beating.

'Can't you see sense, Wesley? What else do you know that you really should tell me?' asked Woodville.

Early on, Wesley had guessed that Mike Armstrong might be the mysterious intruder, but he had decided not to say anything. This was not out of any misplaced loyalty to Mike. Instead, he wanted to surrender nothing to Woodville. The man had all but dispensed with him and Wesley knew it. There was no future for him now, regardless of the *coup d'état*'s outcome. He was dead, finished – but his last secret would die with him.

The blows continued to fall until Wesley hung limp and lifeless from the handcuffs. Eventually, one of the men checked for a pulse but found nothing.

Woodville grunted impatiently and gestured with his hand for the men to leave. He glanced at the bloody mess attached to the metal trellis before spinning on his heel and walking away.

28
EXPLOSIONS AND FERRETS

Mike sat alone in the back of the Land Rover with his boots resting on the lowered tailgate. Libby sat in the front with DM. Both had slid open their windows to allow cool air to pass through as the vehicle travelled along. The stench of Mike's clothes from crawling through the sheep field was overwhelming.

'I hope you found everything you went looking for,' shouted DM back to Mike.

'Yes, but I only got away with it thanks to Libby. Woodville is going to up his security now, and that is going to give us problems,' he replied.

'Don't worry, assistance is arriving tomorrow,' DM shouted back.

Mike was keen to know what form of assistance DM had in mind but was too tired to question him further.

Once back at the safe house, Mike stripped and showered. The malodorous clothes were taken away and replaced with fresh items. Libby shared the shower with him and they made love as if it was their last time together. Both knew what lay ahead, and there was no guarantee either of them would be alive in twenty-four hours' time. They spoke a few words before finally getting a few hours of precious sleep.

* * *

By the time Mike and Libby woke, it was early afternoon on a hot summer's day. The blackout curtains had given no hint to either of them of the strong sunlight trying to burst into the darkened bedroom.

Libby woke first and took a shower to wake herself up. By the time she had finished, Mike had also woken up. He threw back the curtains and let the sunlight wash over his naked body, recognising the familiar need to enjoy every comfort as fully as possible in the prelude to encountering danger. Later, he would feel that each moment was going to be his last. Mike wondered if Libby felt something similar.

'Are you all right?' asked Libby as she pressed her body against his.

'I am now,' he replied.

'Let's get dressed and get something to eat, I'm starving,' she whispered as she nibbled on his ear.

A shiver of pleasure went down his back as he turned and kissed her deeply.

A knock on the door disturbed them, making the pair put on their dressing gowns. Mike answered the door to find Mrs May standing outside.

'I wondered if you would like some lunch. Also, DM would like you to meet a new arrival,' she said.

'We'll need a few minutes to get dressed,' said Libby.

'Oh, don't worry about that. Your guest has never been known to stand on ceremony,' replied Mrs May as she walked away down the corridor.

An intrigued Mike and Libby followed Mrs May downstairs to the bright and airy dining room, where the table had been laid for four.

Mike and Libby instantly recognised the huge figure standing on the patio in the sunshine next to DM.

'Canute! I thought we'd left you in Norfolk laying false trails for Wesley's mercenaries,' exclaimed Mike.

Libby raced over and hugged their friend whilst Mike shook his hand.

'I gave them the slip and decided to come and check on how you were getting on. It seems my timing was just right,' said Canute with a beaming smile and a glance towards DM.

Seeing Canute again raised the spirits of Mike and Libby to new heights, and the small group sat down and talked animatedly about recent events as they ate lunch. Eventually, DM steered them back to the reason for their meeting.

'I hope you are well rested and ready for the main event tonight,' he said, looking towards Mike and then Libby.

The pair knew they could not put off the inevitable, even though they had avoided any serious discussion with Canute and DM so far.

'I just want it all to be over as quickly as possible, so Mike and I can get our lives back,' said Libby, making a point of holding DM's gaze.

'Indeed. This is something Canute and I were discussing before Mrs May went to fetch you,' he replied DM.

Mike glanced at Canute, who smiled back.

'DM has said there is no reason why you have to remain in his care now,' said Canute.

'Naturally, I expect you not to disclose anything to anyone about Woodville and his mistaken adventure. Nor should you talk about myself or what you have seen here,' their host said, with a charming hint of menace.

'I think they fully understand that, DM,' said Canute.

'Good. I would not like to come looking for you. Wesley seemed to find you easily enough, so do not think that I will have any problem doing so either,' said DM.

Mike knew this was no idle threat. He also had no intention of himself and Libby looking over their shoulders for the rest of their lives.

'You really mean we can go from here and the security services will leave us alone?' asked Mike.

'Stopping Woodville is more than enough to gain your freedom and enable you to live as fugitives no longer,' confirmed DM.

'He means it. You really will be free,' confirmed Canute.
Mike and Libby felt an enormous weight lift from them. The chance to live together in total anonymity had finally and unexpectedly come within their grasp.

'Time to get started, then,' replied Mike.

'When you go back to your room you will find a different set of clothing waiting for you. The forecast is for heavy cloud tonight, and having black clothing should provide better camouflage,' said DM.

'We need to do things differently this time. I need to have close cover when I am setting the explosive charges in the headquarters area,' said Mike.

'Yes, I anticipated that,' said DM.

'What do you mean?' asked Libby.

'Get changed and meet us down at the armoury,' said DM, looking at Canute.

Mike and Libby went back upstairs and found the black combat clothing neatly laid out on their bed. They also found high-leg combat boots placed on the floor at the end of the bed. They were a type never seen by Mike, that extended higher up the leg than a standard military boot. A pair of lightweight black balaclavas had also been left out with the clothing. The pair noticed they each had a small container of fresh camouflage cream ready for use. They stuffed the balaclavas in their pockets, along with the camouflage cream, and made their way back downstairs.

On a bench inside the armoury sat two Sterling sub-machine guns. Each weapon had a black cylinder fitted along the length of the barrel.

'The SMGs are fitted with silencers and will be useful if you use them at close quarters,' said DM.

'What about our Smith and Wessons?' asked Mike.

'Take them with you – they both fire the same ammunition,' said DM.

'We might need a lot of it. How are we going to carry it all?' asked Libby.

'Your combat clothing has specially tailored pockets to take the SMG magazines, and you will have this backpack full of spare magazines ready to use.'

Mike looked at a second backpack that was identical to the one carrying the ammunition.

'This second pack contains the explosive charges,' explained DM.

'How do I prime them?' Mike asked.

DM opened the backpack and took out one of the charges, then handed it to Mike. It was about the size of a large bar of chocolate, with two buttons set in the centre. On the reverse were two magnets. DM pointed to a small D-shaped catch set in one end of the charge.

'Flick the catch over to its opposite side and press either the red or green button. The buttons select the timer: red is two minutes and green is four,' he explained.

Mike nodded, glad that the charges were simple to understand and operate.

'Can we test-fire the SMGs?' asked Libby.

'Of course. There's no need for ear defenders and the range is lit ready for use.'

A short while later, the four of them were back upstairs discussing the plan for the night ahead.

'Canute and I intend to distract the attention of Woodville's men by creating a diversion to the north-east of his field headquarters. Hopefully this will allow you to enter the estate from the south-east. As you were not detected coming in on that route last night, there is no reason why you can't use the same approach,' explained DM.

'As you found that the vehicle route being used between the mansion and the headquarters is less secure, it makes sense for you to steal a vehicle and drive into the site,' added Canute. 'This will also save you a lot of time that you may need for your escape.'

Mike and Libby looked at each other. They knew that whatever way they got into the copse, there was a huge risk of being caught. Using a military vehicle reduced their chances of being stopped so they decided to go along with DM's idea.

As the afternoon ended, dark clouds bubbled up from the west until a uniform layer of them completely covered the sky. Darkness in the woods came that much earlier, allowing Mike and Libby to be swiftly dropped off from DM's Land Rover and become almost unseen as they moved deftly between the trees. Their balaclavas and camouflage cream hid the paleness of any uncovered skin, and each carried their SMG at the ready in case they came across Woodville's men. Mike traced his way back to the point where he had left Libby the night before. She followed a few yards back from him and to his right, just as they had practiced in the Canadian forest.

That night the weather conditions were more favourable to them. As they stopped to observe the valley and the river once more, it was much harder to make out any detail. Like a pair of deadly wraiths, they slowly broke cover and headed towards the river. Once across they carefully climbed the gentle slope of the valley to search for a vantage point from where they could observe the mansion.

Libby and Mike carried light-gathering binoculars rather than the heavy night sight. As before, the mansion obscured the view of Woodville's headquarters, but they were able to make out the shapes of vehicles parked outside the front of the mansion.

Mike tapped Libby's shoulder gently. This was the prearranged signal for moving forward to the mansion and taking a vehicle. They slowly rose up to a crouch and went forward over the skyline and down towards the mansion. With the knowledge that there was very little chance of encountering a sentry or a patrol, they arrived safely at the mansion's periphery. They then traced their way along the walls of the building until they were just yards away from the vehicles.

Taking no more chances, Mike dropped on to one knee and Libby followed suit. He soon spotted two sentries standing amongst the vehicles. Each smoked a cigarette and seemed to be totally at ease.

Using hand signals, Mike indicated to Libby to shoot the man on her right, and he the man on his left. Silently, they raised their SMGs and took aim. The shots made an almost synchronous thud and the men dropped instantly. The pair raced over to the dead men and dragged them into the cover of some nearby ornamental bushes, then jumped into the nearest Land Rover.

Mike checked his watch – it was nearing midnight. They had made it just in time and now sat still. With nerves set on edge, they waited for midnight to arrive.

Exactly on cue and to their north-east, the first of a series of explosions began. DM and Canute had begun their intermittent diversions. Libby had placed her ammunition backpack on the floor of the vehicle between her knees, then put the backpack containing the explosives on top of her thighs. Within minutes, Woodville's men rushed out of the mansion towards their vehicles. As soon as the first staff car pulled away, Mike gunned the engine of his Land Rover and kept close behind. Mike and Libby drove straight through the checkpoints as soldiers recognised the lead car and waved the rest through, ignoring all the occupants as all the cars headed to the command centre.

DM and Canute's noisy diversions had galvanised the command centre, making men run to and fro between the caravans. Mike and Libby ducked down and waited for the commotion to stop. Within minutes the car park was deserted once Woodville's men were at their positions.

'The caravans are just in front. Cover me from here whilst I set the charges,' Mike whispered into Libby's ear.

She nodded, and the pair gently pushed down on the door handles and stepped out of the Land Rover. Libby passed the explosives backpack to Mike, then slipped on her ammunition backpack. By the time she had taken a firing position, Mike had disappeared into the darkness.

An eternity of minutes lapsed as she waited for him to put the explosives in place. Outside the headquarters, and in the distance, the sound of moving vehicles reached her ears. It was clear the vehicles were not focusing on the north-east, as both DM and Canute had hoped. It sounded like a curtain of soldiers and steel had surrounded the whole communications complex. Suddenly a hand rested on Libby's shoulder and she jumped with fright before realising Mike had returned.

'All the charges are set, so we need to get out now. The timers are on two minutes and the first ones are set to blow,' he whispered into her ear.

'They've sealed off the place tighter than a drum, Mike!' she replied.

'Yes, I heard them, but I think it's a reaction to DM and Canute, not us,' he replied.

'So what are we going to do?' she asked.

'Follow me,' said Mike.

The sentries posted near to the car park spotted the pair moving towards the exit, which was now sealed with barbed wire and pickets. The men challenged Mike and Libby to stop, then seeing they were being ignored, they opened fire.

The pair returned fire with their silenced weapons, killing their targets instantly. They reached the perimeter of the trees and Mike rushed forward into the open ground and was gone. With her heart in her mouth, Libby ran forward in the same direction. She heard Mike calling her and ran towards his voice in the dark. Some of Woodville's other men had started shooting and bullets zipped past, narrowly missing her on either side. She continued to sprint forward and suddenly felt herself manhandled downwards.

'Got you,' exclaimed Mike as he dragged her into a fire trench that had been prepared by the very soldiers who now lay dead at the opposite end of the trench to Mike and Libby.

'Keep below the parapet and stay still,' he warned.

Machine-gun fire ripped away at the edges of the trench, spraying earth and stones over them. The firing stopped, followed by a buzzing sound that kept repeating.

'It's a field telephone. The soldiers are trying to call the trench to find out what's happening. Keep down,' warned Mike.

The buzzing stopped, and seconds later they heard a parachute flare being launched. The flare popped before spinning lazily around as it slowly returned to earth. The trench Mike and Libby had found was plain to see, even though they were hidden out of sight within it.

'Lie down right at the bottom,' said Mike.

Libby lay down and Mike lay on top of her. Two dull thuds were heard. One on each side of the trench. Mike knew they were grenades and that thankfully the throwers had just missed their mark. However, there would be no second chance for him or Libby once the grenade throwers adjusted their aim.

Seconds later, the exploding grenades rocked the ground, throwing more stones and earth over the two of them. Mike checked his watch, and to his relief it was then that the carnage began.

A mixture of incendiaries and explosives rippled through the headquarters complex as the charges blew up with hideous orange-flamed efficiency. The communications caravans were shattered, fragments of metal ripping into the bodies of the men caught inside. The incendiaries set the site ablaze, making men run for their lives, unable to save their comrades from being incinerated at their posts. Men staggered out of the carnage into the fields surrounding the headquarters. Some were still burning, whilst others seemed almost stripped of their clothes, their blackened skin illuminated by the raging fires. The whole site, now set ablaze, became a focus for the troops who were firefighting or giving first aid to others. Mike knew the site was finished for good.

In the continuing confusion, Mike and Libby slipped over the ragged parapet of the fire trench and headed for the darkness of the distant fields. Finally getting into a patch of dead ground, they shared out some ammunition between them.

'Do think we are safe now?' whispered Libby.

'That depends upon whether or not we were spotted getting away,' he replied.

'It looks like they have their hands full back there,' she said, trying to sound hopeful.

'I'll only feel safe once we are off the estate. We'll head south, then west back to the pickup point.'

The pair moved off, keeping to the formation they had used when moving through the woods earlier that night. Libby kept looking back and scanning the ground to see if anyone had followed them.

Mike spotted movement to his front, and at the same time Libby heard a vehicle pull up in the dark, followed by the sounds of dismounting troops. The pair dropped down, looking and listening to see what the troops were doing. They had formed extended lines and were advancing towards Mike and Libby, trapping them in a pincer movement.

'We can retreat to our left,' Mike whispered. 'Fire off a magazine to cover our movements. You first.'

Libby darted off to the left behind Mike. He fired an extended burst at the men approaching from the front. By the time he emptied his magazine it was Libby's turn to open fire and keep the troops' heads down. Mike ran behind her, changing his magazine at the same time. By the time she had emptied her magazine at the troops, he was ready to cover her movements.

The men had not returned fire, and this puzzled Mike. The answer to this question came as he and Libby crested a small rise and found themselves caught in the headlights of two Ferret armoured cars. There was nowhere to run. Each vehicle was armed with a Browning machine gun, leaving Mike and Libby outgunned.

29
DUEL

Mike and Libby slowly lowered their weapons and placed them on the ground. Two pairs of soldiers ran forward and moved the sub-machine guns out of the captives' reach, then began to search them. Wordlessly, they removed their Smith & Wesson pistols, along with all the spare magazines and ammunition. Their hands were secured behind their backs before they were taken up to the mansion.

Mike and Libby remained as silent as their captors. Apart from a gasp of surprise when Libby's balaclava had been pulled from her head, revealing that they had captured a woman, the soldiers had acted impassively and professionally.

Mike knew that the men had been given orders to capture and not kill them. They could have been shot at any time from the moment they put down their weapons. He realised that meant they were probably going to be interrogated by Woodville. He would want to know to what extent his coup had been compromised, and what countermeasures he may have to take. This gave Mike a sliver of hope that both he and Libby might still get out of the situation alive.

The captives were taken to a square courtyard bounded by the mansion and the stables. The only entry for vehicles was a single large arch flanked by the stables alongside one side of the square. To Mike's amazement, the area was jammed with military vehicles. Woodville had set up another site in case his main command centre was destroyed. Mike swore at his own stupidity, realising he was right all along that the mansion could be used as a command centre. The only difference was the back-up, and not the main. The whole set-up took its electrical power from the mansion, so it had not needed to use noisy generators.

A single large communications caravan had been shoehorned through the archway and set up in the centre of the courtyard, with smaller ancillary vehicles and stores filling the rest of the space. Mike and Libby were taken to the large central caravan, where they waited outside with soldiers maintaining a grasp on each of their arms. Their hands remained tied behind their backs.

A short while later a cabin door opened on the caravan and Woodville stepped out into the night. His face, lit by arc lights, was triumphant.

'Mr Mazarin, Miss Mancuso. What effective agents you both are. You have been a considerable nuisance to me,' said Woodville with menace.

Mike and Libby remained silent. Woodville rested his elbow in one hand and his chin in the other as he looked down on his captives. He appeared to be contemplating what to do with them next.

'Wesley is dead, so please do not harbour any false hopes that he will send in the cavalry to save you,' he said.
Mike and Libby remained stone-faced and silent.

'My only interest is finding out who else you have been talking to. The question is relevant, because after I get into power I will need to decide which department of the security services I need to purge,' he continued.

Mike and Libby remained stubborn in their refusal to answer Woodville, who nodded to one of the men who had interrogated Wesley. He stepped forward and punched Libby fully in the face. The blood from her mouth splattered over Mike's face, and he exploded with anger as he tried to shake off the soldiers holding him.

'A reaction, at last. Why don't you tell me your real names, and who sent you?' asked Woodville with a smile.

The blow had stunned Libby, and she had slumped forward with blood dripping from her mouth and nose on to the courtyard cobbles. Woodville nodded at the man once more. This time the man violently struck Libby in the stomach. She doubled up, but the soldiers forced her to remain standing.

Mike could see that Woodville had absolute authority – he intended to have Libby beaten until Mike finally gave in. Mike also knew that once he did so, and Woodville had what he wanted, he would have them both killed. He therefore chose to remain silent, and Woodville's face clouded with anger.

'This is your last chance. Tell me who you are and who sent you!' roared Woodville.

Nothing. Woodville was right that no one would come and save Mike and Libby. DM would have seen and heard the destruction of the main command centre and assumed they were successful in their mission. He would be waiting for them to arrive at the pickup point outside the Hindhead estate. The only way out of the mess now was to place uncertainty in Woodville's mind.

'You have been played,' said Mike finally. 'I suppose we all have.'

'At last, the man speaks. Do go on,' said Woodville.

'Wesley was a double agent working for Moscow. The Soviets want the coup to succeed and destabilise the country, leading to a split in NATO. You will be assassinated within days and replaced by one of their own. A sleeper agent, who is in government right now,' said Mike.

'A fantastic and obviously desperate story,' countered Woodville.

'You think so? I have nothing to lose by telling you this, seeing as you are going to kill us anyway,' said Mike, desperately trying to sow a seed of doubt in Woodville's mind. He knew there was no way to check on this story, as Woodville had already killed Wesley.

He studied Mike's face. 'We shall see. Kill her,' said Woodville.

Mike struggled with all his might but was helpless to stop the execution. The man who had beaten Libby drew a pistol and placed it against her head. He squeezed the trigger and it was over. Mike exploded with fury and managed to escape the men holding his arms. He headbutted the others before rushing forward to attack Woodville. Suddenly, everything went dark.

* * *

A massive aching sensation forced its way into Mike's consciousness. His arms felt as if they had a massive weight pulling them down, and the back of his head ached painfully. He then became aware of a dim orange light to his front. His surroundings were dark and silent. He shook his head from side to side to try and clear the ache, but that only made the pain worse.

More alert now, Mike realised that his arms were strung up above him and the pulling sensation was from his own body. He opened his eyes fully and focused on the wall light directly in front of him. His sight soon improved, and he looked to his right along the dimly lit corridor. Then, to his left, he saw an iron latticework barrier fitted with a gate that had been left open.

Hanging from the latticework was a man whose face had been pulverised, leaving it bloody and virtually unrecognisable. Mike could still tell it was Wesley, though, and he looked to be dead from the beating he had taken.

Mike shivered at the thought that he could be next. He looked down at a body that was slumped against the wall opposite next to Wesley and groaned in despair. It was Libby, also bloodied and motionless. The cold, dark rage that had possessed him earlier when he tried to attack Woodville returned. A rage that could only be sated by cold-blooded revenge.

Mike's hands had been tied together with a short length of rope that had been hung over a hook extending from the wall above him. The rope allowed him just enough length to stand on tiptoe, confirming to Mike that he could expect an interrogation. He looked more closely at the rope and saw that it had not been tied to the hook. That meant that all he had to do was somehow flick it off the hook. An impossible task, as he was already at full stretch.

Mike looked around for something to stand on and raise himself. There was nothing, but he noticed the wall was roughly constructed from stones and offered plenty of purchase points for his hands. The gaps in the old latticework barrier looked to Mike to be wide enough to provide a foothold, so he stretched a leg across and found that it reached.

He twisted himself towards the wall and looked for a stone that jutted out just far enough for him to hold on to. Choosing the best purchase point he could find, he pushed his left palm against a stone then slowly raised himself by pushing against the metal latticework.

Time after time, Mike's hand slipped off the stonework and he fell against the wall, painfully gouging chunks of skin off his hand and face. His efforts began to exhaust him, so he decided to make one last-ditch effort before being forced to rest. This time his hand held, allowing him to flick the rope off using his free right hand, and he dropped to the floor.

He lay still for a few seconds to regain his breath before standing up and undoing the rope. He then crouched down beside Libby's body and held her limp hand, vowing silently to avenge her death.

Mike followed the dim lights back along the passageway before climbing the stone steps back up into the mansion. He made his way along the opulent corridors, standing motionless every time he heard sound or movement. Despite his fear of discovery, the mansion seemed devoid of people in the small hours of the night.

He checked his watch and realised that he had only a short time before sunrise. After finding a door that led to the backstairs used by the household staff, he made his way up to the first floor. From there he looked down into the courtyard, which was still lit by arc lights. Even though no one was moving outside, Mike knew the command and communication vehicles shoehorned into the courtyard were full of Woodville's men.

The cloud-filled sky still held back the coming light of day, providing Mike with a multiplicity of shadows for him to hide in amongst the vehicles. He retraced his steps downstairs to look for an exit into the courtyard. Minutes later, he was crouching in the shadow of a small petrol bowser. He guessed there had to be others prepared to go in case the mobile command centre had to move in an emergency, so he searched amongst the densely packed vehicles and found four other bowsers. All were full to the brim with fuel. Mike searched among the tools that were strapped to the outside of some of the military vehicles and found an axe.

After taking a final glance around the crammed-in vehicles, he swung the axe down on to a large tap that was fitted on to the base of a petrol bowser. Petrol spewed out on to the cobblestones, running off in all directions whilst its stench filled Mike's nostrils. He rushed from one petrol bowser to the next, smashing off the taps to swamp the courtyard with petrol. The petrol fumes had become overwhelming even to the occupants of the vehicles and the command caravan, resulting in men appearing from all directions.

Mike waited in the shadows for one of them to pass close by to him. When a soldier did so, he leapt out, grabbed the man's head and viciously snapped it to one side. The soldier noiselessly dropped dead on to the cobbles.

Wasting no time, Mike retrieved the man's pistol then searched his pockets, praying he was a smoker. His prayer was answered in the form of a Zippo lighter that he pocketed for later.

More and more soldiers had been drawn to the small of petrol and were alerting others of the danger. Mike knew it was only a matter of time before they discovered him. Moving as quickly as he dared, he headed back to the door that he'd used earlier to leave the mansion. His last act before bolting the door shut was to throw the ignited Zippo lighter into the courtyard. He then sprinted back up the staircase to watch the fiery mayhem.

A sea of flames had already engulfed the courtyard before Mike could reach an upstairs window to view his handiwork. Fuel tanks on vehicles started to explode, adding to a now-raging fire. There was no escape for the men evacuating the flaming vehicles as they jumped into the surrounding sea of flames and certain death. Burning figures ran in all directions, adding further chaos to the hell on earth that was unfolding outside. Mike watched impassively, his finger resting on the trigger of the pistol he had taken from the dead soldier. He watched the main command caravan, waiting for Woodville to appear.

Mike remained rooted to the spot, not wanting to leave until he knew Woodville was dead. He had to have proof positive after promising to Libby that he would kill the man.

Further down the corridor from Mike, a bedroom door suddenly opened. A man wearing a dressing gown appeared, followed by a woman in a night gown. The man gazed down into the courtyard, apparently mesmerised by the fiery carnage. The flames lit up the man's face and Mike realised it was Woodville.

More muffled explosions took place as petrol tanks ignited, and Woodville shook his head from side to side in disbelief. In one hand he carried a revolver, the other was held by the woman who shook with horror as she witnessed men dying horrifically in the flames.

'How does it feel to see your great plan going up in flames, Woodville?' shouted Mike.

The two shocked onlookers turned towards his voice. Woodville raised his pistol and fired into the shadows where Mike was hidden.

'Show yourself!' he ordered.

'Of course,' Mike replied, stepping into the now flame-lit corridor, then dropping on to one knee. He fired a single shot that struck Woodville in his thigh, tearing through flesh and bone. Blood gushed out from a ruptured artery and Woodville collapsed on to the thick carpet. Mike fired a second shot into Woodville's belly, incapacitating the man with immense pain. Woodville dropped his pistol and held up his hands in a plea of mercy.

'Who the hell are you?' he asked.

'I'm the man who loved the woman you had executed, and now it's your turn. Just don't expect to die as quickly,' Mike replied.

Woodville looked down helplessly at the pool of his own sticky red mess and then at Evelyn, who had frozen in horror, watching his lifeblood soak into the carpet. As Woodville began to lose consciousness, Mike took aim for a final time. He squeezed the trigger, then watched Woodville's head snap backwards from the force of the bullet striking him.

The man's body slumped sideways on to Evelyn's feet. His eyes were open wide, his death stare pointed directly at her.

Although unable to move, Evelyn had screamed manically as Mike shot her lover. Watching Woodville die sent her over the edge. Without him, her plans perished as quickly as the burning men in the courtyard below. Her existence was no better than the burning wreckage of Woodville's command centre. Her life was over.

She fell to her knees and grabbed at the revolver Woodville had dropped. With trembling hands, she pointed the pistol at Mike. She managed to get off one shot before he fired at her twice. She died instantly.

Although he was the last man standing, Mike knew he had come away with nothing. All he wanted was Libby, and he knew that could never be. He had doubly avenged her death, but there was no consolation in having done so. He had brought her to her death here at Hindhead. No one else could be blamed for that.

The fire in the courtyard had spread into the mansion and there was no hope for anyone trying to save Woodville's command centre. Mike decided he had cheated death once too often to wait around to see what happened next. He ran downstairs and out into the front of the mansion to where a few vehicles were still parked. He chose a Land Rover and drove as fast as he could towards the river that lay beyond the ridge. Woodville's men were drawn like moths to the massive flames engulfing the mansion and paid no attention to Mike's flight across country.

Mike maintained his speed as he drove down to the river, then accelerated at the last moment. The Land Rover's momentum forced the vehicle through the knee-deep water, causing a mighty eruption of spray all around. For a few seconds the water hit the windscreen, preventing him from seeing ahead.

Staying in low gear, he floored the accelerator to maintain his speed as he drove up the opposite slope towards the sanctum of the woods. At the edge of the trees, Mike stopped the vehicle and leapt out to head for cover. Once hidden amongst the trees, he allowed himself a look back at Hindhead. The mansion was a raging blaze of fire and destruction, the flames complementing the glorious sunrise of a new summer's day.

* * *

Mike, DM and Canute sat together silently eating a late breakfast. Libby's death hung like a pall over them.

Although showered and dressed in fresh clothes, Mike still lacked the sleep he badly needed. Drained of sentiment, he ate slowly and avoided any small talk.

Canute knew there was nothing to be said that might lift Mike's spirits, while DM patiently waited for the right moment to speak. When Mrs May came into the room to check that her guests had all they needed, she too glanced at Mike. It seemed to the others that she understood only too well the emptiness he was experiencing. She also knew enough to be prudent and say nothing.

'What are you going to do next, Mike?' asked Canute eventually.

Mike threw a glance at DM. 'I think that is up to him,' he replied.

'I meant what I said, Mike. Your mission is over, you are free to go wherever you please,' said DM.

'No keeping tabs on me?'

'Not unless you give me a reason to.'

'You needn't worry on that score,' said Mike.

'You will not be called as a witness to any court martial of the commanders that supported Woodville. The military police have more than enough evidence to put these men in jail,' added DM.

Mike appeared disinterested for a moment before speaking. 'What about Libby's body?' he asked.

'We know where to look for her. She will be recovered and returned to her family,' said Canute gently.

'Her funeral?' asked Mike.

'Better that you do not attend,' said DM in a firm voice.

Mike guessed his presence would be an embarrassment to her family and her husband Dicky. He was the outsider nobody wanted to acknowledge.

Canute repeated his question to Mike about his plans.

'I'm leaving, and I have no intention of coming back. I have lost the only woman I have ever loved. There is nothing left for me here,' he said.

Sunshine streamed into the dining room as Mike said his goodbyes to DM and Canute. Mrs May met him at the front door. He said goodbye to her and shook her hand. She held it firmly for a few seconds, her eyes seeming to convey a familiarity and understanding of how he felt.

Mike looked away, then walked out to the waiting car. His new life without Libby had begun and a grim smile crossed his face. When it came to it, he knew she would not have changed a single thing.

MESSAGE FROM THE AUTHOR

A huge thank you for choosing to read my third novel, *The Lions of the North* which is a sequel to *The Masters of the Chandelle*. As a new(ish) author on Amazon I depend massively on readers submitting reviews. If you enjoyed the novel could you spare a few minutes to write a review? Just a few words will help other readers discover my work and raise my profile as a new writer.

If you want to get in touch with me regarding *The Lions of the North*, you can email me at raridleywrites@gmail.com or find me on Twitter @robwritesnovels. I look forward to hearing from you and all messages will be replied to. You can also go to Amazon to see my author's page.

Printed in Great Britain
by Amazon